"Her Unexpected Protector"

Bulbs, Blossoms and Bouquets #8

By Laura Ann

This is a work of fiction. Similarities to real people, places, or events are entirely coincidental.

HER UNEXPECTED PROTECTOR

First edition. October 20, 2021.

Copyright © 2021 Laura Ann.

Written by Laura Ann.

DEDICATION

To my father in law.
We miss you.
We love you.
Thank you for all the memories.

ACKNOWLEDGEMENTS

No author works alone. Thank you, Tami.
You make it Christmas every time
I get a new cover. And thank you to my Beta Team.
Truly, your help with my stories is immeasurable.

PROLOGUE

Rose tried not to become emotional as she watched the handsome police captain, Kenneth Wamsley, dance with her five-year-old daughter, Lily. She tried not to smile when Lily laughed with abandon, much louder than all the other guests at the wedding. She tried not to blush when Ken looked her way, his eyes brimming with longing and attraction.

She tried.

But she failed.

For almost five years, Rose had been holding off the attractive police officer. She had come to Seaside Bay to escape a man, not invite another into her life. But the more time went on, the more Ken got under her skin.

He was tall, handsome, and a wonderful leader...all things that would attract any woman. But it was his gentle kindness that had Rose struggling the most. That and the fact that he treated her deaf daughter as if she were his own.

Lily adored Ken. She clung to him at every gathering and looked for him when he wasn't around.

Unfortunately, Rose often found herself doing the same.

Rose shook her head and forced herself to look away. She couldn't give in. Her life was not the kind that she could welcome in another relationship, no matter how much it hurt to keep telling him no.

Nobody, not even her best friends in Seaside Bay, knew why Rose had slipped into town in the middle of the night. She'd shown up with a brand new baby in one arm and a check to purchase an older shop on Main Street. Calling the shop The Hidden Daffodil had been Rose's way of starting a new life, since daffodils were symbolic of new beginnings.

She had always been fascinated by flowers, but had never been allowed the opportunity to pursue a degree in the floral arts. Well, now she could. Now, she could do anything she wanted because she was free.

Mostly.

So far, Rose had managed to stay under the radar, but the feeling that one day she would be found along with the secret she kept, had never quite dissipated.

That feeling was the main reason she always turned down Ken's invitations. She'd had a good long run in Seaside Bay. She'd started a wonderful business and had the best group of friends, who were more like family than anything else. But someday, she knew she'd have to run again. And how could she do that if she was attached to the police captain?

"Mama!" Lily yelled, unable to recognize quite how loud she was being.

Rose turned her attention to her daughter and automatically pasted a smile on her face. She put a finger to her lips. "A little quieter, Lily."

Lily nodded enthusiastically. "Sorry," she said, though her face said the exact opposite. "You should come dance with us." Her pronunciation of the words was slightly off from the average person, but the older Lily got, the easier she was to understand. Rose was so proud of all her wonderful daughter had accomplished.

"You should." Ken's deep voice came from over Rose's head and slowly, she looked up.

She was an adult. She could handle this. Her smile became one of cold politeness. "Maybe another time."

"No!" Lily stomped her foot. "Uncle Benny and Aunt Ally got married. You have to!" she whined.

"Now, Lily—" Rose began, but Lily started up again.

"You *never* dance," she complained. "Uncle Ken says he'll dance with you." She looked up. "Isn't that right, Uncle Ken? Don't you think my mama is beautiful enough to dance with?"

Rose was frozen in place. She couldn't look away from his intensely blue eyes, even to reprimand her daughter for being so forceful. Tantrums and demands were something new Lily had been trying out lately and Rose was struggling to hold her headstrong daughter back. This time, however, Lily had gone too far.

"I'd love to," Ken said, his voice huskier than before. He finally looked at Lily, allowing Rose to suck in a much needed breath. "Why don't you go sit with Aunt Charli?" he said, giving the little girl a gentle push in the direction of their friends. "She's too tired to dance because of the baby in her tummy. So, you keep her company while I take your mom to the dance floor."

Lily squealed in delight. "You're gonna have so much fun, Mama!" Without another word, she rushed over and hopped on Charli's husband, Bronson's lap. Rose followed her daughter's progress, too dumbfounded to speak.

Bronson gave them both a thumbs up, then promptly began playing a game with Lily.

"I think that's our cue," Ken said, taking Rose's hand and pulling her to her feet.

"I can't—"

"Yes, you can," Ken interrupted. His voice was firm but still soft. "One dance, Rose," he implored. "That's all I'm asking."

Her heart began to race when a slow song came on and goosebumps broke out across her skin when Ken grinned and pulled her in close. He kept them in the old-fashioned dance position, with one hand to the side, but Rose's hormones screamed that it wasn't enough.

"I feel like I've been bulldozed," she muttered, trying to break the spell that was quickly causing her to melt.

Ken chuckled, the sound reverberating through her. "Lily has that effect on people."

Rose furrowed her brows. "I don't think it was just Lily."

Ken shrugged, slowly turning them in a circle. "Think what you will, but she's the one who brought it up."

Rose sighed.

"Is it really that bad to dance with me?" Ken had never been the type to struggle with confidence and anyone who saw him in action as an officer could see that. But right now there was a vulnerability to his tone that nearly killed Rose.

"That's not it," she rasped.

He pulled her infinitesimally closer. "Then what is?"

Rose's bottom lip trembled, but she bit it between her teeth and looked away.

Ken huffed. "Why won't you let one of us in, Rose?" he pressed. "Even if it's not me." He pulled a little more and brought her temple to his cheek. "I just want to see you happy."

"I am happy." The lie tasted like bile. Her daughter was a ray of sunshine in her life and her friends were more like family, but Rose was never truly happy. She was too scared to be.

Ken shook his head ever so slightly. "Let me help."

Three simple words said in a quiet plea.

Yet they were enough to send Rose into a panic. She could lie to herself all she wanted, but Rose knew full well she had fallen in love with Captain Kenneth Wamsley. And it was that love that kept her away.

No one could protect her, but she could definitely protect him.

As soon as the music ended she pulled back. "Thank you for the dance," she said curtly. Spinning on her heel, Rose walked to her table and grabbed her purse. It jolted, letting her know she had a text.

Keeping an eye on Lily, Rose pulled out her phone and clicked on the icon.

You have something I want.

The church had been far too warm only two seconds ago, but now it felt like she'd been submerged in ice. Her head swung from side to side as she tried to see if she was being watched.

She had no idea how her ex-husband had found this number, but she knew it was the start of the end. She swayed slightly, her vision blurring as she realized she wasn't breathing.

Grabbing the table, Rose took in several large breaths.

"Rose, what is it?" Ken's voice was close to her ear.

"Lily," she choked out. "I have to get Lily."

Ken didn't move right away and Rose felt like she was about to scream when he finally said, "Hang on. I've got her."

The twenty seconds it took for him to come back were torturous, but Rose didn't have enough strength in her legs to go herself.

"Come on," Ken said, holding out his hand. He held Lily in one arm, up against his chest. "I'll take you home."

Love tried to overcome the panic and fear racing through her system, but Rose ruthlessly pushed it away. Love would get her or someone else killed. "I can do it," she said, reaching out for Lily.

Her daughter put up a fuss, but Rose was insistent.

"We'll see you another time. Thank you."

Leaving her heart and any chance at happiness behind, Rose walked away from her friends' wedding and the only people in her life who had ever truly cared for her.

Leaving would be horrible, but she had survived it once. She could survive it again.

CHAPTER 1

Rose felt like she hadn't slept in days. Every noise made her jump and her nerves were about to burst through her skin. After receiving the text from her ex-husband, she had had every intention of leaving Seaside Bay, but it hadn't been as easy as she'd planned.

The bags of clothes in her closet were old and Lily's bag held the wrong size. The food she had put away was close to expiring. The shop needed to be handed off to someone else and right now she didn't have a person to do that, since her only worker was on vacation.

In other words, she had gotten lazy. Lax. Unprepared.
Comfortable.

Rose sighed as she scrubbed the few breakfast dishes in her sink. Lily sat at the table, kicking her legs, completely at ease with the world around her as she waited for her mother to walk her to school.

Rose, on the other hand, was waiting for her world to end. The need to run was itching under her skin, but she kept hesitating. She could pack newer clothes. She could raid her pantry for fresher food. She could turn the 'closed' sign on the shop and never look back.

But she didn't want to.

Leaving the place where she had grown up and her family had been seemed far less difficult than leaving the place where she had created a family from the ground up. Leaving Caro, Brook, Genni and Charli, plus the others, was going to break Rose in a way she wasn't sure how to handle.

The knowledge that she might need to leave had always been in the back of her mind. But as time had passed, as her relationships had strengthened, as her friends had rallied around her over and over again, Rose found herself more and more conflicted about leaving it all behind.

Her hands hung limp in the cooling water, suds stuck on her wrists and arms as her mind replayed every moment of support and love she had experienced since showing up in Seaside Bay with almost nothing.

She saw the first time Charli had held Lily so that Rose could grab a nap.

The day Melody brought over smoothies because Rose hadn't eaten since the night before.

The moment Rose realized all her friends were learning pieces of sign language so they could "speak" to Lily who had been born deaf.

Tears dripped down Rose's face and into the cold water, the splash almost nonexistent against the banging of Rose's heart against her chest.

"Mama!"

Rose jerked and sniffed hard, wiping her face on her sleeve. She waited just a second to make sure her face was clear before turning around. "Yes?" She made her sure she was looking straight at Lily. The hearing aids helped, but reading lips was Lily's best way of communication.

"It's time to go," Lily said, in her slightly garbled tone. She pointed to the wall clock, a wide smile on her darling face.

Rose glanced up to confirm. "Okay," she said, keeping her plastic smile in place. She grabbed the prepared lunch, her purse and keys, and walked to the door. "Let's go!" Rose tried to make her voice sound extra perky. Whether they ended up running or not, she wanted to spare Lily as much of the heartbreak as possible.

She held out her hand and Lily skipped over, her red curls swinging with each hop. She grabbed her mother's hand and looked up, smiling like the porcelain doll she was.

Rose's heart pinched in pain. How could she do this to her daughter? Rip her from everything she'd ever known. From the idyllic childhood they had created in a small town on the Oregon coast.

From the home where they had been accepted without question or qualm. A lone, broken woman with a disabled baby.

It took more strength than Rose knew she had to keep her smile on her face as they walked down the stairs and onto the sidewalk. It was about a ten minute walk to the school and usually it was full of sunshine and smiles from everyone they passed. There wasn't a person or shop owner on Main Street that didn't love little Lily, and Lily loved each of them in return.

With each wave and greeting, Rose's heart broke a little more. *Maybe he doesn't know where we are yet. Maybe he just found the number.*

The thoughts were wishful thinking. Rose knew full well if he had her number, it was only a matter of time before he found where they were located. Too many things were traceable.

What if you just changed your phone?

"Morning, Lillers!"

Rose jerked her head upright.

Caro's friendly wave slowed. "Rose?" Caro frowned. "Are you all right?" She looked down and smiled and gave Lily a high five. "How's my favorite girl?" Caro signed carefully as she spoke.

Lily let go of her mother's hand to sign and answer back. Much to Rose's relief, their conversation carried on for several minutes.

Rose put her hand on her daughter's shoulder to get her attention. "We have to hurry," she spoke and signed. "School is going to start in just a few minutes."

Lily took her mother's hand and waved an enthusiastic hand at Caro. Caro waved back, but then her eyes went to Rose, her worry evident.

Rose pasted on a practiced smile and began to walk. She couldn't talk to anyone about this and Ken was already suspicious. Putting her head high, she kept up a purposeful walk all the way to school, dropping Lily off with a kiss and an internal prayer for safety.

Walking back to the apartment, Rose barely noticed when a car pulled into a parking spot right behind her.

"Rose!"

She stumbled slightly before righting herself. Her heart was racing in excitement, while her stomach churned in regret. This was definitely not what she needed this morning. Not when she was already struggling so hard to keep it together.

"Rose, please."

Squeezing her eyes shut, she slowly turned around. "Good morning, Captain."

Captain Kenneth Wamsley stood in the morning light like an avenging angel, yet it was a role Rose could never let him play. He put his hands on his hips, his aviator sunglasses keeping her from seeing whether he was angry or inviting, but the tightness of his shoulders told her all she needed. He took off his sunglasses, furthering her conviction that he was definitely angry. "I think we need to talk." His voice was low and strong.

Rose pulled her phone out and glanced at the screen as if looking at the time. "Actually, I have to get back to the apartment so I can freshen up and open the shop." Her fake smile faltered as his brows furrowed further.

"Don't make me do this in an official capacity, Rose."

She forced her pulse to stay inside her throat and pushed her eyebrows up in surprise. "What do you mean?"

Ken stepped forward, his stature allowing him to tower over her, blocking the morning sun. "I'd rather ask questions as your friend," he said. "But if you force me to, I can certainly use the badge, Rose. Your choice."

Her jaw clenched. "Have I done something wrong?" she asked tightly.

He slowly shook his head. "No. But I still have some questions."

"Fine." Rose spun on her heel. "Meet me at the shop in a half-hour," she tossed over her shoulder.

*****

Ken felt as if his chest were a hollow cave. Watching Rose walk away from him sent a shooting pain straight to his core. Something was wrong. He knew it. He just didn't know what *it* was.

He hated pulling the police officer card on her, but what else could he do? Something had spooked her at the wedding a couple days ago and he'd been sending extra patrols around her shop and apartment ever since.

Nothing suspicious had come up, but Rose's paranoia had certainly been plain. Each time she came outside, Ken or his officers noted that she seemed agitated. Her eyes never stopped moving. Her usual friendliness was stiff and she had been even more protective of Lily than usual.

If Ken knew Rose's backstory, he probably wouldn't be quite so worried about her, but no one in the entire town knew anything about Rose's life before she had arrived in Seaside Bay.

She'd shown up, newborn in arm, and opened a flower shop before anyone could figure out who she was. Between her beauty and her kindness, she'd quickly become an integral part of the community and no one had ever bothered to question her.

Ken had been too dazzled by the woman to push for answers. All these years, almost five of them, he'd watched her, losing his heart a little more each day. Not only was Rose the most beautiful woman he had ever seen, with an elegance that was unmatched, but she genuinely cared about people. Even when she had almost nothing to her name, she'd gone out of her way to help others. Particularly women.

It didn't matter if it was five dollars, a bouquet of flowers, a warm meal, or a soft bed, Rose was always willing.

As a single mom, her life couldn't have been easy, even with the help of the small town they lived in, but no one would ever be able to see that Rose struggled in any way, shape, or form. The woman was a saint and a rock all in one. She never faltered, never gave up, and never said no.

Except in one area of her life.

Ken was the only person Rose ever said no to. But as far as he knew, Ken was also the only man who continued to push for more than friendship.

With Rose out of sight, he slapped his sunglasses back on his face and got in his patrol car, going straight to the shop. She was more than likely hoping he would get busy and forget about coming to question her, but Ken was at the end of his rope.

He had seen genuine fear on her face at the wedding and it had been eating at him ever since. He loved her too much to let this go. For once in her life, Rose was the one who needed help and Ken wasn't about to let her go unassisted. It didn't matter if she never gave him a chance romantically. It didn't matter if he eventually had to watch her be with someone else. It didn't matter if Lily, whom he loved like a daughter, was never his.

Rose Ingalls needed him. And Ken wouldn't let her down.

He turned off the radio as he waited in the parking lot for Rose to arrive. He watched the front window, noting that she sighed in defeat when she saw him sitting outside. She turned the sign to 'OPEN', unlocked the door and walked away, leaving Ken to come in on his own.

A small bell rang above his head and he went inside, grateful that no customers had been waiting. "Rose?"

"I'm in the back," she called out.

Ken walked into the backroom where Rose did her arranging. "Is Susan still gone?"

Rose kept her back to him but nodded as she took some vases and buckets of flowers out of a cooler. "Yes. She'll be back in a couple of days."

Ken grabbed a chair and spun it around so he could straddle it. "Then I guess it's just us this morning."

"I suppose so," Rose murmured, still not meeting his eyes.

He desperately wanted her to look at him, but the fact that she wasn't, was just another sign that something was wrong. "Rose," he said softly. "What happened at the wedding?"

"I don't know what you're talking about," Rose said coolly.

Ken held back an eyeroll. "Don't lie to me."

Rose spun, her jaw dropping open. "What did you say to me?"

Ken stood up, unable to relax enough to sit down anymore. "I'm not stupid, Rose," he said in a fiercer tone than he meant to. He did his best to back off. "I'm asking, Rose...as a friend...for you to let me help." His heart nearly snapped in two when she turned away just before a tear trickled down her cheek. Before he could stop himself, Ken stepped forward and reached out to pull her chin back his way.

He'd never managed to touch her like this. Holding her on the dance floor was as close as he'd ever come. But there was something about the smooth, perfect lines of her face that felt more intimate than having his arms around her.

She must have been too shocked at his boldness because Rose didn't even try to pull away. Instead she turned her bright blue eyes up to Ken and froze.

Without permission, Ken found his thumb tracing her jawline. How could anyone's skin be that soft? Lily was often compared to a porcelain doll and it was no wonder when her mother looked perfect. But it wasn't Rose's looks that kept Ken's attention. It was her strength, determination, and goodness. The looks were only a bonus.

Right now, however, Ken was so caught up in the beautiful woman's spell that he almost forgot what he had come for. Slowly, ever so slowly, he pulled her chin up and brought his face down. The anticipation was as horrible as it was exciting. They were in new territory with each other.

Ken had definitely gotten the vibe that Rose had feelings for him, but she always held back. Right now though, her guard was obviously down.

"Rose," he whispered, the sound nearly inaudible. He could feel her rapid breathing wash over his face, the warmth of her mouth was almost—

Rose jerked back, breaking the connection and bringing Ken's mind back where it belonged. He cursed himself mentally. That wasn't what he'd come here to do. This woman made him lose his head. He groaned and pushed a hand through his hair. "Sorry," he croaked, then cleared his throat to get rid of the emotional tone in his voice.

Rose was standing several feet away, hugging her middle and looking far too frail. "Me too," she whispered.

Ken held out his hand and tried to step toward her, but when Rose tucked more into herself, he stopped. His fingers curled into a fist and dropped to his side. "I just want to help, Rose. It's obvious something is scaring you. You have friends here. Family. Let us do for you what you've done for so many of us."

Rose was shaking her head before he ever finished. "There's nothing anyone can do," she said, her voice slightly stronger, but still quiet.

"You don't know that—"

Rose held up a shaking hand, waiting until he stopped. "*You* don't know," she said tightly.

"Then tell me," Ken growled, his frustration once again mounting.

Rose straightened her shoulders and backed up a couple more steps. "Thank you for stopping by, Captain Wamsley," she said, sticking her chin in the air. "But my life is my own. I'll handle the problems that come along."

Ken could hear his teeth grinding as he worked his jaw back and forth. Stubborn woman. How could she throw away his help? Or anyone's for that matter? What in the world had her so scared that she felt she couldn't talk to anyone about it?

The idea of doing a background check on her flashed through his mind, but he dismissed it. He wanted Rose to come to him. He refused to violate her privacy that way without a true cause. Right now all he had was his concern as a man who was in love. Nothing a jury or judge would find credible.

Until she gave him no other choice, Ken would do his best to wait her out. "Fine," he said, stepping back toward the door in order to give her room. "But I'm here, Rose." His shoulders drooped. "I'm *always* here."

Turning quickly, he walked out. Every protective instinct and loving muscle in his body screamed he was going the wrong way, but what else could he do? She was right. This was her life. And if she never chose to let him in...then he'd just have to learn to live with that.

He just hoped she came to her senses before whatever had frightened her became a reality.

CHAPTER 2

Rose's hands hadn't stopped shaking since Ken left. She knocked over two pitchers of water during the day and ended up mopping the floor multiple times. It was probably the cleanest her floor had ever been.

Finally, she was able to turn the sign on the door to 'CLOSED' and take a deep breath. She'd made it through one more day. Lily was safe in the apartment with her nanny and Rose had an hour and a half before her arrangement class.

A deep weariness began to filter through her body. Rose had never cancelled the arrangement class before, not since starting it several years ago. She'd never taken a vacation, never closed the shop when it wasn't supposed to be closed. She'd stayed the course, made a good life for her and Lily. And now it was all for nothing.

With Ken pressuring her and the fear that Alexander was around every corner, Rose knew she couldn't continue to stay. She was going to have to pull roots and run. It was the only way.

Somehow she would make it up to Lily. She was young enough, she would forget in time...hopefully.

Rose glanced at the wall clock. If she hurried, she could still get a hold of everyone before they left. She walked to the front desk and pulled up her appointment calendar, making sure she had all the ladies coming for the evening, and slowly began working her way through the list.

It took a full hour to finish and some of the conversations had been more difficult than others. In particular, her friends.

Caro, Charli, and all the others had all tried to ask questions and Rose was a little concerned that eventually they would come give her grief about it. She would have to be quick.

Her eyes went to the ceiling and Rose said a quick prayer for courage. Lily wasn't going to understand, but maybe if Rose made it sound like they were playing a game, her young daughter would go along with it.

Rose walked to the back of the store and stepped into the alley so she could go up the stairs to her apartment. Before entering, she took a shaky breath, steadied her shoulders, and spread her lips into a semblance of a smile.

"Mama!" Lily ran to the door and wrapped her arms around her mother's legs. "I made a picture!" Dashing away before Rose could react, Lily grabbed a long piece of paper from off the dining table and brought it up, holding it proudly.

Rose had to bite her cheek to keep from crying. Tearing her baby away from the only home she'd ever known was more than she could bear, but everything, their very lives, may depend on it. "It's beautiful," she signed, squatting down to her daughter's level. "Let me talk to Mrs. Hennessey for a moment, okay?"

Lily nodded enthusiastically and skipped down the hallway to her room, more than likely to post her picture on her bulletin board.

Rose felt like an eighty-year-old woman as she straightened to her feet. Her whole body felt brittle, but she had to keep going. She had to. "Thank you, Mrs. Hennessey."

"Oh, it's always a joy," the elderly woman gushed. "Lily is just the sweetest thing." She began to gather her coat.

"Hold on," Rose said, grabbing her purse. "Let me get you paid."

Mrs. Hennessey paused. "I was paid last week," she said with a frown.

"I know," Rose replied. "But we'll be out of town for a bit, and I don't want to forget."

"Oh? Going somewhere fun?" Mrs. Hennessey put on her coat and waited while Rose counted the cash.

"Hm? Oh, yes. Somewhere fun." Rose looked up. "Here you go. I'll call when we get back."

Mrs. Hennessey took the money. "Thank you," she said with her usual warm smile. "I'll be excited to hear Lily's stories when you get back." She waved. "Night!"

"Goodnight," Rose responded. She quickly locked the door after the nanny had left.

"Mama?"

Rose turned from the door, her smile perfectly in place. "Guess what, sweetheart? We're going to go on a trip!"

Lily's baby blue eyes opened wide. "Really? Where?"

"What if we went somewhere warm?" Rose asked, doing her best to be enticing.

Lily frowned. "It's warm here."

"No...I mean much warmer." Rose walked over and crouched down again, stroking her daughter's silky skin. "Warm enough to wear your swimsuit all day."

"Can we go swimming?" Lily's hands were flying as she signed.

"Of course!" Rose stood and held out her hand. "Let's go get packed."

"When are we leaving?" Lily swung their hands as they walked down the hall.

Rose let go as they got to the hall closet and started pulling out suitcases. "Tonight," she said.

Lily squealed in a high pitched tone and bounced up and down. "Can I take Mr. Pinky?"

"Oh, we never go anywhere without Mr. Pinky," Rose assured her daughter. Rose walked over and grabbed the well-loved rabbit. His fur was all but gone and one of his eyes had been sewed back on, but there was no denying that he held a certain type of charm. The type that would only appeal to a small child.

Lily grabbed her favorite stuffed animal and held it close, the same place it had been for years. "Will Aunt Caro go with us?"

Rose's head shake was jerky, but somehow she managed it. "No. This will just be you and me." She tweaked her daughter's nose. "How does that sound?"

Lily shrugged. "What about Uncle Ken? He likes us. He'll miss us if we go."

Lily's innocent comment struck Rose's heart harder than a bullet. There was no denying that Ken would be upset about her leaving. He'd probably be furious. But hopefully once she was gone, he could eventually move on. He could marry some local girl who could give her heart away without worrying that the person she loved would end up hurt...or dead.

Rose's chest was tight as she answered. "Yes. I'm sure he will miss us. And we'll miss him. But it won't be forever." The white lie tasted bitter, but Lily was young. She would come to accept it in time. It was probably too much to hope that eventually she'd understand.

Lily pouted, her bottom lip hanging down. "I want Uncle Ken to go with us. He keeps us safe."

Rose froze. "Do we need Uncle Ken to keep us safe?"

Lily hugged Mr. Pinky. "He's big."

Rose nodded. "Yes, he is."

"He's strong."

Rose nodded again. "Yep."

Lily's eyes were wide and innocent. "Amy said her daddy keeps her family safe. Can't Uncle Ken keep us safe?"

How many times could one heart break before it ceased to function? Rose was sure hers would stop beating one of these days. It had been abused too many times. "That would be nice to have a daddy, wouldn't it?" Rose forced herself to say. "But don't worry." She knelt and hugged Lily. "We're big and strong too," she whispered against Lily's hair. "We can keep ourselves safe."

*****

Ken sat in his dark car, tapping his fingers against his steering wheel. Call it a policeman's intuition, or just the fact that he was in love with Rose, but something in his gut told him she was planning to run. The fact that her shop was dark on a night when she should have been holding an arrangement class only fed his concerns.

The problem was...Ken knew full well he didn't have any authority to keep Rose from leaving. She wasn't a criminal, nor was she his spouse. Ken had nothing but his own protective worry to fight her with. Well...that and the fact that he loved her, but she hadn't been listening to that argument for five years. Why would she start now?

Still, if she really was planning to run, Ken wanted to know why. He thought he deserved that at least. So did Caro, Charli, and everyone else in their group of friends. They deserved a chance to talk her out of it, or at least know why she would leave in the middle of the night the same way she had come into town.

Every bit of his protective instincts were screaming that something needed fixing and he wanted to know what. This is what he did. He fixed things. He put criminals behind bars. He stopped people from speeding. He protected the innocent.

That same instinct that told him Rose was going to run, told him she was just such an innocent.

His phone buzzed, taking his attention from the shop. Ken grabbed it and paused when he read the text. While he was reading, a call came through.

"Felix?" Ken answered, recognizing the number.

"Ken. I think we have a problem," Felix said, his tone more serious than usual.

"What's going on?" Ken sat up and prepared to start his car.

"Hadlee said Rose cancelled her flower class tonight."

Ken pinched his lips. "Yeah? Her shop is dark, so I wondered."

"You're at the shop?"

Ken nodded, then spoke out loud. "Yeah. Rose has been acting weird lately, so I've been doing extra patrols in her area."

"Weird? How?"

That was so like Felix. Straight to the point. That was part of why he and Ken got along so well. "Agitated. Jumpy. But she refuses to speak to me."

Felix huffed. "She's always refused to speak to all of us. It's not just you, Ken."

The words should have helped Ken feel better, but they didn't. There was something more personal about the fact that she held him at bay. The fact that he was almost positive Rose had feelings for him, yet still refused to let him in made this hurt much worse than just a friend clamming up.

"Yeah...sure," Ken responded.

"Ken..." Felix drawled. "Come on, man. Don't let it get to you. Right now we're all worried about a friend. Let's keep it at that for the moment."

"I know."

"So what are we going to do?"

Ken's phone buzzed again. "Hang on. I've got another call." He switched over without seeing who it was. "Captain Ken Wamsley."

"Ken? It's Charli."

Ken sighed. "Hey, Charli. I've got your brother on the other line."

"Good. I think we all need to talk. Are you at the station?"

"No. I'm camped out in front of Rose's shop."

"Perfect. Hang on. We're coming."

Her line went dead and Ken held in an eye roll as he switched back. "It sounds like Charli is gathering the gang. I think she's bringing them here."

"Apparently, Hadlee isn't the only one concerned. We'll see you in a few."

"See ya." Ken hung up and dropped the phone in the passenger seat. His fingers immediately went back to drumming, only the beat was faster now. He wasn't sure how he felt about this becoming a community affair, but since Rose had kicked him out of the shop, he probably needed all the help he could get. Maybe one of the girls would be able to get through in a way he hadn't.

It took a good fifteen minutes for everyone to arrive, but soon they were blocking the sidewalk as most of the crew huddled into a group. Only a handful of them were missing. It took another ten for Ken to explain what he knew.

Caro folded her arms over her chest and tapped her foot impatiently. "Just what are we going to do here? We've let her go too long without telling us everything."

"We did it because we love her," Charli shot back. "We can't go in there and just demand her backstory. Rose'll jet for sure."

"She's got a child," Hadlee inserted. "She can't just run."

Felix put a hand on his wife's neck and rubbed soothingly. "If what we're thinking is true," he said in a low tone, "she ran here with a child. I don't know that Lily will hold Rose back. In fact, as a mother, she might be even more determined to get somewhere safe."

"Here is safe," Caro shouted.

Her husband, Jack, put an arm around her shoulders. "No one is disputing that, Caro. But if Ken's intuition is right, something frightened her and she doesn't feel safe anymore."

Caro wiped at her eyes. "We can't let her leave. We just can't. We'll take care of whatever it is."

Ken held up a hand. "While I appreciate the sentiment, we need to be careful here." He raised an eyebrow at Caro. "None of you have any authority to do anything but be her friend. If there's any protecting to do, it falls to me and my office."

Caro huffed, but didn't argue.

"I don't want to have to arrest anyone for overstepping their boundaries."

Caro made a face. "I make no promises," she said.

Ken shook his head, but didn't say anything further. He couldn't blame Caro for her words. Even if he wasn't a police officer, he would feel the same. Luckily, he had the law on his side.

Hadlee stepped forward again. "I think maybe we need to talk to Rose," the scientist said softly. "Law or not, this is all her decision. We have no right to hold her to anything if she feels she's acting in the best interest of her family."

Heads nodded around the group.

"Come on." Caro tilted her head toward the back of the building. "You didn't see her leave, did you Ken?"

Ken shook his head. "No. She closed up and, I'm assuming, went home. I wasn't watching the back."

"Her car is out here," Jensen pointed out. "If she's planning to leave, she'll need it."

"Right." Caro started marching. She was definitely the shortest of their group, but her spunky personality more than made up for her petite stature. Everyone else scurried to catch up as they went to the back of the building and began climbing the stairs.

Ken forced himself to stick to the back of the group. Rose wouldn't be happy to see him. He knew that. But he wasn't about to sit this out. Someway, somehow, he had to get through to her. She didn't need to carry this burden alone. Ever. And even if she didn't want to explore the chemistry between them, he would still be her friend and help her.

He just prayed for once that she would listen.

CHAPTER 3

"Okay. Looks like we're ready to go," Rose signed just before finishing zipping the last suitcase. She'd packed all she could think of that would get them started. It was more than she'd had when she came to Seaside Bay.

The next step would be getting rid of her phone and cutting all ties to Seaside Bay so that nothing could be forwarded in her new direction. A searing pain nearly split her chest in half.

Closing her eyes, Rose breathed deeply through her nose, trying to ease the sensation. The first time she'd run, she'd been scared. This time it wasn't just fear, it was heartache. There'd been nothing left for her in Boston. Now she was leaving everything.

Sniffing back tears, Rose reached out one hand to Lily and grabbed the biggest suitcase. "Why don't we run down to the shop and put together a couple of gifts. Then we'll go, hm?"

Lily nodded eagerly. "Gifts for who?" she signed, yawning as she did so. It was past her bedtime at this point, but that only meant the little girl would sleep in the car, making Rose's job easier.

"For Aunt Caro and Uncle Ken and everyone else." They walked into the family room. "We'll make everyone a small bouquet so they won't miss us as much." One of the few things Rose took pride in was her ability to speak in flowers. She had become a serious student of the language and her friends had all been recipients of it at one point or another.

While Rose might not be able to leave a forwarding address, it wouldn't hurt to take twenty minutes to put together a few flowers to send them a message. One of gratitude, friendship...and love. Maybe it would ease the shock of her disappearance.

"I want to give Uncle Ken a rose," Lily signed excitedly.

Rose nodded. "Sure. We can do that." She set down the suitcase and began to reach for the doorknob when she heard voices on the other side. An immediate panic ran through her and Rose gasped, dragging Lily away from the door.

"Rose?" a voice called out, followed by a strong knock. "It's Caro! We need to talk to you."

Rose's eyes fluttered as all the adrenaline that had just shot through her system immediately began to drain. She hated being so fearful. Still...even though it was Caro, Rose knew she couldn't open the door. Trying to explain why there were several suitcases packed and ready to go wouldn't be easy, and Caro wouldn't buy the story of a vacation. She knew Rose too well.

Lily, however, had other ideas. For the first time in her life, Rose found herself frustrated at how well the child's hearing aids worked, when the five-year-old threw open the door without a moment's hesitation, all before Rose could stop her. "Aunt Caro!" Lily threw herself at the petite candy maker.

Caro smiled brilliantly down and immediately picked Lily up, putting the girl on her hip. "How's my Lillers? Did you have a good day at school?" Caro spoke slowly and faced Lily, since she didn't have two hands to sign with.

Lily nodded and began talking loudly.

Rose's eyes widened as the doorway behind Caro began to fill up and more and more people filed into her small apartment. "What's going on?" she whispered hoarsely. Her heart nearly stopped altogether when Ken stepped in and closed the door behind him. His golden brown eyes met hers and locked into place.

"Rose." Charli spoke hesitantly, which wasn't like the bold woman at all. She stepped forward, wringing her hands. "We're worried about you. We wanted to come and offer our help."

Rose frowned and forced herself to look away from Ken. Gathering her wits, she prepared herself for the performance of a lifetime. "Help? What do you mean?"

Before anyone could answer, Rose pressed on.

"Is this because I cancelled class?" Her laugh was stiff to anyone who bothered to pay attention, but it was all Rose could manage. "I just needed a break for the night. I've been doing that class for years, you know. Once in a while even the arranger needs a break."

Caro's lips were nearly white as she pinched them together. "Lillers," she said, turning back to Lily. "Can you go read in your room for a bit? I need to speak to your mom."

Lily must have started to pick up on the tension in the room because her bottom lip trembled as she looked around. The whole front room was full of people that she loved and who adored her in return. They were the only family the child had ever known. Those bright blue eyes went over the crowd until they met Ken. "Uncle Ken?" Lily asked, her voice much softer than normal.

Ken pushed from the back and held out his arms. "Come on, Peach."

Lily went willingly into his arms. The sight of the large man cuddling the tiny child stole Rose's breath. She wasn't strong enough to do this. She couldn't pull Lily away from everyone and everything. The chances of them finding this kind of support group again were slim to none.

But are your lives worth the risk? Are theirs?

The words were a sobering reminder of why Rose needed to be strong. Alexander would never stop. Rose knew that. The law hadn't been enough to stop him before, and the odds were it wouldn't be enough now. If she stayed, Rose knew she was risking not only her own life, but that of her daughter and that of her friends. Anyone who stood up for her would be considered a target.

It was a wonder she was still upright and breathing.

Her legs, at that moment, decided she couldn't be upright anymore and Rose's knees buckled.

"Whoa!" Bronson, Charli's husband, leapt forward and caught Rose. "Hang on. Let's get you to the couch," he said kindly.

"Thank you," Rose whispered. They were only a few feet from her sofa, so it didn't take long for Rose to be sitting.

Her eyes were unfocused as the group slowly settled in around her. When the seat to her left sunk down, Rose didn't bother to look at who it was, but the instant heat from the person caught her attention.

"Mama," Lily whispered.

Looking over, Lily was tucked under Ken's chin, her face red with tears and one arm reaching out. Rose took her daughter's hand, still feeling disconnected from her own body, but it was enough for the little girl.

They must have made quite a picture, but Rose had no time to enjoy it, since Caro pressed on.

"Rose. We love you. We're here for you. But you *have* to tell us what's going on."

Rose closed her eyes and sighed. "I can't, Caro."

"Can't or won't?"

Rose looked up and met Caro's determined gaze. "Both."

*****

Ken kept his mouth shut, but it was hard. Lily was burrowed into his chest and he could feel her tiny body reacting to the overwhelming emotions in the room. Instead of arguing the way he wanted to, he rubbed her back and stayed quiet. When the right time presented itself, he would intervene, but for now he would let the others handle it.

"At least tell us why, Rose," Caro argued. "We're your friends. Your family. We want to help."

Rose shook her head. "No one can help," she rasped.

Caro snorted. "That's where you're wrong. We *always* help each other."

"Rose," Charli spoke up. "You know as well as the rest of us that when things get tough, we work together to overcome it." She tilted her head and waited for Rose to acknowledge the truth of that statement. "Then tell us why you feel that you can't share with us. Do you not trust us?"

Rose's face contorted into something painful. "Not trust you? Really? After all we've been through together?"

Charli held her arms out, palms up. "What do you expect us to think? You've never told us where you came from before you arrived in Seaside Bay. And because we trust and value you, we've never pushed you about it. But now it's obvious something's wrong. Something you're refusing to share. If you trusted us, wouldn't you let us help?"

Rose's head was shaking harder and harder at this point, anger starting to mix with the simmering emotions of the room.

"Peach," Ken whispered in Lily's ear. "Will you turn off your hearing aids for me?"

Lily leaned up and frowned. "Why?" she asked.

Ken gave her a reassuring smile. "Sometimes grownups have to talk about things that are hard for children. I promise to hold you and keep you safe. But will you do that for me?"

Lily's frown remained. "You'll keep me safe?"

Ken nodded.

"And Mama too?"

He nodded again.

Lily reached up and fiddled with her hearing aids, then tucked herself back into his chest. It wasn't until she was lying back down that Ken realized the whole room had stopped to listen to their exchange. He supposed it was hard to speak to a deaf person without catching attention.

Rose's eyes were red-rimmed as she looked at him. "You can't promise her those things," she said thickly.

"What? That I'll keep her safe?" Ken asked incredulously.

Rose nodded.

His own anger mounting, Ken leaned in. "I don't know what's going on, Rose, but if you think for one moment that I wouldn't give *everything* to keep Lily or yourself safe, then you haven't bothered to get to know me very well."

"I believe you," Rose stammered back. "The problem is, I won't let you."

"Rose." Bronson, who was normally very easy going, was scowling heavily. "You're making it sound like by keeping quiet, you're protecting us."

After a moment's hesitation, Rose nodded. "I am."

The room broke out in loud arguments and Ken was more grateful than he could say that Lily had turned off her hearing aids. She could probably hear a tiny amount of the noise, but she wouldn't be able to understand any of it. He rubbed her small back, reveling in the feel of her in his arms. If things went south, this might be his last time playing father to this little girl, and his future looked more than bleak if that was the case.

"Who is Lily's father?"

The loud question brought the entire room to a halt. It took Ken a split second to realize he was the one who had actually asked the question. It was something he had asked himself many times, but never had the guts to bring up to Rose. Now, however, it was the best lead-in he had as to why Rose was running.

Rose's face paled but she didn't answer.

"We all see the suitcases, Rose," Ken said, making sure to keep his tone as calm as possible. He didn't want Lily any more upset. "You showed up here without warning and now you're leaving without warning. Obviously there's someone in your past who's haunting you. Someone who has a hold over you." He raised a challenging eyebrow. "I might not be a big city cop, but I know a few. In cases like this, it's most likely an ex or a child's parent. Which is it?"

Rose was practically vibrating, she was shaking so hard. "Both," she said through a clenched jaw.

"You were married?" Charli clarified.

Rose jerked at the question. "Of course. How could you think otherwise?"

"You've never told us anything," Charli defended herself. "And lots of women have children without being married."

Rose scowled. "And after all this time, that's what you think of me? That I would live that kind of lifestyle?"

Hadlee leaned forward. "No, Rose. But we only know the Rose from Seaside Bay. We've never met the Rose from your previous life." She held up a hand before Rose could argue. "Who you were before doesn't change how much we love this Rose, but that doesn't mean they weren't two different people."

Rose's shoulders straightened ever so slightly. "Well, they are two different people. Once upon a time I allowed others to dictate my life. Now, I own it. And since I get to make those decisions, I've decided Lily and I need to move. It's in everyone's best interest."

Arguing broke out again and Ken sighed. This wasn't helping anything. "Why won't you let my office help you?" he said, turning his head toward Rose.

Rose's face could only be described as defeated. "Because not everyone abides by the law."

"That's why I'm here. We take care of those who don't," Ken pressed.

She shook her head. "Only if you have proof."

Caro was suddenly kneeling at Rose's feet. "Rose," she said tightly. "I'm begging you. As a friend, as a *sister*, to reconsider this. If this phantom ex tracked you here, who's to say he won't track you at the next place you'll go?"

Rose dropped her gaze to her lap. "Then I'll just have to keep moving."

"And is that the life you want for Lily?"

Rose's cheeks flared red. "What kind of question is that? Of course, it's not. But if it keeps her safe, then I'll do it."

Caro nodded slowly. "And we understand that, but where does it end? When does she get to simply grow up? Or find roots and friendship?" Caro shook her head. "You can't maintain that kind of lifestyle forever, Rose." Caro grabbed Rose's hands and squeezed them tight. "Here you have support. Friends. Even law enforcement on your side. Please, I am begging you to stay. If not for yourself, then for Lily. You don't have to tell us everything, but at least here you're not alone. Here you have people to keep an eye out, to report suspicious strangers, people to run to in the middle of the night without question." Her big blue eyes filled with tears. "Here you're not alone no matter what. Please. *Please!* Give it a little more time. You know I would never ask you to risk Lily's life, but I feel with everything in me that you will never be safer than you are here."

The entire room seemed to collectively hold their breaths. Caro's speech was exactly what Ken was hoping would happen tonight. He needed someone to be able to break through Rose's icy exterior, someone she wasn't holding at arm's length. Caro was the perfect person to do that.

Tears dribbled down Rose's cheeks, but Ken kept his hands to himself. This wasn't about his feelings at the moment. It took a full minute before Rose answered, though it felt like an eternity.

"For now," she said hoarsely. "I can't guarantee I'll stay forever, but for now, I can see you're right."

Caro got up on her knees and threw her arms around her friend. Soon Ken had to scoot away so the women could have their little hugfest without smothering him and Lily. It was heartbreaking and wonderful at the same time. The outcome was good, but they were still no closer to getting Rose to tell them anything.

One step at a time.

He forced himself to take deep breaths and keep soothing Lily. The small victory of keeping her in town would have to be enough...for now.

CHAPTER 4

Rose did her best to stay focused through the next couple days of work, but it was difficult. Part of her was regretting giving Caro her word that she would stick around town. She had managed to avoid spilling her backstory to everyone, but it had come at a cost.

Despite still being edgy and ready to run, the rational part of Rose knew her friend was right. There was nowhere else on this Earth that Rose would be as protected as she was in Seaside Bay. Complete strangers would be far less likely to help Rose, if she needed it, than her friends in Seaside Bay.

On the other hand, Rose was less worried about strangers being hurt in the process. Her friends were fair targets.

No matter how many customers she helped or how many flowers she arranged, Rose's mind couldn't seem to settle. She flip-flopped between running and staying all day long.

Luckily, she hadn't had any more ominous text messages. Rose was positive that if Alexander had sent her any more notes, she wouldn't be able to stop herself from running, promise or not. For now, she had turned off GPS tracking and doubled her prayers that that was enough.

A flash of blue caught her eye as she helped check out a customer and Rose pinched her lips together. Every ten minutes or so, she saw a police car drive by. Ken had been deadly serious when he said he would do anything to keep her and Lily safe. And apparently, he was using every resource at his disposal. Including his patrol officers.

Rose wasn't sure whether she should be angry or flattered. She wasn't ready to admit it out loud, but she was just as bad as Lily. Ken made her feel safe. Just his presence in a room made her feel better, but at the same time, it only gave her one more person to be worried about.

If something were to happen to Ken while he was trying to protect her, Rose wasn't sure she'd be able to survive it.

Her ex-husband, Alexander, had been a suave businessman who had swept Rose off her feet and flattered her with gifts and compliments until Rose's head had spun.

After the mega wedding and a long, luxurious honeymoon, life had settled into a more normal routine and it wasn't until then that Rose realized something...she wasn't in love with Alexander. She was dazzled. In awe. And truthfully, completely fooled.

At first she had tried to ignore it. She had put her time and attention into making him happy, into building an emotional connection that she seemed to be lacking. Surely she could love someone who threw everything money could buy at her.

But it didn't work.

Another flash of blue brought Rose out of her maudlin thoughts. It was better not to get stuck in the past. This time she was grateful for the distraction. As she rearranged the vases in her display case, Rose noted that the patrol car hadn't passed by. It was parked across the street. That could only mean one thing.

Ken was in the car.

Sighing, Rose closed the display case door. Noting that she had no customers at the moment, she headed to the back and grabbed a bottle of Gatorade out of her mini kitchen. Keeping one eye on her door for customers, she walked across the street and knocked on the dark window. It made a soft humming sound as it slowly descended.

"Ms. Ingalls," Ken said formally.

Rose rolled her eyes. "I think we're past that, aren't we?" She held out the Gatorade. "Thought you could use a refresher."

A small smile quirked on his lips and it sent a little thrill through Rose's stomach. "Thanks," he said. That deep voice of his was deliciously smooth and right now Rose was feeling like a ridiculously young fangirl rather than the mature adult she was.

Feelings like this were something she had always dreamed of, yet never felt with Alexander. How unfair was it that she finally found the perfect man, but giving into him would mean risking not only hers, but Ken's life in the process.

"I'm starting to get the feeling that you're spending more time driving past my shop than behind your desk," Rose teased, raising an eyebrow at him.

Oh my...

A soft pink blush crept up Ken's neck and the tips of his ears turned red. What was it about a big strong man looking like a kid that was so attractive to the female population?

"Things are pretty slow right now," he hedged. "I figured it wouldn't hurt to make sure you were taken care of."

"And how do your officers feel about that?"

He chuckled. "Taking turns watching a beautiful woman? Not a one have complained."

This time it was Rose's turn to blush and her lily-white skin showed it off all too well. "Aren't all your officers married?" she shot back.

Ken's grin grew. "Yes. Which is why I know I can trust them around you."

"You're incorrigible," Rose huffed.

He shrugged. "There are worse things."

"Ken," Rose said seriously. "You don't need to do this."

"I know," he answered gently. "But I want to."

"I don't expect my friends to set aside their own lives for whatever might or might not be coming," Rose argued.

"You were pretty sure something was coming the other night," Ken pointed out.

Rose paused. "Yeah...I suppose you're right. But that doesn't mean I want you all involved."

"We're your friends, Rose. We're involved whether you want us to be or not."

Rose had no response for that. She knew her friends and she knew he was right. Any of them would go out on a limb for her. "What if I don't want you to be involved?"

His brows furrowed over his glasses. "Why not?"

Rose had to choose her words carefully. If she let him know what her ex was capable of, Ken would only go into a stronger protection mode, not ease off. But she couldn't tell him how much he meant to her. She couldn't tell him that the idea of him being hurt, hurt her worse than anything else she could think of besides losing Lily. "Because I'll be fine," she finally lied.

Ken shook his head slowly. "If you were going to be fine, why were you so dead set on leaving? What would be the point if you were going to be *fine?*" An edge of frustration was leaking into his tone. "What about Lily? Will she be fine?"

"That's not fair," Rose snapped. "You don't have the right to bring my daughter into this as if you care about her more than I do."

Ken grabbed the handle of the door and slightly opened it, waiting for Rose to move aside so he could step out. He didn't speak until he was standing over her, his bulk blocking the sun and his glasses blocking the emotion Rose was sure was in his eyes.

"And you don't have the right to tell me who I can or can't care about."

Rose swallowed hard. She shouldn't do it. She couldn't ask it. It would only hurt more. "And just who do you care about?"

*****

This was the type of opening Ken had been waiting for for years. Only he hadn't planned on it happening out in public with cars and pedestrians swirling around them. Why couldn't it have happened in a location where they were alone, and he could take full advantage of her question? "I think you know the answer to that," he said softly. His hands clenched into fists to keep from touching her.

Rose fell back just slightly until she was leaning against the patrol car. "We can't do it," she rasped.

"Give me one good reason why." Okay, apparently they were doing this here. He watched her swallow, the movement audible even with the noise of the town around them.

"I can't."

"Can't what? Can't give me a reason? Or can't give in to what you feel?" He'd never pressed her like this, but something in Ken's gut told him time was running out. He was going to lose her...and Lily...if he didn't make a move. Why was this woman so stubborn? What could have her so frightened that she refused to acknowledge what was between them?

"Both."

Ken sighed and pushed a hand through his hair. "That's not good enough, Rose. I've been patient. Heaven knows I've been patient. But now you're threatening to run and I..." He put his arms on either side of her, gripping the edge of the car and hanging his head in between. "I don't know how to let you go."

Rose's hand was slightly clammy as she reached out to cup his cheek and pull him up until he was looking at her. He could feel her fingers shaking, but nothing had ever felt so amazing as her touching him. "I'm sorry," she whispered. "I wish I could give you everything. But I can't."

"Tell. Me. Why," he ground out.

Rose's hand fell and Ken immediately mourned its loss. She turned away, refusing to look him in the eye. "I need to get back to the shop. I'm still by myself and I haven't been paying attention to whether or not someone went inside." She cleared her throat and shifted her body, waiting for him to move his arms.

Ken deflated, and obeyed. His arms fell to his side. She started to move when he finally found his voice. "I won't give up, Rose." He didn't touch her, but he didn't have to. He knew she could feel the pull between them as much as he could. Her ability to walk away, however, was much stronger than his. "What we have is rare and beautiful. I love Lily like my own daughter and whenever you give the word, I'll show you exactly how I feel for you as well."

His eyes tracked her as she darted back across the street and disappeared behind the glass doors of her store. She wouldn't come out again today. She wouldn't risk another emotional encounter such as the one they'd just had.

Ken knew this because he knew he could only handle so much before he broke, and even as strong as she was, Rose also had a breaking point. He'd seen himself get close to it several times over the years, but always he had held back just enough to keep from cracking through her wall. He didn't want Rose because he broke her. He wanted her to choose to break the wall herself.

He didn't mind thinning it and making it easy for her to step outside its boundaries, but what good was love and affection if not freely given?

His radio squawked and Ken swore under his breath as he slipped back into his car. "This is Captain Wamsley," he said into the mic.

"Cap, we've got a fender bender out on Powerline Road. No reported injuries, but apparently both of the involved parties are sure they aren't at fault."

Ken sighed. "On it. I'll be there in five." Buckling up, he threw the car into reverse and made his way to the residential neighborhood.

It took forty-five minutes for him to clear things up and get people on their way. Tired, hot, and ready to go home, Ken got back in his car and started to head to the station for lunch.

He glanced down, seeing the bottle of Gatorade, and paused. Growling at himself, he turned right instead of left and cursed himself the whole time as he drove all the way through town, being sure to pass Rose's shop before he landed back at the station. He was an idiot. Why couldn't he just let her go?

Why did this whole situation have to be personal for him? He could protect her as a friend, as an officer of the law, but it was more than that and he wasn't sure how to separate the two.

She'd been holding him off for years, but instead of doing the smart thing and letting it go, Ken was obviously too dumb for his own good because he kept coming back for more. Rejection after rejection. No matter how many times she walked away, he stayed put.

If he was smart, he would learn to keep his emotions on a tight leash.

Yet even as he pulled into his assigned parking spot, he knew he'd never manage it. Rose was too deep inside of him and he knew, he *knew*, it was reciprocated. Someday, he would figure out what was keeping them apart, but until then...he'd just go on being a fool.

CHAPTER 5

"Mama?"

Rose's head jerked up. "Yes, sweet pea?"

Lily was sitting at their little dining table, her legs kicking beneath her. "Why aren't you happy?"

Rose froze, her wooden spoon pausing in mid air. "What?"

Lily's bottom lip popped out. "You never smile."

As if to refute her claim, Rose pushed her mouth out to the sides. "I smile. See?"

Lily shook her head. "You look weird."

The grimace fell and Rose sighed. "Sorry, hon. Mama's had a lot on her mind lately."

Lily scrunched up her tiny nose. "And it's making you sad?"

How to answer? Lily was too young to understand, but obviously she wasn't oblivious. "No. Not sad," Rose began. "Just...busy. Sometimes mamas get busy and they forget to have fun."

"We can have fun tonight," Lily signed, perking up in her seat. "Aunt Caro will have fun with us."

Rose actually did smile this time, though it was small. "Of course she would. But Aunt Caro is a busy woman. She might not have time for us tonight."

Lily shook her head. "Aunt Caro always has time for us. And treats. She always has treats for us."

Rose huffed a laugh. "I see. You don't want Aunt Caro. You just want the desserts she makes."

Lily shrugged. "They're good."

Rose nodded. "Yeah...they are." She went back to stirring the pasta. Caro made absolutely delectable desserts, but none of them would ever give Rose nearly as much pleasure as being close to Ken Wamsley did. That man ought to come with a warning label. How different her life would be if she had met him first. If she hadn't been born on the East Coast. If she had left for college instead of falling into the hands of a madman.

Her eyes darted to the side. *But then you might not have Lily. And she was worth it all.*

Memories of her time with Alexander had been flooding Rose's brain lately. She'd done such a good job of blocking those thoughts for the past five years, but now with that text making her edgy, it seemed she'd lost all control.

She'd flirted with and touched Ken, for one thing. That had opened a whole can of worms Rose wasn't sure how to handle. And every time things got quiet, her mind went back to *before.* Before she was divorced. Before Lily was born. Before she knew what love truly was.

Her brain was going to implode one of these days. How could one body hold so many turbulent emotions? There were times when she was sure she was going to burst apart from the constant struggle of it all.

Those were the times when it was hardest to ignore Ken's offer to help. When she was tired and wanted to set down the load and let someone else carry it for a while. But she couldn't. She couldn't risk someone else getting too involved and becoming a target.

Ken's words yesterday were still floating through her mind and Rose wanted to grasp them and hold them close. She wanted to let him help. She wanted to feel his arms around her the way he wrapped them around Lily. To let him scare all the monsters away and make her feel safe.

But that wasn't realistic.

She wasn't a five-year-old girl who trusted so easily and didn't re-alize monsters were more than creatures in a picture book.

A tug on her shirt brought Rose back to the present and she looked down to see Lily frowning. "Aunt Caro is coming."

Rose jerked a little. "What? How?"

Lily held up Rose's phone. "I texted."

Rose's eyes grew wide and she scrambled for the phone.

Mama iz sad.

Sure enough, the text had been sent to Caro's number. It had quickly been answered.

I'm on my way.

"Lily," Rose said carefully, trying to contain her ire. "When did you learn to text?"

Lily scrunched her nose. "I don't know."

Rose hung her head. How did children pick up on things so quickly? Lily could barely read, yet she had managed to send off a text to Rose's best friend. Now Rose understood all those jokes about kids teaching their parents about technology. "Lily. Next time, please don't use Mama's phone without permission, okay?"

Lily's bottom lip trembled. "I'm sorry," she signed.

Rose deflated and fell to her knees, opening her arms. It took all of point-two-seconds for Lily to throw herself in them.

"I don't like it when you're sad," Lily blubbered against her mother's shoulder. The words were barely understandable between the tears and her natural way of speaking, but Rose caught them anyway and they reached deep inside of her.

Something needed to change. She couldn't live life like this. Lily couldn't live life like this. But what to do? Leaving wouldn't necessarily bring them any more peace than they had, Rose would just be looking over her shoulder the whole time. Staying brought the possibility of happiness, but the reality of putting those she loved in danger.

How could one person be expected to survive this?

A knock on the door had Lily straightening up and wiping her nose on the back of her hand. "Aunt Caro!"

"Wait!" Rose stopped her daughter from opening the door. Instead, she carefully walked over and put her ear to it. "Caro?"

"It's freezing tonight, Chica. Better open up or I'm not sharing these truffles."

Rose sighed and unlocked the deadbolt, letting in her friend. Caro immediately swallowed Rose in a tight hug.

"You and I will talk later," Caro threatened in a whisper. She pulled back and her eyebrows rose in expectation.

Rose nodded in defeat. "All right."

Caro's smile was almost a smirk of triumph. She spun and held her arms wide for Lily. "Where's my best girl who always eats my chocolate?"

Lily jumped up and down with her hands clasped at her chest. "Me!"

"Perfect!" Caro took Lily's hand and they began to walk toward the couch. "Have you had dinner yet?"

Lily shook her head. "No."

"Even more perfect," Caro said through a giggle. "That makes chocolate taste even better."

Rose went to the stove and turned off the overcooked pasta. As scared as she was, she was grateful Caro was there. She couldn't tell her friend everything, but Rose needed help. It had never been more clear than now that she couldn't do this on her own. Lily...and Rose herself...deserved more.

*****

The knock on his office door made Ken want to break something. Why couldn't everyone just leave him alone?

"What?" he roared, not bothering to look up.

The door creaked open. "Are you going to shoot if I come in?"

Ken looked up and sighed. "Hey, Felix."

Felix came in the rest of the way and closed the door behind him. After settling in a chair, he folded his arms over his stomach and stared Ken down.

"What?" Ken made a face.

"I'm trying to decide what's going on in that granite head of yours."

Ken huffed and shook his head. "Well, when you figure it out, be sure and let me know."

"Talk to me."

Ken glanced up. "What?"

Felix leaned forward onto his knees. "Come on, Cap. You're so tightly wound that somebody is gonna get a bullet in them before the end of the week if you don't let out some of that steam."

Ken just stared.

Felix, who was known for being the stern person in their group, softened. "We're worried about you," he said. "And judging from the amount of gratitude I got as I walked back here, it was with good reason."

Ken threw his pen down on the desk and leaned back. "Yeah? And just what have my men been saying?"

Felix put his hands in the air, straightening his back. "I'm not here to get anyone in trouble. I'm here because I'm worried about a friend."

"I'm not the friend that needs help."

Felix nodded slowly. "And we're working on helping Rose as well. With as stubborn as the two of you are, it's a wonder you haven't both imploded by now."

Ken shook his head. "It doesn't matter. Rose is the one who needs help. Save your speeches for her."

"I'm letting the women give Rose the heavy words. In fact, Jack texted that Caro is over there tonight. Something about Lily asking for help."

Ken shot to his feet. "What? What does Lily need?"

Felix once again put his hands up. "Ken. She's taken care of. Sit down."

Ken obeyed, but his whole body was stiff. "Explain."

"I don't know it all, but Lily asked Caro to come over and she went. If they need more help than that, I'm sure Caro will let us know." Felix chuckled. "It's not like Caro's shy about handling that kind of thing."

Ken forced his back to bend slightly. He knew Felix was right, but he wanted to be the one there. Now more than ever. He couldn't sleep. He couldn't focus. He couldn't get himself to do anything without thinking about Rose and how he could save her.

Felix whistled low under his breath. "Man...and I thought I had it bad. I can't imagine what it's like looking at it with a policeman's perspective."

"I'm not worried about her because I'm a cop," Ken growled. "I'm worried about her because..." He cut off. Those weren't words Felix needed. The person they were meant for didn't want them, and Ken wouldn't give them to anyone else.

"Because you're in love with her," Felix said on a sigh. "I know. We all know." He frowned. "We've all been watching the two of you for years. I gotta tell ya, I think Rose feels the same."

Ken fought the blush that made his ears burn when he was embarrassed. He hadn't thought about the fact that his horrible love life had been on display for their entire group of friends since the dawn of time. Nothing said "I'm a man" like being rejected every day for five years straight. "Yeah, well, if she does, she has a funny way of showing it."

Despite those harsh words, Ken knew full well he wasn't ready to give up. He was certain that Rose only held him off because she was scared. But of what? That was the million dollar question and had an answer that not a single person, other than Rose herself, knew.

"Take it easy," Felix said. "I know you're hurt. But I'm sure Rose has her reasons."

Ken snorted and went back to the paperwork on his desk. He didn't want to talk about this anymore.

"When's your break?"

Ken shook his head. "I got off duty a couple hours ago."

"I thought so. Come on."

Ken watched his friend stand up and head to the door. "What?"

"Come on," Felix pressed. "You need to step away from all this."

"And do what? Go home to an empty cabin?" Ken wanted to bite his rude tongue. Felix was trying to help. He knew that. But right now, Ken didn't care. He was so fed up with waiting, worrying, wondering. Rose didn't trust him. He wasn't sure why, but Rose didn't trust him with the truth and it was eating Ken up from the inside out. He couldn't save her if he didn't know what was going on. He couldn't even count how many times he had to stop himself from running a background check. Now more than ever, Ken was convinced this had to do with her ex-husband. It would take so little effort to find out who he was and how Rose's marriage had fallen apart.

It was only Ken's love and respect that kept him from doing it.

Felix crossed his arms over his chest and spread his legs. He wasn't quite as tall as Ken, but he was nearly as wide. "Stop being a jerk and get up," he snapped.

Ken raised an eyebrow. "Oh? And if I don't?"

"Then we'll both go home tonight with black eyes and nothing will have gotten any better."

Ken let out a sarcastic laugh. "I don't know," he drawled as he stood up. "Giving you a black eye might at least make me feel better."

"Yeah, well, right now the feeling's mutual." Felix held the door open. "You're being an idiot. Snap out of it."

"Is this what they call tough love?" Ken asked as he walked past Felix. "Because I gotta say, I didn't know you felt that way about me."

"You spend too much time with Bennett," Felix grumbled, shoving Ken's back. "My truck is out front. Get in."

The men were silent for a few minutes while Felix pulled out onto the street and took them to the marina.

"Am I finally going to see those cement shoes you brag about so often?" Ken asked as he slammed the truck door.

"Don't tempt me," Felix growled. He stomped up to the *Morwenna*, his boat, and began tossing ropes around. "Don't just stand there. Help me."

Ken grumbled, but did as he was told. Not that he was ready to admit it, but getting out of the police station was probably a good thing for him. Ken couldn't seem to stop stewing and it was affecting how he treated everyone. He was normally a good guy but lately, he was snapping and shouting like a grizzly. He knew it, his staff knew it, and apparently his friends knew it.

"What are we doing?" Ken finally asked as they slipped out onto the water. He was standing in the doorway of the wheelhouse while Felix maneuvered them out to sea.

"We're shutting up and fishing." Felix said over his shoulder. "It's called quality time. You should try it sometime. Good for the soul."

Ken grunted, but gave a half smile. Caro was probably prying every secret available from Rose's lips right now, but Felix? He didn't come to talk. Somehow he knew that Ken didn't need to rehash everything, he just needed a break. A chance to decompress without doing anything to rekindle the fire in his belly.

For the millionth time since he moved to Seaside Bay, Ken was grateful for his friends. He had left his family behind to start fresh, but it was the family he'd built that ended up being the key to helping him find a life worth living.

CHAPTER 6

Rose set the bananas in her cart before shoving the handle hard enough to make the back, left, squeaky wheel move to her next destination. Why was it that she always managed to get the grocery cart that had at least one wonky wheel? It never failed!

She glanced at her phone. "Broccoli, apples, juice..." Sighing, she kept pushing through the store. Their grocery store wasn't huge, but it was enough for her usual essentials. Once a month or so, Rose would drive an hour south in order to hit a bigger chain store to buy nonperishables in bulk, but most of the time she shopped local.

It had been a few days since Caro had come over and Rose was starting to feel a little better. She didn't tell her best friend everything, but just enough to help ease the burden.

Caro now knew that Rose was doing her best to stay away from her ex-husband and Caro knew that Alexander had sent Rose a text during the wedding.

There had been no more texts and with everyone on the lookout for any suspicious tourists...Rose was starting to relax. It was possible that Alexander didn't know that was her number. He could have been sending out a mass message, hoping for a hit.

She had done everything she could to cover her tracks when she had fled Boston. The odds of Alexander looking for her in a small, Oregon beachtown were slim to none. It was the exact opposite of their flashy, luxurious lifestyle.

"He wouldn't be caught dead over here," Rose muttered to herself as she put a box of crackers in her cart. She needed to hurry. This little trip to town had taken longer than she'd expected and Mrs. Hennessey had an appointment soon.

Rose shoved her unruly cart to the front counter and paid for her groceries before heading outside. She popped the trunk on her sedan and began to put the bags inside. The humming of an expensive engine caught her ear and Rose froze. Slowly she leaned around the trunk hood and looked toward the sound. A black Jaguar sat in a parking spot, looking completely out of place among the more reasonably priced sedans around it.

Her heart began to pound and her breathing grew shallow. "It could be anyone," she whispered to herself. "Alexander isn't the only one who likes Jaguars." Her eyes wouldn't move, nor would her body. It was like spotting an accident and being unable to look away from the horror. Rose waited for any kind of movement or confirmation that that car belonged to someone other than her ex-husband.

Finally the engine shut down and the door cracked open.

Rose was sure she was going to faint. Her muscles tightened and without warning, her body jumped into motion like a spooked jackrabbit. With jerky movements, she threw the rest of the groceries inside her trunk and slammed it shut. For the first time in her life she didn't put the cart away, but shoved it to the side just enough that she could get her own car backed out.

Once in the driver's seat, she forced herself to pause long enough to wait for the driver to step out of the vehicle. A man in a suit stood. Rose didn't recognize him, but that didn't mean much after five years. Especially when he stopped by the back window and waited for it to roll down.

She couldn't quite see the face of the person in the back, but she could see tanned skin and dark hair and the collar of an expensive suit.

That was all she needed. Rose peeled out of the parking lot, only grateful several minutes later when she realized she could have hurt someone if there had been pedestrians around when she had backed out.

She hit the brake as she parked in front of the shop, her car jerking with the movement. Trembling hands turned off the key and Rose took a moment to catch her breath. She could barely breathe.

"It wasn't him," she told herself over and over. "It wasn't him." Even from her odd angle, Rose had been able to tell that the man's dominant nose was nothing like her husband's. He was more than likely some business man passing through from Portland, who had forgotten something for the commute. It happened once in awhile.

Her reactions had been knee jerk and Rose was deeply ashamed at them, but she literally had had no control in the moment. Sweat poured down the back of her shirt and she felt close to hyperventilating.

"Rose!" A fist pounded against her window and Rose screamed before she could stop herself.

Plastering her hands over her mouth, she breathed through her nose, but it was much too fast. Stars began to burst in her vision and even when she saw Ken's concerned gaze, she couldn't quite bring herself under control.

Years, *years,* she'd worked to set up a life for herself. To be strong and in control, and all it had taken was one short moment in time for every fear, every feeling of helplessness, every nightmare to come rushing back so strongly she had completely lost herself.

"Rose," Ken said more softly. "Open the door, sweetheart. Open the door."

Rose couldn't seem to stop trembling, but she managed to press the button. As soon as the lock clicked, Ken practically tore the door off before he reached for her. Sagging into his chest, she let him hold her. This was so different than when they had danced. His arms were bulky and strong and though they had cradled her during the wedding party, right now they were completely holding her weight. Rose's legs felt like mush and she knew if Ken let go, she would crumple to the ground.

"What is it?" he whispered in her hair. "What happened?" He shifted her until she was set more firmly against his chest, and Rose ate up the affection like a dying man in the desert.

"I thought..." She swallowed hard. "I thought I saw someone."

Ken stiffened. "Who? Your ex?"

Rose nodded.

"Thought you saw? Was it him or not?" Ken leaned his head back and looked her in the eye.

Rose jerkily shook her head. "N-no. It wasn't."

"So you're telling me that just seeing someone who *looked* like your ex had you speeding down Main like a maniac and screaming in fright?"

Rose blinked rapidly as tears filled her vision. She didn't know how to answer him. How to admit that all the progress she'd made in the last few years was for nought. Unable to find the words to express herself, she buried her face in his chest and gripped the back of his shirt.

Ken tightened his hold, apparently understanding without words her predicament. "Come on, sweetheart," he said. "Let's get you out of the public eye."

Rose followed blindly, not questioning him at all. When a burst of cold, damp air hit her face, she knew they had gone inside her shop.

"Oh my goodness!" Susan gasped. "Rose! Are you all right?"

"She's fine, Susan," Ken said easily. "Just a little shaken up. But I'll take care of her. Thanks."

Her feet knew the steps even if her eyes weren't watching and Rose knew they were going into her backroom. But it was Ken's words that stuck in her brain. He would take care of her. How she wanted those words to be true, but the possible consequences were still terrifying. How could she choose?

*****

This wasn't exactly how Ken had planned his first chance to truly hold Rose, but he wasn't about to turn up his nose at it. She was clinging to him like he was her hero, and he would give anything for that role.

He led her over to one of her folding chairs sitting around the room and sat down, pulling Rose into his lap.

She jumped slightly and pushed back against his shoulders. "Ken!"

"Shh..." he soothed. "Just sit and let me help you calm down. We can talk about it in a few minutes." He could see the hesitation in her eyes, but ultimately the weariness in her face won over and she collapsed back against him. "We're going to get through this," he continued, rubbing her back. "You're not alone. We'll get through this together."

Rose gave a shaky sigh and relaxed further into him.

They were quiet for several minutes, Rose's breathing slowly calming down and Ken just enjoying the fact that her impenetrable wall was in shambles.

Finally, she took a deep breath and sat up. "Thank you," she whispered, wiping at her face. "I'm sorry I was such a mess."

Ken shook his head, immediately sorry that she was standing up and moving away from him. "There's nothing to be sorry for."

Rose laughed sarcastically and pointed at his chest. "The big tear stain on your shirt would suggest otherwise."

Ken glanced down and rubbed at it. "It's nothing. I've definitely had worse."

Rose pulled up a seat and sat across from him. "You rescue damsels in distress often, huh?"

Ken shrugged. "Maybe, but I don't offer any of them my shirt."

Rose's face flushed even redder than it already was. She turned away and cleared her throat.

"Rose," Ken started. He was about to break the tentative truce they had going, but something had to change. They couldn't continue like this without someone eventually getting hurt.

Rose put up her hand. "Stop," she said. "I know what you're going to say."

He folded his arms over his chest. "You do?"

She nodded and finally turned back to look him in the eye. "And I'm ready to say you were right."

Ken straightened. "Just so we're on the same page, what exactly was I right about?"

Rose huffed a soft laugh. "I can't keep all this to myself. I need help."

He nodded. "I would say that's a good start."

"A start?" Rose jerked back a little. "What else are you suggesting?"

"Knowing you need help is great," Ken said, "but I think you need to start at the beginning." He tilted his head in sympathy. "We need to know everything, Rose. Everything." He paused when her face blanched. "What all did you tell Caro the other night?"

Rose threw back her head and groaned. "This is why small towns are so horrible," she complained.

"It's also why small towns are so wonderful."

Rose looked at him again and the tiredness in her gaze pinched his chest. She nodded. "True enough." Sighing, Rose stood and began to pace the area. "I only told her a few things. Just enough to make me feel less alone, but not enough to put Caro in danger."

"You think that by telling us what's going on, we're going to be in danger?" Ken stood up and met her across the room. "Just what is going on here?" he demanded. "Every time I get a bit of information from you, my what-if scenarios get worse and worse. Are you in trouble with the law?"

Rose shook her head. "I'm not, but if it ever caught up with my ex, he would be."

"But your hands are clean?"

Rose nodded. "Yes. Believe it or not, I was found innocent of all charges," she snapped. "Happy?"

Ken shook his head. "No. Because I need to know why you were even a suspect in the first place."

Rose went back to pacing. "It's all such a mess," she murmured. "And by coming here, I thought I left it all behind me." Her arms flung out to the side. "When will I ever be free?"

Ken caught her outstretched hand. "Hey, hey, hey," he said in a soft tone. "You're not alone, Rose." He put her hand against his chest. "You don't have to ever be alone if you don't want to. And I'm not saying that as a police officer."

Her eyes filled up again. "I know, Ken. But I'm scared."

"About what? That your ex will find you?"

Rose shook her head and stepped close enough to rest her other hand on his chest. "No. I know it's inevitable that he'll eventually find me. He has too many resources for him not to."

"Then why would you want to run away?" Ken argued. "Why leave everyone and everything that will help keep you and Lily safe?"

"Because of what you just said," Rose explained. "Seaside has everyone and everything that I love."

It took Ken a second before the light bulb hit. "You're worried he'll hurt one of us." It was a comment, not a question.

Rose nodded. "Yes. If Lily and I are on our own, the amount of people I have to protect is much smaller."

"You don't have to protect me," Ken said hoarsely, stepping slightly closer. They were toe to toe now. He wondered if she could feel the tension humming between them.

"Don't we always try and protect those we care about?"

Ken closed his eyes and hung his head. He'd been waiting five long years to hear those words. They'd been hinted at. He'd read them in her eyes, but it wasn't until now that she was finally admitting out loud that she felt something for him. It was almost more than he could bear. "Rose," he groaned.

Her fingers curled against his shirt. "Ken. I know I've hurt you and for that, I'm truly sorry, but it was in your best interest." Her grip tightened ever so slightly before she let go and stepped back.

Ken wanted to stop her and pull her back. He wanted to finish talking about them, but now wasn't the time to lose his head. "I get that we need to focus on your situation first," he said, his tone lower than normal. "But once it's done...you and I are going to talk."

Rose nodded. "If it's ever done."

"It will be," Ken vowed. "I refuse to let it be otherwise."

CHAPTER 7

"Thank you for coming tonight," Rose said. Her knuckles were beginning to ache from how much hand wringing she was doing, but she couldn't seem to stop herself. After her chat with Ken that afternoon and the scare with the man at the grocery store, Rose was ready to tell her friends everything.

She couldn't continue to live like this, and it wasn't fair to ask Lily to live like this. She also couldn't continue to keep her friends in the dark and expect them to stay by her side. That's not how friendships worked.

"We're glad you called," Charli said, her dark brows furrowed. "We've all wanted to help for forever, and now we can finally do something about this whole situation."

Rose shook her head. "Other than possibly helping keep an eye out, I don't want you guys involved," she hurried to say. "My situation is dangerous, and I'm not sure I could live with myself if any of you got hurt on my account."

"Why don't you just tell us the whole story," Ken interrupted. "We can talk about any plans afterward."

Rose nodded jerkily, her gaze falling to her lap. She had let herself get too close to Ken today, but it had been so hard to resist what he had so willingly offered. Still...she knew she needed to pull herself up by her bootstraps and get back in control. Using Ken for protection wasn't an option. Alexander would take him out first.

"The first thing you probably should know about me is that I was raised in the foster care system," Rose said. Her voice was smaller than she would have liked, but at least the words were coming out. "I was left at the hospital door as a baby, so there was no record of my birth or my parents, and I was immediately declared a ward of the state."

Sniffles brought Rose's eyes up and she gave Mel a commiserating look. Those pregnancy hormones were no joke, Rose knew from experience.

"You were never adopted?" Caro asked.

Rose shook her head. "No. There were so many of us in the system and we were often shuffled around," Rose said. "But I was okay. I kept my head down and got through school without creating any major problems." She took a deep breath. Here was the hard part. "But as soon as I left the protection of the system, I found myself floundering." Her hands began to shake. "I was working as a waitress at a small coffee shop when I thought my salvation walked through the door."

A sarcastic laugh broke free, but the dark memories in her mind required no less. "Alexander was tall, handsome, and very, very charming. He started showing up at the cafe every day, just to leave me a massive tip and chat with me." Her smile fell. "Sometimes he didn't even drink anything. Just gave me a tip for my time and the use of the table."

Charli whistled low. "That must have seemed like a dream come true."

Rose nodded, careful to keep from looking at Ken. She couldn't bear to see how he was reacting to this at the moment. He more than likely thought she was the stupidest person on Earth and Rose already knew that. Right now she didn't have the strength to hear it from someone else.

"Anyway, soon the chats became date invites and within the span of just a few weeks, he had swept me off my feet, and put me in the church where we were married in a huge ceremony that included guests from the wealthiest and most influential families in Boston." A teacup was pressed into her hands and Rose took it, grateful for the warmth, though she was sure she couldn't swallow anything. "Thanks," she said softly.

"Go on, sweetie," Caro said, rubbing Rose's back. "We're not going anywhere."

Rose nodded. "We took an extended honeymoon in Europe and Alexander showed me everything I had been missing in life, spoiling me rotten in the process." Knowing she was getting to the worst of it, Rose forced down a sip of the hot brew to ease her tight throat. "It wasn't until after we had been home for about six months that I started to notice things were...odd."

"What do you mean?" Ken asked quickly.

Rose couldn't help but glance up from under her eyelashes. He was stiff as a board in his seat, his eyebrows pulled so close together they almost looked like one. "Like how I never got a straight answer about what he did for a job. Or why his buddies always came over late at night rather than during the day. Or why we always had bodyguards with us wherever we went."

"Are you telling me the man you married was some kind of mob boss?" Charli's jaw was completely slack. "No way! I thought that kind of thing only happened in movies."

Rose felt color rising in her cheeks, which was better than the faint feeling she had been struggling with earlier. "Me too," she responded. "But no...they really do exist." She closed her eyes. "Apparently, Alexander was into acquiring businesses. He basically turned himself into a bank, giving loans to people under the table, then requiring outrageous amounts of interest, *or* taking majority shares in their businesses. I can't even begin to tell you how many he had weaseled his way into over the years."

"Let me guess." Ken's voice was so dark Rose jumped when he spoke. "Somehow, in all his dealings, people got hurt, but his hands always stayed clean. Making him untouchable for the police."

Rose slumped against the back of her seat. "It sounds to me like you've dealt with this before."

Ken shook his head. "No. But I've heard the stories and seen the case files." His hands were clenched so tightly they were devoid of color. "Their specialty is preying on people who are naive or unable to function the normal way of things. Immigrants needing loans but having no collateral." He nodded toward Rose. "Beautiful, young women who have never really experienced life and would be content to sit by while he handled all the finances."

Rose snorted. "That's a nice way to put it."

"What happened next?" Caro pressed. "We know you managed to get divorced, but if news stories are to be believed, men like that don't let go of what they consider their property very easily."

Rose huffed. "That's putting it mildly. I spent the next two years slowly discovering more and more of his business practices and growing more and more frightened by what I learned. Especially after..." She swallowed hard, trying to keep from throwing up.

"Especially after you realized you were expecting."

Rose looked at Mel, who had spoken, and nodded with tear-filled eyes. "Yes."

Mel rubbed her small baby bump. "I think any good mother would feel that way."

Rose shrugged. "By then, Alexander and I weren't as close as we were. I had purposefully been putting distance between us, waiting for an opportunity to break free, but I was afraid no one would believe me. I mean, I was just an orphan kid from the wrong side of the tracks."

"Never," Caro said fiercely.

Rose gave her bestie a grateful smile. "Thanks for the vote of confidence, but Alexander was basically untouchable and I worried that serving him papers would make him go crazy." She took a deep breath, the tears starting to fall. "He took the news of my pregnancy well, even using it as an opportunity to take me away again and try to buy me back with all sorts of gifts." The tears flowed harder. "But when I miscarried at ten weeks, it all fell apart."

"Oh, Rose." Caro wrapped her arms around Rose and squeezed tight.

"What did he do?" Ken demanded.

Rose forced herself to look up. She wasn't proud of this part of the story, but it was part of what they needed to understand. "That was the first night he hit me."

*****

Ken squeezed his eyes tight and leaned forward with his fists against his eyelids. He could feel his teeth grinding as rage, stronger than he had ever felt before, flooded his system. He wanted to kill this Alexander guy. He wanted to do it with his bare hands, and Ken didn't care the slightest bit about whether or not it was legal for him to do so.

"Easy," Felix said, squeezing Ken's shoulder.

Ken nodded, but didn't look up.

"You gonna be okay?" Felix continued.

Ken nodded again. "Keep going," he croaked.

Rose cleared her throat and her voice was a little stronger as the story went on. "He told me I had failed him and it took a while for us to get back on a civil footing with each other. Of course, he eventually apologized, and showered me with more gifts in order to clear the air between us, but I wanted nothing to do with it."

"Good girl," Charli said under her breath.

"It took me almost another year, but I finally found a lawyer who would take my case for divorce."

Ken growled low in his throat. This man obviously had more power than Ken could imagine if even the lawyers were afraid to go against him.

"By then, however...I was pregnant again."

Ken's head shot up. This story was getting worse and worse. Rose had been abused, gone through medical trauma, and even while trying to get divorced, had had to play the role of dutiful wife. How did this woman ever endure?

"I didn't tell Alexander. Instead, I did all I could to rush us through the divorce process so that he would never find out. It happened to land during a time when a case was being brought against him for being a loan shark, so the divorce case was able to move through a little faster because Alexander had his attention elsewhere."

"You said you were found innocent in court," Ken managed to get out. "Is that the case you were talking about?"

Rose nodded and took in a shuddering breath. "The police were casting as wide a net as possible, but when they put me under the microscope, they couldn't find anything that tied me to the loans."

Ken nodded. It made sense. Trying to take down mob bosses wasn't easy and the police often had to use every resource within their disposal.

"The biggest hold up came from the fact that Alexander needed to pay me money." Rose shook her head. "I didn't want much, but coming from being a waitress to being one hundred percent dependent on him, if I didn't get anything, I wouldn't have a single penny to my name." Her bottom lip trembled. "I would have been fine, but not with a baby on the way."

Caro leaned her head on Rose's shoulder. "There was nothing else you could do," she said. "That bozo owed you a lot more than just enough to get by."

Rose nodded. "The judge and my lawyer were constantly telling me to ask for more, but I didn't want Alexander to have any more reason to slow things down or to come after me later. I only wanted enough to start a new life with my child. Plus, I had no way of knowing whether the courts would seize all his assets during the trial."

Ken huffed and leaned back in his chair. "So you ran from Boston, gave birth, and what? Kept traveling until you reached us?"

"Something like that," Rose said softly. She tucked a piece of hair behind her ear. "I ended up driving the 'Big Daddy,'" she said with a dark chuckle. "It's actually a highway from Boston to Newport. But I stopped several times along the way to work. I wanted to save as much as I could from the settlement so I could start a business and pay for the birth when the time arose." She stopped to drink some more tea. "Lily was born in Idaho and she was only two months old when I landed here after finding an ad for the shop and attached apartment."

Caro stood and walked over to grab a box of tissues, bringing them back to Rose, who smiled her thanks.

"I had determined during all my driving that I wanted to open a flower shop. It was a hobby that I had picked up while Alexander and I were married, and it was the only thing that brought me joy after we started to fall apart." Rose wiped her eyes with a tissue. "I named my daughter Lily, which means purity, sweet, and innocent. All things that were perfect for her." She sniffed and wiped her eyes again. "And I named my shop The Hidden Daffodil."

"Because daffodils stand for new beginnings or rebirths," Ken spoke before he could stop himself. He had figured out a long time ago that Rose was hiding something, and her expertise in flower language caused him to do some research.

Rose's eyes widened and she nodded. "Yes," she whispered.

Ken shrugged. "Call it a policeman's curiosity."

"You knew I was running."

Ken nodded once. There was no point in denying it. He had seen the signs. He hadn't known quite how serious it was, and as time had gone on and his feelings had begun to get involved, he had approached it from a different angle than that of the law.

"But you never said anything," Rose argued.

"You weren't breaking any laws," Ken explained. "Telling us about your past was your gift to give."

Her eyes filled again. "Thank you," she said thickly.

"Thank you for trusting us with it."

"I'm sorry to burst the moment," Felix inserted. "But we need to know what's changed," he said seriously.

Rose nodded. "Right." She sighed. "When I ran from Boston, I did everything I could to not leave a trail. I changed my name back and went by Rose instead of Rosalinda." One side of her mouth quirked up. "I know it's not much, but I couldn't quite bring myself to fully rid myself of my name. Rose can stand for anything from secrecy to balance and love," she explained. "But I was careful about using my name, so I wasn't as trackable. I didn't bother getting a new phone until I was settled for good, which was right after I arrived here. I paid cash for all my transactions and have managed five whole years of semi-peace."

Caro squished her lips to the side. "Do you really feel like he's still after you after all this time? Why not just cut his losses and move on?"

When the blood drained from Rose's face, Ken knew her answer wasn't going to be pretty. "Because he nearly killed me the night before our divorce was final," she said hoarsely. "The only reason I'm alive is because my lawyer happened to show up just as Alexander was waving a knife in front of my face." She shook her head as the room sat in stunned silence. "As he disappeared, he promised me he would never stop until I was back where I belonged." Her lips trembled. "I was gone from the city before the ink was dry on the documents."

Ken stood and began to pace. "Why didn't you report his threat to the police?"

"He had too much power!" Rose cried. "Didn't you hear me? I had to go outside of Boston just to find a lawyer who was willing to go up against him." She shook her head. "And honestly, if that man hadn't been ex-military and as big as a barn, I'm not sure I would have found anyone at all. I simply got lucky on that score. Plus he was already being charged. I prayed that he could be convicted and I wouldn't have to worry about him anymore. But it didn't work. He was convicted on lesser charges and only spent a few years in prison instead of the maximum sentence."

"You're not in Boston anymore," Ken snarled, facing her. "We're not under his thumb."

Rose jumped to her own feet. "No, but you're my friend. And tossing you in his path would be putting your life in danger!"

"I'm a policeman," Ken argued. "My life is always in danger."

"Seaside Bay danger is a far cry from Boston crime ring leader," Rose said, stomping toward him. "It's like apples and oranges."

"The law is on our side," Ken said, his voice dropping as she got closer. "You have the power to fight him now."

Rose shook her head. "He has more resources than you can imagine. And when he finds out I've been hiding a child from him..." Rose let the words trail off. She didn't need to finish them. After everything she had just shared, it was clear that if Alexander found her, she was in serious danger.

CHAPTER 8

Felix cleared his throat. "I'm sorry to do this, *again,* but we still don't know why you're suddenly ready to run, Rose."

Rose shook her head to clear it from the argument with Ken. "I got a message during Benny and Ally's reception."

"What did it say?" Caro asked breathlessly.

Rose slowly reached for her phone. She had kept the message as a reminder. "I don't know if it's from him and I don't know if he's actually figured out where I am." She pulled up the words.

You have something I want.

"You don't know who sent it?" Ken asked, taking her phone and pulling up the sender.

Rose shook her head. "No. But the words sound like something he would say." She laughed shakily and went to sit back down. "I can just see him showing up and demanding I pay him back what the courts took. Or offering me a deal by coming back with him. Just like he does with the business owners."

"But this isn't a loan," Charli said through a clenched jaw. Her husband, Bronson, put his hand on her neck and gave her a soft squeeze.

"Hang tight, Char. We'll get this figured out. It sounds like this guy hasn't played by the rules in a long time. He probably doesn't even know the meaning of the word at this point."

Charli nodded and leaned into her husband. "We're not letting this guy get to you, Rose."

"And what spooked you this afternoon?" Ken asked, handing her phone back to her.

Rose put her elbows on her knees and buried her face in her hands. "I'm sorry about today. I saw a man in a Jaguar at the grocery store." She looked up at Ken's intense stare. "Alexander prefers those as well. He was more than likely some business man from Portland

"

driving through, but he had a driver and his coloring was similar to Alexander. It sent my flight reaction into overdrive."

Ken nodded. "Understandable."

Rose shook her head. "No. It's not. I've spent five years redefining myself. Learning who I was and working to protect my handicapped daughter. There is absolutely no excuse for me to turn back into a scared rabbit as if I were still fresh out of the foster system."

Caro sat down again and rubbed Rose's back. "Sweetie, your body has a learned response when it comes to this man. It makes sense that your first..." She eyed the phone. "Second real scare would send your body back to those responses. But don't worry. Between your own gumption and our united front, you're covered."

"But that's just it!" Rose cried. "This is exactly why I've kept you all from this all these years!" She pinched her lips together and her eyes automatically went to Ken, though the words were meant for everyone. "I didn't tell you because I didn't want you all to become targets." Rose forced herself to look from face to face. "You all are the family I never had and if anything happened to any one of you, it would kill me inside."

Ken knelt at her feet, bringing his face to her level, and Rose sucked in a breath. She loved this man so much. Why was life so cruel? She'd been abandoned as a baby, collected by a criminal, and now that she was on her own, she couldn't give her heart to the man it beat for.

"Rose Ingalls, you listen to me and you listen good," Ken said. The room hushed as if Ken's words were those of a king speaking to his subjects. "You are an amazing woman. You've carried a heavy burden, rising from the streets to being a full-time mother and business owner, and you've done it with a grace and beauty that most women envy."

A sob slipped through Rose's lips and she pressed against the sound with her fingers. Her heart was pounding painfully against her chest and her vision was clouded with tears.

"But you. Are. Not. Alone." He said each word with a heavy emphasis. "You've got a family now. And yes, we understand you don't want us hurt. But *you* have to understand that we're not just willing to help you, we're willing to help each other." Ken purposefully looked around at the people standing over his shoulder. "I'm not just willing to protect you, I'm willing to protect Mel and the baby. And Charli. And Caro." One side of his mouth quirked up. "And even Jack."

"Hey!" Jack called from the back of the group. "Just because I bake cookies doesn't mean I'm weak!"

A soft chuckle ran through the group and Rose's muscles relaxed the tiniest amount.

"Point is," Ken continued, "we're here to help, but doing so doesn't mean we're hanging ourselves out to dry. Caro was right the other night when she said that you were stronger and better protected if you stay. Alexander has no power or contacts here. My station isn't under his control, and I've got friends down half the coast that I trust with my life if the occasion calls for it."

"I've got access to the best lawyer on the West Coast," Bronson offered, speaking of his brother who lived down in California. "I'll bet he could help us."

Rose's blurry vision cleared as the tears flowed down her cheeks. Each of her friends began offering their own expertise to the situation, causing a swell of gratitude and love to fill her core.

"I can install a security system," Charli said.

"I'm not much good for protection, but I'm an easy babysitter," Caro offered. "Lillers can spend her afternoons in the kitchen with me so she's not left unprotected."

"And I'm there to protect them both," Jack said.

"When Benny gets back, he can keep us informed of any mail that arrives for suspicious names," Felix said. "And I'll keep my cement shoes handy."

Charli rolled her eyes and slapped her brother's shoulder. "The point is to put him in jail and keep the rest of us out, idiot."

Felix folded his arms over his chest. "Ken doesn't have to know."

"Too late," Ken said, climbing to his feet.

"I don't know what my knowledge about fish does to help the situation," Hadlee said, "but like Caro, I'm always available to help with Lily. I can even take her up to the museum if getting her out of town would help."

Rose wiped at her face, but it was a losing battle. The tissue was quickly dissolving and her determination to protect everyone was as well. She knew they were right. She could do this. She had won once, she would win again, and this time, she had much more than a single judge and lawyer on her side.

"I wonder if Grayson has access to a security firm that might help?" Caro asked, speaking about their friend Brook's movie star husband. They split their time between homes and weren't currently in Seaside Bay.

"That won't be necessary," Ken replied.

"Don't you think it would help if she had a constant bodyguard?" Caro asked, putting her hands on her hips.

Ken nodded. "It would. Which is why I'm going to be moving in with her."

*****

Ken watched a variety of emotions play over Rose's face after he said those words. He probably should have mentioned them to her in private, but he also needed the support of the group if he was going to have any chance of convincing her his plan was sound.

"You can't move in with me!" Rose shouted. Her face was flushed so red that Ken wasn't sure if she was embarrassed or angry, but it didn't matter. She was under heavy emotional stress at the moment, anyone could see that.

Ken did his best to hide a smirk. When she wouldn't meet his gaze, he knew she wasn't mad as much as embarrassed. She wasn't completely immune to him physically and he figured that played a role in her feelings on the matter.

"Actually," Caro started, "I think that would be a great idea."

Rose jerked away from her friend. "You can't mean that," she said fiercely. "He can't live with me."

Caro shrugged. "You could always live with him."

"Are you sure you know what you're doing?" Felix's voice was low in Ken's ear, not meant for the rest of the group to hear.

Ken nodded subtly. "It's the best way to keep her safe. Even with extra patrols, she'd be vulnerable during the night."

Felix sighed and scrubbed a hand down his face. "I get it, I really do. But it worries me."

Ken frowned and turned. "Why?"

Felix raised a single eyebrow. "You're in love with her."

Ken hated it was such common knowledge, but there was little he could do about it. "So?"

"So...can you live with her and not let your feelings get in the way?"

Ken opened his mouth, then shut it. He didn't want to admit it, but Felix had a point. It was hard being close to her once or twice a week. Living with Rose would only make his life a constant state of purgatory. "Keeping her safe is the top priority," Ken said. "Nothing else matters."

Felix slapped Ken's back. "Then you've got my vote."

They turned back to the arguing women.

"What will people say?" Rose argued. "This is a small town. Everyone's going to assume we're..." She waved a hand toward Ken and her words died off when she caught his gaze.

Ken held it steady and strong. He knew what it would look like, but he wanted her to know she was safe with him. He hadn't risen to the rank he was at the department because he was undisciplined.

Cooper cleared his throat and stepped forward, looking slightly sheepish. "While I understand what you're getting at, Rose," he grinned slightly, "I think Genni and I can tell you from experience that the town can be very forgiving if the circumstances call for it."

He was referring to the fact that he and Genni had lived in the same house for several months when he'd first arrived in town. Both of them had inherited half the house when their grandparents died, and neither had been willing to give an inch in regards to moving out. It had been difficult for a while, but eventually the two had fallen in love, and it no longer mattered.

What I wouldn't give for that to be our outcome, Ken thought wryly. He kept that particular thought to himself. It would only add fuel to the fire.

Rose huffed and puffed, but eventually her shoulders drooped. "Is there no other way?" she asked.

The tears in her voice tugged at Ken's heart. "Could you guys give us a minute?" he asked, his eyes fixated on Rose.

"On it," Felix said, ushering his wife and the rest of the group out into the front of the shop.

The room was deathly quiet after everyone else had left, leaving Ken feeling decidedly uncomfortable now that the others weren't there to buffer the situation between him and Rose.

"Rose," he said softly.

She glanced at him sideways before dropping her eyes to the floor again.

"Would it really be that horrible?" The question was meant to help break the tension in the room. The crowd was gone, but the emotions certainly weren't. "I don't make messes, I can take out the garbage, and I promise I don't snore."

Rose huffed. "You better not be close enough that I could hear you snore, anyway," she retorted.

Ken grinned and stepped a little closer. "We both know how I feel about you. I've never worked to hide it," he said. "But that's not what this is about." When she still didn't look up, he reached out to touch her chin, bringing her eyes to his. She needed to see his sincerity. "I promise I'm not doing this to try and take advantage of your situation." He took in a fortifying breath at the wariness that was in her gaze. "This isn't about me, or how I feel. This is about you, Lily, and protection. While Grayson might be able to help us find you a bodyguard, I know you well enough to know that walking around with a stranger shadowing you isn't going to help you feel safe."

Rose's bottom lip began to tremble and Ken rubbed it softly with his thumb.

"You know me." He took her hand and put it against his chest. "You might not want to admit to it, but you also trust me. No matter what I feel and you don't feel, I will always have your best interests at heart. Yours and Lily's."

Her fingers curled against his T-shirt.

"No one will work as hard to keep you safe as I will," he whispered, his thumb moving to her soft cheek. "You know that."

Rose closed her eyes and a single tear slipped out.

Ken quickly wiped it away.

When she opened them again, her blue eyes were bright with determination. "I know," she answered hoarsely. "I know you'll keep us safe, but I don't like...I struggle to..." She sighed and pulled away from him, wringing her hands together. "I've learned the hard way not to trust anyone but myself."

"You trusted your lawyer," Ken pointed out.

Rose nodded. "You're right. I did."

"You trust Mrs. Hennessey and Caro and all of us with Lily."

Rose's shoulders fell. "You're right again." She gave a harsh laugh. "I suppose I've slipped into it without noticing."

"Do you trust me to keep you safe?" Ken needed to hear her say it out loud. For some reason the words were necessary, not just the inner understanding.

Rose took her time answering, but to his Ken's surprise, when she did, she came right up to him and put her hand back on his chest. "I don't know that there's anyone else I trust more," she whispered thickly. "But the idea of you getting caught up in this trouble terrifies me."

Ken savored her words and allowed himself to cup her cheek when she didn't move away. "I'm trained for this exact thing, Rose. If you trust me to keep you safe, trust me to keep myself safe as well."

She broke his touch when she let her forehead fall forward and land on his sternum. "That's one of the problems," she said into his shirt. "I know you *can* keep yourself safe. But I also know you well enough to know you'll put our safety first."

Ken wrapped his arms around her and rubbed her back. "I can't fix that one," he said. "You and Lily will always come first." He paused. "One of the problems? What are the others?"

She brought her head up. "I trust you to be a gentleman," she said softly. "But if we're living in such close quarters, I'm not sure if I can trust *me*."

Ken groaned and let his head fall back. "You better bring in the others before I do something that'll only make things harder." The need to kiss her was about to consume him. He had no idea how he was going to survive living with her, but somehow he would do it.

If he was going to have any chance of winning her later on, he needed to keep his head on straight. Keep her safe. Eliminate the threat. Then win her heart.

It sounded so easy in his head, but after five years of watching her from afar, Ken knew full well this was going to be the hardest thing he had ever done.

CHAPTER 9

Lily danced around the small bedroom she and her mother would be sharing while they stayed with Ken. It had been decided that since his cabin was larger than her tiny apartment, it was a better fit for the situation, though Rose was beginning to regret her decision.

Everything in this place reminded her of Ken. From the bachelor style furniture to the smell of the linens. Ken, Ken, Ken.

How in the world was she going to survive this, keeping her heart intact at the end?

If Alexander is out of the picture, you won't have to guard your heart.

The fleeting thought made Rose catch her breath. The words were true, but also frightening. She hadn't let a man in since Alexander, though the struggle with Ken had been real. It wasn't until recently that he had even touched her as more than a friend, and with each caress, each mention of his feelings, each flutter in her stomach...Rose knew she was falling harder and harder.

It seemed weird to be in love with someone she had never kissed or even gone on a date with, but there it was. Ken was everything Rose wanted in a man, and everything she couldn't have.

Yet.

Maybe after this was over, they *could* start from the beginning. They could try a few dates and see if their feelings stayed the same. She smirked. Wouldn't it be crazy if after all these years pining for each other, they spent time together and discovered it wasn't what they hoped?

But first you need to be rid of Alexander.

And that was the catch. Rose's smile fell. How could she ever be sure she was rid of the man who wanted her dead?

"Mama?" Lily tugged on Rose's shirt.

She looked down and signed. "Yes?"

"I'm hungry."

Rose bit her lips between her teeth. She knew that Ken would have something to feed Lily, but it felt weird to ask. Rose would need to talk to him about splitting the grocery budget or maybe just doing all the shopping.

"Let's go see if Uncle Ken has a granola bar, huh?" Rose held out her hand and Lily took it, then proceeded to skip at Rose's side as they walked out into the sitting area.

The cabin wasn't large, but it was enough. Three bedrooms and two baths were more than they needed for their little brood. At least in the short term.

"Ken?"

He popped his head in from the kitchen. "Yeah?" Stepping fully into the doorway, Ken wiped his hands on a dishtowel before slinging it over his shoulder.

Lily squealed and dropped her mother's hand to rush over.

Ken's smile was captivating as he caught the little girl and swung her into the air before nestling her against his chest. "Whatcha need, Buttercup?"

Lily scowled. "I'm not a buttercup."

Ken tapped his lips thoughtfully before signing again. "Really? I thought you were a flower?"

Lily rolled her eyes and Rose got a glimpse of what she would look like in ten years. "I'm Lily, not buttercup!"

"Oops. Sorry." Ken tweaked the girl's nose. "What can I do for you, Lily?"

"I'm hungry!"

"Lily," Rose warned. "Manners please."

The eyeroll, apparently, wasn't going to just be a teenage thing. "Uncle Ken, do you have anything I can have for a snack?"

"I think we can rustle something up," he said with a wink. "Let's go see what we can find."

Rose stood rooted to the spot. If any man was hoping to win her heart, interactions just like that with her daughter were the best way to do it. There was no way for Rose to hold onto any part of her heart when a man treated her daughter that way. She could hear giggling and chuckling from the kitchen and part of her longed to join in the fun. The other part of her was worried she wouldn't be able to maintain any kind of self control if she walked in to see them together.

Why was a man with a child so attractive?

Slowly, Rose forced her feet to move. The laughter stopped and she could hear Ken whispering as she approached the door. For some reason, Rose found her heart pounding as she got closer. There was something significant about this moment, though Rose wasn't sure why.

Ken and Lily had been close for a long time now. This shouldn't have felt special, but it did.

Lily's giggle once again floated through the air and Rose caught her breath. Her daughter was so happy, so carefree. It was a life Rose was slightly jealous of, though she was grateful to have created it for her daughter. Rose's carefree moments had been fleeting. With any luck, Lily's would never be gone.

Rose finally arrived in the doorway and her heart nearly jumped out of her chest. Ken and Lily were sitting at the small bar, heads together as they both ate a bowl of ice cream.

"My mom always said, life's short. Eat dessert first," Ken said to his partner in crime.

"What's that mean?" Lily signed before stuffing an extra large bite in her mouth. Even from across the room Rose could see a smear of chocolate sauce on her daughter's face.

"It means you're being naughty," Rose said in an extra loud voice so Lily would hear.

Their heads whipped around and Ken groaned. "Caught," he complained. "Red-handed."

Lily kicked her legs. "Hi, Mama! We're having ice cream!"

Ken's ears turned slightly red, letting Rose know he was embarrassed. "I can explain," he started to say.

Rose folded her arms over her chest. "Why do I have the feeling that moving in here just means I'm taking care of two children instead of one?"

Ken's right eyebrow quirked up. "You think I'm a child?"

Rose waved a hand toward the bowls. "Creating a secret rendezvous with a five-year-old so you can have ice cream in the middle of the day certainly doesn't sound like a police captain."

Ken held her gaze as he slowly stood from his stool. His presence filled the room until Rose felt like she was struggling to breathe. Her heart was in her throat and her hand unconsciously fluttered up to it, as if that would stop it from bursting from her body.

Ken stood toe to toe with her, his body caging hers in. "A child, huh? Do I look like a child to you?"

Rose did her best to regather her dignity, but it had flown the coop. Her hand went to his chest as if to push him away, but the warmth of his body stopped her. "You've got chocolate on your upper lip," she whispered. "Definitely a child."

*****

Ken had no idea if she was telling the truth, or if Rose was just trying to make a point, but right now he didn't care. Reaching behind his back, Ken spelled out "napkin please" with his fingers.

The screeching of the barstool let him know Lily had gotten the message. She was still giggling when she came up to his side and held one up.

"Thanks," Ken said, giving the girl a quick wink. To his surprise, she kept going, skipping right out of the kitchen and out of sight. When his eyes came back to Rose, hers had widened, as if realizing the only thing keeping him in line had fled the room.

Ken held the napkin up between them. The joke had gone from being funny to something more. "If I'm such a child, I'll let you clean my face."

Rose was breathing heavily as she took the napkin. "Should I wet it down with my spit?" she asked.

Ken knew she was trying to lighten the tension, but instead, the words just brought his eyes to her lips. He was too close. They had only been at his house for a couple of hours. This was probably not a good way to start off their time together. "Whatever you need to do," he whispered.

Rose brought up the napkin and wet it against her tongue. Then raised it to his own mouth before quirking an eyebrow. "Are you sure?"

Ken's lips twitched. "I'm not scared of a little saliva."

Rose laughed softly as she began to dab just above his lip. After a second, her other hand came up to hold his face in place. "I can't believe you filled her with sugar," she scolded softly.

"I can't believe you thought I wouldn't." He kept watching her as she cleaned him up. When the napkin finally came down, her other hand remained.

"You didn't shave this morning," she whispered.

"Nope," Ken responded. "I'm sure I'm a little scruffy."

Rose's fingertips gently moved along his face. "I like it." The words were so soft, they felt like an admission she hadn't wanted to say out loud.

Ken allowed himself to move closer. He shouldn't do it. He shouldn't. But how to say no when Rose was egging him on? "Rose?" he paused just beyond her mouth.

"Hmm?" Those blue eyes came up to his.

"I..." The words stuck in Ken's throat. He shouldn't be doing this. He wanted to...but he shouldn't. Not to mention he'd promised he wouldn't take advantage of her. Stiffening every muscle in his body, Ken squeezed his eyes shut and began to back up.

"Don't," Rose said quickly.

Ken's eyes popped open.

The hand on his cheek slowly slid down to his chest. The touch was like a branding iron against his shirt. "I haven't kissed anyone in years," she admitted.

"I promised I wouldn't take advantage," Ken reminded her.

"Is it still taking advantage when I'm asking?"

His eyes widened. "Are you asking?"

Rose leaned forward, bringing their mouths close once again. "Ken," she breathed. "Will you kiss me?"

"Rose, I..." Resistance hurt. Like a knife in his chest, it hurt to hold back. When had the tables turned in their situation? She was always the one running and now it was Ken. He didn't want her to feel like he was forcing anything. He didn't want to create a weird situation while they were staying together. He wanted her, badly, but he wanted her happy more.

"You don't want to." Rose's voice had gone flat and she'd settled back onto her heels.

"Nothing could be farther from the truth," Ken said so fast he didn't even think about the words.

"Then what's holding you back?" Rose asked. The hurt in her tone was audible, and it only made the pain worse.

"You've been running from me for five years, Rose," he replied, tucking a piece of hair behind her ear. "What's changed your mind?"

Rose huffed. "Honestly? I'm not sure." Her eyes darted to his lips, then back up. "Is it wrong to be curious?"

"Curious?" Ken frowned. "What do you mean?"

She looked away. "Curious as to whether or not your kiss will be as amazing as I think it will."

He couldn't help the hopeful tone in his voice any more than she could help the sad one in hers. "You think it'll be amazing?"

Rose tilted her head and gave him a wry look. "I don't know," she snapped. "That's why I was curious. Just because I want it to be, doesn't mean it—"

That was the last thing Rose got out before Ken decided to give her all that she was wondering about. She wanted to know if their chemistry was more than just unrequited longing? Okay. He could deal with that.

His mouth captured hers, while his hand went around her low back to pull her closer. The bolt of lightning that hit his system as soon as she began to kiss him back told Ken he'd bitten off more than he could chew, but he didn't regret it for a second.

Her slim fingers slid up and around his neck and she molded into his chest with a sigh, allowing Ken to deepen the kiss.

His free hand automatically went to her hair. He loved her hair. Long, silky with some curl and a vibrant red that looked like the sun rising over the ocean. Having her in his arms gave him the perfect chance to run his fingers through it and enjoy to his heart's content. The ponytail she had come into the kitchen with was quickly gone and Ken let his fingers tangle in the luscious strands.

She responded in kind, one of her hands going up to the back of his head and gripping his hair.

"We need to stop," Ken rasped, taking his lips to her jawline.

"I know." Rose gasped.

"Are you still curious?"

Rose stilled and Ken froze with her. Slowly, they both brought their faces back so they could see each other. "No," she said carefully. "I think all my questions were answered."

"Then what's the consensus?" Ken dared to ask.

Rose gave him a sad smile. "That you're dangerous...in the best of ways."

Ken chuckled and brought their foreheads together. "I'm sorry if I got carried away. I've waited a long time to do that."

"I've waited a long time to let you," Rose replied.

There was a catch at the end of her words, as if she wanted to say more, but wasn't sure how to do it. "But?" he pressed.

"But we probably shouldn't do that again." Rose's voice was slightly stronger, and after a moment, she brought her hands down to push against his chest.

Ken obeyed, knowing she was right, but not liking it a single bit. "I know," he admitted. His blood was still thrumming through his veins. More than ever, he wanted to catch this Alexander jerk and get this all behind her. Rose was meant to be his. He knew it and he prayed that after that kiss, she knew it.

Now that he knew exactly what he was missing, Ken was aware he wouldn't be able to hold out forever, but he could hold out long enough to make her safe. That would be the goal. Get rid of the danger and then convince Rose she never needed to leave his cabin. Two things. Only two things.

Easy as pie.

CHAPTER 10

Rose hurriedly finished the messy bun she had slapped on the top of her head before rushing to the kitchen to see where Lily had disappeared to. They had only been at Ken's for two days and her daughter was settling in a little too well.

Not that Ken seemed to mind, but Rose certainly did. Yes...she had given into her curiosity...okay, her desires...and kissed him, but they had both walked away from the situation knowing it couldn't happen again.

But you want it to.

Rose shoved the voice aside. It didn't matter if she wanted to, she couldn't. Not while Alexander was hanging over her head. She'd received another text from the same number, but this one had been fishing, as if he wasn't quite sure where she was and was hoping to push her into answering him.

"Lily," Rose scolded, her signing sharp. "Please remember, this isn't our house. We can't just walk around and take whatever we want."

Lily made a face and put the cereal back in the cupboard.

Rose made a mental note to get to the grocery store. She really needed to purchase her own food so she didn't feel so bad every time they ate.

"What's the issue?" Ken asked, stepping into the kitchen as he rubbed his head with a towel. "Did you not find breakfast?"

"Oh, she did," Rose drawled, ignoring the way his wet and messy hair made him look too enticing. "But she doesn't have permission to eat it."

Ken frowned. "What? Of course she does. She has permission to eat anything in the house."

"We can't just eat all your groceries, Ken!" Rose said a little too loudly. Even Lily would be able to hear her at that level.

"That's exactly why I bought them," Ken said slowly, as if talking to a child. "So they would be eaten."

"But not by us," Rose pressed.

"Why not?" Ken demanded, dumping his towel on the counter. "Why does it matter who eats it?"

Rose threw up her hands. "We didn't move in here so you could take care of us financially, Ken. I'm perfectly capable of paying for our groceries. I've been doing it for years."

"No one is disputing that," Ken argued right back. "But until you get to the store, why does it matter?"

It mattered because Rose didn't want to be dependent on him. It was all too easy. Let him protect them, let him pay for the groceries, let him drive her to work... Soon Rose would have nothing of herself left. Everything she'd worked so hard for the last five years would be gone in a matter of days if she wasn't vigilant. "It just does," she said through clenched teeth.

Ken deflated and hung his head before looking back at her. "Rose. I'm not Alexander. I'm not going to demand something in return."

She stiffened. "How did you know he did that?" Though Rose had shared a lot the other night, she hadn't shared all the nitty gritty details of her life. Alexander had been a negotiator through and through. When he gave, he expected a return, and that included from his wife, family, and anyone else in his life.

Rose suspected that was part of why he was still after her. Yes, he had threatened her life, but she was almost positive that in his mind, he was simply taking back what was his. She just wasn't sure if he would want the money or her. Considering the way he had acted the last time she'd seen him, it was more than likely her.

Ken sighed and looked down at Lily, who was standing with a stricken look on her face. Her eyes were filled with tears as she looked back and forth between Rose and Ken.

Rose's heart lurched. She hadn't thought about what a fight with Ken would look like to her daughter. Lily worshiped the ground Ken walked on. But Rose wasn't used to having a man around. She wasn't used to having to check with someone else or get permission. She'd been making decisions for the two of them since Lily was born. A couple's fight, even if they weren't a couple, was a completely new concept to the tiny girl.

"How about you get a bowl of cereal and you can watch a cartoon while you eat breakfast?" Ken signed calmly before walking into the family room to turn on the television.

His ability to keep his emotions in check was amazing to Rose. Her entire body was humming with a mix of anger, attraction, and fear. How could he act as if nothing had occurred? She felt as if she would fall apart at any moment.

Lily wiped her face and looked at Rose, who nodded, doing her best to smile. "It'll be just like a Saturday!" She tried to appear eager, but Lily still looked upset when she finally padded into the sitting room to watch whatever was on the television.

Ken came back in and rested his hip against the counter, folding his arms over his chest. "Now...what was it you wanted to know?"

"I want to know how you knew about Alexander," Rose said carefully. Lily was out of hearing range unless Rose yelled. She'd traumatized her daughter enough for the morning. She didn't need to make it worse.

Ken pushed a hand through his drying hair. "I didn't," he said. "I only made an educated guess."

"An educated guess?" Rose argued. "How can you guess about something like that?"

"Rose..." he said softly. "I'm a police officer. Do you really think I haven't dealt with criminals like him before? Or haven't read and heard about their MO?" He shook his head. "This guy has 'sleazy loan shark' written all over him. I've seen his type. I've arrested his type."

It was Rose's turn to shake her head. "You can't begin to understand the amount of power he has."

Ken stepped up closer, his voice low but intense. "That's where you're wrong," Ken argued. "He doesn't have power. Not unless we give it to him. He has resources and maybe he has more than others, but at the bottom of it all, he's just a jerkwad with a bunch of cash, and he uses it to buy favors. Those favors are what keep him at the top."

"Maybe so," Rose whispered. "But that also keeps him out of range of the little guys. We can't compete."

"You're not one of the little guys," Ken said. "And you've got me, our friends, and the entire precinct of Seaside Bay at your disposal. Trust me...this guy doesn't stand a chance."

"If only it were that easy," Rose said thickly. She was so tired of being emotional. It almost felt as if she needed medical help as the pendulum of her emotions seemed to be running on extremes. From the fear and sadness of Alexander's impending arrival, to the highs of Ken's kiss. There had to be something wrong with her...but she wasn't quite sure what.

*****

Ken had a feeling they had definitely started this little adventure on the wrong foot. He should never have kissed her, even if he still couldn't seem to stop thinking about the moment. It played on a loop in his head, distracting him from everything.

And now she was fighting with him about the groceries. Who cared about the stupid cereal? It was just cereal! Lily was welcome to eat it and more. Ken wasn't trying to count every penny between them. If he had his druthers, he and Rose would have been married ages ago and what's his would already be hers.

He sighed and scrubbed his face with his hand. "Okay...let's just agree that food isn't going to be an issue and stress over things that actually make a difference, okay?"

Rose's shoulders fell slightly, which let him know she was giving in.

Thank goodness.

"Okay," she said. "But I'll still pick up some food later this afternoon."

"Fine," Ken said, backing away. "Pick up anything you want. But you both have permission to eat anything in the house."

Rose quirked an eyebrow. "Anything?"

Ken stopped moving. "Yes?" He wasn't quite sure where she was going with this, but he was willing to play along.

"Even the candy stash in the freezer?"

He scowled. "Been doing some snooping?"

Rose laughed, and the sound broke all the unpleasant tension of the room. "I had no idea you were such a fan of Sour Patch Kids."

Ken put his hands on his hips. "What can I say? I know what I like." When Rose's cheeks flushed, he knew she had gotten his message.

"Well...despite your permission, I'll be keeping Lily away from that particular corner of the freezer."

Ken grinned. "And maybe I'll make sure she knows where it is."

Rose spun and headed back to her room. "Your candy loss!"

"But it'll be you dealing with the sugar high!" he hollered. He continued to snicker when he heard Rose grumbling under her breath. Stepping forward to grab his towel he'd forgotten on the counter, Ken went back to his own side of the house to finish getting ready.

As captain of the precinct, he had put his men on alert for Alexander, and then worked his schedule to accommodate Rose's. He would drive her to work, Lily to school, and pick them all up. At least for now. The hope was he could continue this until Alexander was taken care of. If that ever happened.

Rose had received another text message yesterday, but it was just as vague as the first. It left Ken wondering what the man knew. Today at work, he planned to do some digging. There would easily be a rap sheet a mile long and notes from the case, prison sentence, and subsequent release.

He tossed his towel in the hamper of his bathroom and headed to his bedroom, only to bite back a curse and fall against the wall with a thud.

"Ken?"

He could hear Rose rushing his way. "I'm fine!" he croaked, clenching his fists for a second. By the time Rose rounded the corner, he was glaring at the ground.

"What happened?" she asked breathlessly.

Ken bent down and picked up a small toy. "I'm not quite callused enough to handle children's toys yet." He wiggled the sharp block at Rose with a smirk.

Rose slapped her forehead. "You've got to be kidding me."

He chuckled and bent forward to pick up the rest of them. "Nope. I've never actually had to watch for landmines in my own home, so I definitely haven't ever stepped on one before."

"I'm so sorry," she gushed, stepping forward to take the blocks from him. "I'll see it doesn't happen again. I'm sure Lily didn't realize—"

"Rose." Ken grabbed her shoulders gently. "It's fine."

She shook her head, obviously still flustered. "No, she needs to take more responsibility for her things."

Ken looked skyward and sent up a prayer for patience. This woman was driving him crazy in multiple ways. "She's five," he said more firmly. "It's fine. I don't expect her to not make messes, and I don't expect her to not play. Just because I'm not used to having it around doesn't mean I can't adapt." He grinned. "Truthfully, having someone to eat ice cream with in the middle of the morning is a definite perk."

Rose sagged against him and Ken automatically put his arms around her. "You're too good to us," she whispered against his shirt.

Ken rubbed her back. Rose had been strong for so long, he couldn't imagine what this must be like for her. Being chased by her crazy ex, moving in with the man who loved her, raising a deaf child by herself, running a successful business... The more he thought about it, the more in awe he was. "That's not possible," he said, kissing the top of her head. "You're an amazing woman, Rosalinda Ingalls. It's been an honor to get to know you over the years."

She shivered slightly before straightening up and pulling away.

Ken felt the loss immediately, like always. How he hated when she pulled back. It was never just a physical thing. It was emotional as well, and it hurt like the dickens. Even after five years, he couldn't quite stop the pain from slamming into his chest.

"I'll talk to Lily," Rose said softly as she turned to leave.

"Please don't," Ken said just as softly.

She stopped, but didn't turn around.

"I want her to feel safe and comfortable," Ken continued. "Which means, I promise not to fight with you anymore and I promise not to complain if there are toys or hair curlers or even princess underwear strewn around the house."

Rose laughed and turned. "You can handle princess underwear? What'll they say at the precinct?"

Ken shrugged. "Most of them are already dads. I think they'll get it."

Rose's humor faded and she swallowed hard. "You're going to make a wonderful dad someday."

Ken smiled sadly back, noticing very well what hadn't been offered. "Maybe that day is sooner than we know."

Her cheeks flushed once more as Rose slipped back to the kitchen, and Ken had a thought. Why did it matter if he tried to win her heart while they were living under the same roof? He could keep her safe while still trying to woo her. One didn't have to be separate from the other.

In his heart, he already felt as if Lily was his daughter. He had the desire to protect, to love, to play, and to watch her grow. His feelings for Rose were more complicated, but just as sincere.

It seemed stupid not to make use of the situation that had fallen into his lap. They both believed in boundaries as far as intimacy was concerned, but why should that stop him from trying to encourage her to break down the last wall of her objections?

There was nothing that said Ken couldn't put Alexander behind bars and still maintain a relationship with Rose.

He took in a deep breath, his path decided. She felt something for him and at the very least, she was attracted to him. It was a good starting point. Now he just had to use their time together to make it more.

Easier said than done.

CHAPTER 11

"Thank you, Officer," Rose said with a tired smile as she got out of the patrol car. Ken had been picking her up from work for the last couple of days, but he'd been off and watching Lily, so he'd sent another in his stead.

Her legs felt like stumps as she walked up the small sidewalk. Today had been one of *those* days. Rose had been on her feet the entire time. Apparently, the entire town of Seaside Bay had decided they needed flowers, and they needed it now.

Rose wanted nothing more than to crawl under the covers and sleep the night away. Her stresses, her burdens, her worries... All of them needed to just disappear.

Unfortunately, that's just not how life worked.

Three more texts had come in today and Rose needed to report them to Ken. Each time she saw another message, it made her heart stutter and her feet want to run, but she had been working to push back the sensation.

I want what's mine.

You'll pay me back in full.

Make this easier on yourself and call me now.

With each new text, Rose was more and more positive that Alexander wasn't sure *where* she was. And if she never answered, he might not even know for sure this was her number. He was more than likely waiting for some kind of response to fill in the gaps.

"Ken, I..." Rose trailed off as she entered the front door to one of the oddest but most endearing scenes she had ever laid eyes on.

"More?" Lily asked, holding up a plastic teapot.

Ken nodded. "Sure," he signed.

Rose put her hand over her mouth to stifle a giggle.

Ken glanced sideways at her and shrugged. "What are ya gonna do?" he asked softly. His extra large body was folded down on the floor with the coffee table between him and Lily. She was up on her knees handling the food and drinks.

A red liquid came out of the teapot and Rose assumed it was the Gatorade Ken kept in his fridge. But seeing a large, strong man on the ground wasn't what had her holding back laughter. It was the way he looked. Apparently, Lily hadn't just roped him into playing tea party. She had also demanded a certain dress code.

Ken's hair had been pulled back with barrettes and bows and headbands, and it looked like an accessories shop had thrown up on his head. His blond hair poked up in an array of directions and was mixed with purples, pinks, and glitter in abundance.

His T-shirt was gray, but that hadn't been enough, since he also wore a pink tie that Rose hadn't even known he owned. And lastly, a handful of necklaces hung off his wrist. More than likely the actual bracelets had been too small for his size.

"If you can't say something nice," Ken warned with a raised eyebrow, "don't say anything at all."

Rose pressed harder against her lips, but the giggle still slipped out. She slowly pulled her phone out of her back pocket, determined to get a shot of the precious scene.

"Don't even think about it," Ken growled.

Lily frowned and looked at her mother. "What's wrong?" she signed.

"Nothing," Rose said clearly, since her hands were busy. "I just thought we might want to document this for posterity." She pulled up her camera app.

Ken jumped to his feet. "You mean for blackmail," he said, rushing her.

Rose squealed as Ken grabbed her around the waist and pulled the phone from her hands.

Lily jumped to her feet. "Mama!"

"Don't worry," Ken said loudly to Lily. "Your mama is just fine." He pulled her back against his chest and Rose lost her breath. "Aren't you?" he whispered in her ear.

Rose nodded. "I'm fine, honey," she signed to Lily.

Lily grinned. "Are we taking pictures?" She pointed to Rose's phone.

Rose felt Ken stiffen behind her and she smiled. "I think pictures would be a great idea!" she signed and spoke, glancing over her shoulder.

Ken groaned and hung his head back. "How do men survive?" he mumbled.

Rose laughed and turned in his arms. She did her best to ignore how good it felt to be pressed up against him and snatched the phone out of his hand. "Come on, Lil," she said, reaching out to her daughter. "You come over and we'll take pictures of you and Uncle Ken together."

"Not so fast," Ken said, snatching the phone back. He bent down and balanced Lily on his arm, against his chest. "If we're doing pictures, your mama needs to be in them too, right?" he said carefully to Lily.

Lily clapped her hands. "A family picture!"

Rose felt her eyes widen and she met Ken's shocked gaze. His golden brown eyes slowly heated and Rose felt her temperature match his intense stare. Without warning, Lily snagged an arm around Rose's neck and tugged her in until they were all nestled together.

There was no way to miss the slight shake in Ken's hand as he held the phone out in order to capture all of them. Nor could Rose ignore how well they all fit together. Blond with brown skin mixing with two pale faced redheads. The contrasts were strong but complementary.

"Say cheese!" Ken shouted before grinning wildly for the camera and Rose found herself responding in kind. Lily looked like she was on cloud nine and it was hard not to enjoy the little girl's enthusiasm, even if it was misplaced.

When all was said and done, Ken set Lily on the ground and handed the phone back to Rose. "Do with those what you want," he said in a slightly hoarse tone. "But would you mind sending one to me first?"

Rose nodded. "Sure. I can do that." Her eyes fluttered back to the screen. She couldn't seem to stop looking at how happy they looked together. If only it could last more than the few seconds it took to take.

Lily skipped out of the room and Ken quickly pulled all the decorative pieces out of his hair.

"You're wonderful with her," Rose said before she could think better of it.

Ken shrugged. "I have sisters. I know how this works." He paused and glanced up at her. "Though I have to admit there isn't any evidence of the stupid stuff I did for them."

Rose laughed and put her phone in her pocket. "Pity. I would've liked to have seen that."

"I'll bet you would," Ken grumbled good naturedly. "If you decide to use those for blackmail, by the way, I have to admit I'll arrest you before I let you get away with it."

"What...this?" Rose took her phone back out and shook his. "Didn't you just ask for a copy of the picture?"

Ken nodded. "Yes. But that's for my own personal memories, not so I can show them to anyone else."

Rose pursed her lips to stop from laughing as she put her phone back in her jeans pocket. She clasped her hands at her waist. "Well...I suppose we'll just have to see how our living arrangement goes then. I make no guarantees I won't use them to get what I want."

Ken stepped up and crowded her space. "And what exactly do you want?" Their playful banter was gone instantly and Rose swallowed hard.

You.

"Freedom," she fibbed. Only, it wasn't exactly a fib. She did want freedom. From Alexander, from fear, from stress and worry...but she absolutely did not want that more than she wanted Ken. Nothing in life, other than Lily, made her feel the way the police captain in front of her did.

Unfortunately, she couldn't have one without the other and freedom wasn't going to be as easy as it had been to give her heart to Ken.

*****

Ken ran his fingers through his hair and backed away from Rose. "Freedom, huh? We live in America, right?" he quipped. He knew exactly what Rose was referring to, but the words were more than a little uncomfortable. He really struggled to pin down her feelings. One moment, he was positive that she returned his feelings, the next she was shutting him down without batting an eye. What was a guy to do?

Shut up and take it, he told himself.

Which is exactly what he had been doing for the last five years. He'd been quiet, loyal, caring and anything else Rose had needed, but he'd also worked hard not to step on a single toe as he did it.

Lately, that had been slowly changing. With the idea that she was in possible danger hanging over their heads, he had pushed her boundaries...more than a little. But Ken found he was growing tired.

Tired of the whiplash from her being receptive one minute and cold the next. Tired of holding back what he felt so he wouldn't scare her away. Tired of her being unavailable to him because of a past ghost. Tired of watching all his friends get the women they wanted...except for him.

He stepped back into her space, which must have shocked Rose, since she jumped at his nearness. "I have to know," he began.

Rose's blue eyes darted back and forth between his. "What?"

"About this freedom." His hand rose, seemingly of its own accord, and he trailed a finger along her jawline. "Am I on the list of things you want to be free from?" He swallowed hard. He desperately wanted her to answer one way, but was terrified she would answer another.

"I..." Rose's mouth opened and closed a few times.

Ken could practically see the wheels moving in her head and the emotions churning in her eyes. Fear, want, wariness, longing... The bundle nearly made *him* dizzy as he watched her try to settle herself.

"No," she finally admitted in a whisper. "I don't want freedom from you." She put her hand on his chest when he tried to lean down. "But you also scare me, Ken."

He froze. "I scare you?" he asked in surprise. "Me?"

Rose nodded. "At the risk of digging a little too deep too early, I'm scared that by taking another man in my life, I'll..." She looked away as if to gather her courage. "I'm afraid I'll once again lose myself in the process." Her eyes were misty when she looked at him again. "It has taken years for me to pull myself back together. I'm not ready to lose that again."

"Sweetheart," Ken said, sliding his hands along her waist until they were resting on her low back. "That's not how a real relationship works," he said. Knowing he couldn't have exactly what he wanted at the moment, he appeased himself by kissing her forehead, lingering just a little in order to breathe her in.

Rose slumped against his chest, letting him take her weight.

Ken tightened his hold, pressing his lips against the top of her head before resting his cheek against her hair. "In a real relationship, two people become the best versions of themselves," he whispered. "They don't lose who they are." She tried to lean back, but Ken held her in. "I don't want you to lose yourself," he said. "You're the most amazing woman I've ever met, and it was that woman I fell in love with."

When she pressed against him again, Ken let her lean back until they were looking each other in the eye. "How do you know that?" she asked. "How can you be so sure? As long as I've known you, you've never had a serious girlfriend, and I've never heard you say you were married before."

Ken chuckled. "Before I met you, I wasn't interested in a serious relationship," he admitted. "And after I met you, I couldn't look at another woman with anything more than friendship." He kissed her forehead again. "And no...I've never been married."

"Then how can you be so sure that's how relationships work?" Rose asked.

"Have you not paid any attention to your friends?" Ken asked with a grin. "Tell me they aren't all better people for having found their person."

Rose huffed a laugh. "Found their person? That sounds like something a dog would say."

Ken shrugged and resettled his arms against her waist. "It's true though. We find a person who's made just for us and we live happily ever after."

Rose shook her head. "Life isn't a fairytale. I should know."

"No, it's not," Ken admitted. "But there are parts of it that can be." He gave her a serious look. "You were young and inexperienced," he said. "Alexander took full advantage of that. He *knew* exactly what he was doing because he'd made a business out of being a manipulator, and he used the same tactics to get the woman he wanted."

Rose dropped his gaze, studiously staring at the neckline of his T-shirt. "Young and stupid, you mean," she mumbled.

"No, I don't," he said fiercely. "You said you jumped from home to home. Where in the world were you supposed to have learned what a happy family should look like?" Ken tilted his head until he met her gaze. "But even with your background, you can still learn now, Rose. You've already come so far. Why not see what's right in front of your eyes?"

"And what's right in front of my eyes, Ken?" she snapped. "A bunch of texts that may or may not be my ex trying to kill me?"

Ken shook his head. "No. What's right in front of your eyes are a whole bunch of friends who love you like family. A whole bunch of people who have set wonderful examples of what marriages can be if given the proper care." He took a deep breath for courage. "And a man who's more than willing to give that fairytale a try with you if you'll only let down your guard long enough for it to work."

Rose's face crumpled. "Ken...I already told you that I have feelings for you. But as long as Alexander is on my trail, I can't give you what you want."

Ken sighed and brought their foreheads together. "Has it ever occurred to you that this is the best time to start something?"

"What?" Rose pulled back.

Ken knew his next words were going to be harsh, but he had decided earlier that he was going for it. This was that moment. "How long do you plan to let Alexander run your life?"

Rose's face paled. "What are you saying?"

"You said you want freedom," Ken responded, dropping his voice. "But letting Alexander keep you running is the exact opposite. You're not free as long as you're afraid of him."

Rose pushed against his chest. "So what?" she demanded. "I should just not care if he kills me or Lily? Or hurts one of my friends?"

"Rose," Ken said firmly. "You know that's not what I'm saying."

She stilled and drooped against him. "I know," she admitted.

"If you want your freedom," Ken pressed, "take it. You've already done so much. Why not find your happy ever after?"

Rose looked up at him. "And you think you're my happy ever after?"

He couldn't help the small smirk on his face. "I'd sure like to try to be."

Her face was still serious. "And what happens when Alexander finds me?"

"We'll handle that as it comes," Ken answered. "Right now we don't know what he's up to. The texts could be from anybody, or maybe he really is fishing. Maybe he even knows where you are and is on his way, but you can't build yours or Lily's lives on maybe." He squeezed her for emphasis. "Take what you want. Now. You might never get another chance."

Her breathing picked up as she stared at him and for once, Ken couldn't tell what she was thinking. Her eyes were full of indecision and inner turmoil, making him wholly unprepared for Rose to leap up and kiss him.

He grunted, but stabilized himself and quickly took over the exchange. This kiss was entirely different from the "curious" kiss in the kitchen a few days ago. This was full of want and need and involved two people who had been kept apart for far too long.

Rose finally pulled back, but by then neither could catch their breath. "That's what I want," she whispered, bringing her eyes up to his.

"You're allowed to take that at any time," Ken said hoarsely.

Rose laughed quietly. "Anytime?"

"Anytime."

"Are we really going to give this a try?" Her voice had the slightest tremble to it.

"We're not just giving this a try," Ken said, resting his forehead against hers. "We're going to succeed."

CHAPTER 12

Rose closed the door on her shop, locked it, and let out a long sigh. The last few days had been so busy. She wasn't sure why flower fever seemed to have struck the area, but she was selling flowers like crazy, especially since she didn't have a wedding or party on the horizon.

"Must be something in the water," she muttered to herself. The smile that crossed her face after those words couldn't be helped. Despite how tired she was, Rose wasn't sure when she'd ever been so happy.

Ken's speech the other day had gotten to her on a deep level, and for the first time in a long time, Rose had let herself drop her inhibitions and move forward without fear of consequence.

The last forty-eight hours had been dreamy, as she, Ken, and Lily had felt like an actual family. Her phone had been quiet of suspicious texts, Ken was constantly touching her or taking her hand or stealing a quick kiss. Lily was happy as a clam having Ken around all the time and being able to talk him into anything she wanted. The man was a complete pushover. He couldn't seem to tell the girl no.

Rose chuckled as she remembered him with the hair clips in. One of these days she would have to put her foot down about how much sugar Lily was ingesting, but as for the play time? Watching Ken play with Lily only melted Rose's heart further. That, she could do with more of.

"Ready to go?"

Speak of the devil. Rose spun and smiled at Ken. He looked so dashing in his uniform. She'd never thought of herself as the type of woman to fall for a man in blue, but there was just something about it that made her want to kiss him until she couldn't breathe.

Because he was running a different schedule now, he usually picked her up in regular clothes, since he got off when Lily got off school. Rose was glad to see today he hadn't changed yet.

"Mama!" Lily came running from behind Ken and grabbed Rose around the legs.

"Hey, baby girl," Rose said, bending down to hug her daughter. "How was school today?"

Lily's hands were flying. "We used leaves to make pictures, and colored them with crayons." Lily continued to sign about her day, but Rose's eyes were caught up in Ken standing in the doorway.

Forcing herself to look back at her daughter, Rose did her best to concentrate. She couldn't help the yawn that slipped out, however. Rose's days were fantastic, but her nights had been difficult. It was the only downside to her and Ken's relationship. Living with him made her wish for things neither of them were ready for. Not to mention the squirmy toddler who had a habit of kicking in her sleep.

"Do you need a nap, Mama?" Lily asked, her light red eyebrows pulling together in concern.

Rose shook her head. "No, sweetie. Mama's fine." She stood and stretched her lower back. "How was work today?"

"Fine," Ken stated. "Quiet."

"I suppose that's a good day in policeman terms," Rose said with a smile.

Ken smiled back, but didn't make a move to touch her. They were both trying to be careful around Lily, at least for the moment. Rose wasn't sure they were fooling anyone though. Her daughter saw more than Rose wanted her to.

Lily tugged on her mother's hand. "Let's go home," she said.

Rose nodded. "I'm coming. Let me grab my purse and stuff."

"I got it," Ken said easily, slipping into the back room to grab her personal belongings.

Rose took Lily's hand and they followed him into the back room.

Ken came back with the purse and jacket and they all headed out to the waiting squad car.

"Did you come straight from work?" Rose asked as they got inside.

Ken nodded. "Yeah. I needed to stick around a bit today. Extra paperwork." Before Rose could ask any more questions, he responded to her fears. "Lily came to help me at the office today."

Rose looked down at Lily, who was grinning wildly. "You went to the station today?"

Lily nodded before she began signing fast again. "I saw the policemans and the dungeon in the back."

Rose raised an eyebrow. "Dungeon, huh? I thought they phased those out in the seventies..."

Ken chuckled. "She's referring to the holding cells."

"Ah." Rose scrunched her nose. "You should have brought her by the shop. I'm used to having her underfoot."

"Ah, she wasn't underfoot." Ken looked in the rearview mirror and upped his volume. "Were you, Peach?"

Lily shook her head. "No. Next time I'm going to shoot a gun!"

Rose choked on air and took a second to catch her breath. "I'm sorry...what?"

Ken put one hand in the air. "Sorry. One of my deputies got a little carried away. Said he would teach her everything he knew if she just kept smiling for him."

Rose rolled her eyes. "Good heavens. The entire precinct is full of pushovers."

"And proud of it," Ken said with a grin. "Most of my men are fathers. And at the moment, I actually don't have any women on staff, so there was no one to be strong when faced with those baby blues."

Rose shook her head, but smiled.

"Guess what, Mama?" Lily signed as they pulled into Ken's garage.

"What?" Rose helped her daughter unbuckle her car seat and climb out of the vehicle.

"I'm staying with Mrs. Hennessey tonight!"

Rose frowned and turned to Ken. "Why would she be staying with Mrs. Hennessey?"

Ken's ears turned red and he rubbed the back of his neck. "Uh...it was supposed to be a surprise."

Rose folded her arms over her chest. "Oh, really? And just what was this surprise?"

"A date!" Lily cried, throwing her hands in the air and spinning in a circle. "Date! Date! Date!"

Rose turned from her overly excited daughter to stare at Ken. "You want to go on a date?"

Ken made a face. "Yes?"

"Is that a question or an answer?"

"Both?" He shook his head. "I was planning to ask you very politely and with a bouquet of flowers that I have waiting for you inside. Mrs. Hennessey agreed to come watch Lily so I could take you to dinner and let you unwind from a very busy week." He put up his hand to stop her objections. "I still have people watching out for Alexander. I've put some police buddies of mine on notice. If something comes to your phone, I'll be right there to help deal with it." He gave her a hopeful smile. "But in the meantime, while we're waiting to see if he'll make a move or not...why not live...just a little?"

Rose took a deep breath. This was the same conversation that led to her saying yes to testing out a relationship with him. And the words were just as true now as they were then. She couldn't keep living her life in fear. That was how Alexander won. If she wanted her life, she was going to have to take it.

Her heart fluttered as she thought of a night without a child tagging along. A night of romance and a chance to hold Ken's hand without pulling away every time Lily walked into the room. A night that might involve another one of those mind blowing kisses. Was there really any other choice? "Okay," she whispered.

*****

Ken wasn't even sure how long it had been since he'd been on a proper date. The closest he had come were the bonfires he and his friends put together most Friday nights through the summer and fall. Now that everyone was in the stage of getting married, however, the bonfires weren't quite as frequent as they had been, which is why Ken was able to have the night to take Rose on a real date.

He'd made reservations at The Clam Pot, booked a babysitter, and now was spraying cologne on his chest in the hope that he didn't smell like the station anymore. He'd been there long enough that he was sure it was a permanent part of his DNA at this point.

The sound of laughter and cartoons carried all the way into his bathroom and Ken relaxed at the sound. He really did enjoy having Rose and Lily living with him. Although he was unsure how long it was going to last. Alexander had gone strangely quiet, and if he didn't speak up soon, it was probably best for Rose to go back to her apartment. It was already difficult having her around, but her safety trumped his hormones.

If there was no need for protection, though...Ken knew keeping her there would only make keeping their relationship within the right boundaries all the more difficult.

He stepped out into the hallway, trying to keep his crazy pulse under control as he prepared himself to see Rose. She wasn't in the sitting room, however, so Ken sat down on the couch with Lily and tried to relax.

Easier said than done.

"Ken?"

He practically leapt to his feet when Rose called his name from the room entryway. After recovering from his initial shock, Ken's eyes went all the way down Rose, then all the way back up. He couldn't help himself. Nor could he help the fact that his neck was probably just as red as Rose's face by the time he finished. "You look stunning," he said hoarsely.

"You look wonderful, Rose, honey," Mrs Hennessey said from behind Ken.

He closed his eyes and fought the desire to smack his forehead. He'd completely forgotten the older woman was there and he'd just acted like a drooling teenager in front of an audience. When Ken managed to open his eyes again, Rose was fighting a smile.

"Thanks," she said to Ken, then leaned sideways to thank Mrs. Hennessey as well.

Ken walked up and offered his hand. "Ready?"

Rose took a deep breath and put her soft hand in his. "As I'll ever be."

It took a few more minutes to get to the car, since Lily required goodbyes from both of them before they left, but soon enough Ken was driving down Main trying to find a parking spot. "It just occurred to me that I've never asked if you like seafood," he said, his mind racing.

"I don't think you can survive on the coast without liking at least a little of it," Rose said easily. She smiled at him. "I'm not a huge shellfish fan, but I don't mind salmon and halibut."

"Clams?" Ken asked. He and the guys used to go clamming and then have a big boil on the beach, but now everyone preferred their wives to slimy sea creatures. Ken couldn't blame them.

Rose shivered dramatically. "I've never tried them, but they look gross enough that I don't think I want to."

He laughed as he got out of the car and made his way around to open her door. "They don't taste too bad," he told her. "As long as you drown them in enough butter."

"Is there anything that isn't edible if it's been drowned in enough butter?" Rose questioned.

Ken shrugged, tucking her into his side as they walked to the restaurant. "Probably not, but I don't really want to find out."

"Welcome, Captain Wamsley," the host said with a small smile. "We already have your table ready," he said. "If you'll follow me." The young man grabbed two menus and led the way to the back of the restaurant. Apparently, Ken's request had been taken to heart. He and Rose were in a very intimate corner of the restaurant, one that would let them be free from prying eyes and have a quiet, romantic date. At least he hoped that's what it would be.

"Thank you," Ken said, then held out a chair for Rose. He scooted her in and walked over to his own seat. He pulled it a little closer to her side before sitting down and readjusting the place setting.

Rose's pursed lips look amused. "Sitting across the table was too far for you?"

Ken took her hand and played with her fingers. "Any distance is too far." He brought her palm to his mouth and gave it a soft kiss.

Rose's face flushed and she dropped her eyes to the table. "I haven't been on a date since before Lily was born."

Ken chuckled. "That's funny. I was thinking something similar. It's been a long time for me as well."

"You don't seem to be hurting for it," she teased. "You've been quite the Romeo, and we just got started."

"If you mean I was stunned into speechlessness when I saw you in that dress and couldn't get my caveman tongue back in my mouth, then sure...we can go with Romeo."

Rose's laughter was exactly what he'd been looking for. She opened the menu with her free hand. "I've never eaten here before. Have you?"

Ken nodded. "I have."

"Any suggestions?"

Ken thought it over, taking into account what she had mentioned in the car. "Do you trust me?"

Rose stiffened slightly and Ken realized exactly how his words sounded. He hadn't meant them to be quite so deep, but apparently nothing in their relationship was able to sit on the surface. They'd stayed away from each other for too long for anything to be casual.

Her blue eyes looked through him with unwavering intensity. "Yes," she said breathlessly.

Ken wanted to punch a fist in the air or puff up his chest in victory. He'd seen the signs over the years, as he got to spend more and more time with Lily and now as Rose agreed to move in with him. But there was something so satisfying about hearing the actual words that he struggled not to celebrate. Instead, he worked to keep things as light as he could, knowing they would need the break if they were going to survive the night. "Then I suggest the cedar plank salmon with asparagus."

Rose smiled shyly. "Whatever you think best."

Ooh, boy,...it was going to be a long night.

CHAPTER 13

Rose could see that Ken was becoming more flustered by the second. She didn't realize how fun it was to feel like she had power over a man. Tonight, though, since admitting she trusted him, she'd thrown a little bit of flirting his way and suddenly the big strong police captain was fumbling over his words like a teenage boy.

It was absolutely adorable.

Their waiter left, leaving her and Ken all alone, and the tension between them automatically tightened, nearly choking Rose with its intensity.

Ken reached over and took her hand, playing with her fingers. "Tell me what you're thinking."

Rose raised her eyebrows. "Uh..."

He grinned. "It had to be something good. Your face is all flushed."

Rose rolled her eyes to try and distract him from the chaos running through her brain at the moment. "There's a reason we're not capable of reading each other's thoughts," she drawled.

Ken chuckled, the sound low and delicious. "That's why I asked." He leaned in. "It must be good for you to be reacting this way."

Rose shook her head and pulled back just a little. She could hardly control herself when she was around the handsome officer. And since kissing him a couple days ago, she had become a mess of hormones. It was ridiculous. She was a mother and had an ex-husband. She shouldn't be feeling like a young woman in the blushes of her first love.

Ken brought her fingers to his lips. "Okay...mind reading is off the table. How about more about you?"

"More about me?"

Ken nodded. "Isn't that what dates are for? To get to know each other?"

Rose laughed softly and leaned onto the table with her elbow. "We've known each other for five years."

"True," Ken agreed. "But somehow, I have the feeling there's a lot that I still don't know."

Her playful countenance faded and Rose turned away. Yes, she had secrets. More than she should. But they had been in self defense, and had absolutely nothing to do with her date for the night.

"Hey." Ken squeezed her fingers and brought her attention back to him. "I wasn't complaining, Rose. I was simply saying that there are holes I'd like to fill."

He continued to play with her fingers and it was distracting Rose from his words, making it difficult to concentrate. "What would you like to know?" she managed to whisper.

Ken made a considering face. "Your favorite color?"

She laughed. "After all that, all you want is my favorite color?"

Ken shook his head. "No. After all that, I'm starting with the easy questions."

Rose grinned. "Okay. My favorite color is green."

Ken nodded. "Any particular reason?"

She shrugged. "I don't know. I like the way it represents life and growth. I love my flowers, but without the green stems and leaves, they aren't nearly as beautiful. In fact, without the greenery, flowers wouldn't be able to grow at all. The flower heads come and go, but the plant itself is steady." Her voice dropped a little. "I suppose green means strength and resilience to me."

Ken smiled sadly. "So you're less like your name and more like the vines?"

Rose hung her head and laughed a little. "I suppose so."

He shook his head, still playing with her fingers. "You're the whole package, sweetheart. The more I think about your story, the more in awe of you I am. You're that very same strength, resilience and growth, but it's all wrapped up in the most beautiful package I've ever seen."

Rose shook her head. "I didn't realize you were such a flatterer."

"I'm an officer," he quipped. "We don't flatter. We're truth tellers."

"I don't know if I can believe that," Rose challenged.

"Then I'll have to make it my personal mission to convince you."

Rose lost her breath for a moment. How did she manage to hold this man off for so long? The more time she spent with him, the more she realized how much of a miracle that was. "I had no idea you were so romantic."

Ken raised a single eyebrow. "You didn't give me the chance."

Rose pulled away, but Ken grabbed after her.

"I'm sorry," he said quickly. "That was a low blow and I should never have thought it, let alone said it."

"I didn't want to," Rose whispered thickly.

"I know," Ken soothed, gripping her hand between both of his. "I know, sweetheart. I'm sorry that I'm still working through my old-man bitterness."

"Old man?" Rose asked, wiping at her eye. "You know, I'm not sure I know exactly how old you are."

Ken blew out a breath and sat back in his seat. "Thirty-two," he admitted.

Rose shrugged. "That doesn't sound old to me."

"And you are?"

"Twenty-seven."

"You're not bothered by that difference?" Ken asked.

Rose shook her head. "No. Should I be?"

"I'm not," Ken said. "But that doesn't mean others aren't."

"Age is just a number," Rose said. "I've learned the hard way that a person's actions are much more important than how old they are."

*****

"Favorite movie," Ken continued. He didn't want them to dwell too hard on her past tonight. He'd already said some things he shouldn't have, and he wanted to bring the conversation around to more pleasant topics.

"Ugh," Rose groaned. "Right now all I see are Pixar movies, so..."

"Are you telling me that you don't love cartoons?" Ken teased.

Rose grinned. "I probably enjoy them more than Lily does, since I get all the jokes."

"True enough." Ken leaned back. "But for real. Before you were inundated with princesses and talking animals, what was your favorite movie?"

Rose pinched her lips together and thought about it for a few moments. "You know...I think it was *The Princess Bride*."

Ken nodded. "Not a bad choice."

"Not bad?" Rose cried. "It's got action, adventure, pirates, murders *and* romance. What more could someone ask for?"

Ken chuckled, then paused before answering because their food had arrived. "Thank you," he said as the waiter put down their plates.

"Anything else I can get you two?" the young man asked.

Ken looked to Rose, who shook her head. "No, I think we're fine. Thank you."

The server tilted his head, then disappeared.

"I haven't been so spoiled in ages," Rose whispered after they were alone again. She picked up her fork, but leaned in for a sniff. "Oh, my word. That smells divine." Her blue eyes met his. "I'm guessing your recommendation was pretty good."

"I sure hope so," Ken said before trying a bite of his steak. He didn't order steak very often, but tonight he'd wanted to splurge. This date had been a long time in the making. He had no desire to cut corners.

"Mmm…" Rose closed her eyes and hummed her enjoyment. "It's cooked perfectly."

He nodded. "Yeah. I've always liked their salmon."

"So how about some information on you?" Rose queried as she cut another bite.

"What do you want to know?"

"I know you have a good sized family," Rose began. "But I don't know the details." She glanced up from under her eyelashes. "Care to share?"

Ken nodded. "All right. I've got three siblings, all younger than me."

Rose snorted softly. "Why am I not surprised?"

Ken raised his eyebrows.

She tilted her head back and forth. "It seems to me that the oldest child always seems to be the most responsible one. As a police captain, you definitely are responsible and used to being in charge."

"I'm not sure if that's meant as a compliment or not," Ken said, making a face.

"Oh, it's a compliment," Rose clarified. "Being responsible is a great quality." Their table was quiet for a moment while they both ate another bite. "Do any of them live around here?"

Ken shook his head, his eyes on his plate. This is where things got a little tricky… "Uh, no. My parents live in Eugene along with one of my sisters. She's only five minutes away and has the only grandchildren, so they refuse to entertain going anywhere else."

Rose smiled. "How many does she have?"

"Four."

"And she's younger than you?"

Ken nodded. "Yep. They got started right off the bat and her last two were twins, so it adds up pretty quick."

"Oh my gosh," Rose gushed. "I can't imagine having to deal with two babies at once. It would have been insane."

"I don't think she got much sleep during that first year," Ken admitted. "I once heard her complain that she had about three hours a night for the first few months."

Rose winced. "Oh, man...that sounds terrible."

Ken shrugged. "She's fine now, plus my mom did her best to help so everyone survived."

"Where are your other siblings?"

The question was innocent enough, but this was exactly what Ken had been dreading. "Uh, my brother is down in Texas."

"Is he married?" Rose asked.

Ken shook his head. "Nah. He's going to school."

"Cool. And your other sister? I'm assuming she's younger than the one with four children?"

Ken's eyes couldn't seem to leave his plate as he nodded slowly. "Uh, yeah...she was number three."

"Was?"

Ken squeezed his eyes shut. Rose hadn't missed his verbiage, which both made this easier and harder. "Yeah. Miranda, uh, passed away."

"Oh my gosh." Rose gasped. She reached over and grabbed his hand. "That's terrible. What happened?"

Ken didn't answer right away and Rose gave his hand a squeeze.

"Please tell me," she whispered.

Ken sighed and set down his fork, giving Rose his full attention. "It was a hit and run."

Rose's eyes filled with tears. "How old was she?"

"Twelve."

Rose's hand went to her mouth and a couple of tears leaked down her porcelain cheeks. "Oh, Ken."

Ken cupped her face, wiping the tears away. "It was a long time ago, Rose. We're all doing just fine."

"What happened to the driver?"

Ken looked away before meeting her eyes again. "I don't know. He was never caught. She was walking home from school when she was hit. It was presumed he was drunk, since witnesses said the car was swerving widely, but no one was able to remember the plate or anything, so he was never caught." He sighed. "The guy clipped her just right, causing Clara to fall, and she hit her head on a rock with extra force." It took a minute for the next words to make their way out. "She was gone before the ambulance could get there."

"That's why," Rose whispered. "That's why you became a police officer."

It was a statement, not a question, but her assumption was dead on. He put his eyes back on his plate, poking his steak with his fork. "I swore I would do everything in my power to make sure this kind of thing didn't happen to another family. That another idiot who thought he was above the law couldn't take away from those who followed it." He was probably a little fiercer in his delivery than he needed to be, but this was a nerve that had never quite healed.

Their table was quiet long enough that Ken was sure Rose had left. He finally looked over, but instead of an empty chair he found a woman with tear-stained cheeks and adoration in her gaze.

It caught him off guard, not having expected his story to create that kind of response. "Some first date, huh?" Humor probably wasn't the best response in this situation, but Ken was wrung out. He needed a change of subject. Now.

Rose laughed through her tears and used her napkin to clean her face. "Actually, I was just thinking that this was the best date I've ever been on."

"Because I made you cry?"

Rose shook her head. "No. Because of the company."

CHAPTER 14

Despite the difficult topic of conversation during their dinner, Rose was telling the truth that this was the best date she had ever had. The food was good, the atmosphere romantic, and her companion more like a superhero than a normal human.

Ken finished signing his name on the receipt and handed the copy to the server. "Ready?" he asked Rose.

She nodded and began to stand, but he hurried around to pull out her chair. "Thank you," she said, giving him a smile.

"My pleasure," Ken said, returning her grin. He put his hand on her lower back as he guided her out of the restaurant. Once outside, he took her hand instead. "Would you like to take a walk? Or are you anxious to get back to Lily?"

Rose's heart stuttered at his consideration. The first half of her life had been an absolute disaster. Now...there was some hope on the horizon, which Rose desperately wanted to take advantage of. There was still a small part of her that was waiting for the other shoe to drop. That this lovely moment in time was just that...a moment.

"I'm all right with a walk," Rose replied, feeling the heat creep up her neck. She hadn't spent this much time with a man for years. Especially without Lily. But tonight she was caught up in the cozy feeling of the evening, the warmth of Ken at her side, and she found she wasn't at all anxious to go home to her responsibilities.

Ken's smile was slow and heart-flutteringly beautiful. "Sounds good to me." He slapped his firm stomach. "Besides, I think I need to walk off how much I ate."

Rose laughed and tucked a piece of hair behind her ear. "I hear you. I haven't had so many calories in ages."

Ken began to walk, then tugged Rose a little closer and wrapped his arm around her. Being so close forced her to put her arm around his waist in return and she wanted to sigh in contentment.

"Want to walk by the water? Or stay on the boardwalk?"

Rose considered. She loved the water at night, especially when the moon was bright, like it was at the moment. But walking in the sand meant she would have to take off her shoes, which wasn't quite as romantic as it sounded.

Ken chuckled. "Can't decide?"

Rose shook her head. "I love being near the water, but I hate getting sand in my clothes."

"Sounds like quite the conundrum."

Rose gave him a look. "It is. These are some of the nicest clothes I own." His eyes traveled over her the same way they had done when she'd first gotten ready. The flush she felt had obviously not been a fluke since it happened again.

"And it would be a shame to damage any of them." He leaned forward to kiss her forehead. "Have I told you how amazing you look tonight?"

Rose gave his side a squeeze. "Only one or twice."

"Well, let me make it three times." He dropped his voice into a husky whisper. "You are the most beautiful woman in Seaside Bay."

"You can't say things like that," Rose complained, putting her free hand against her cheek.

"Why not?"

"Because it makes it harder for me to be smart about us."

Ken frowned. "Are we not being smart?"

Rose groaned quietly. She didn't want to fight with him, nor did she want to ruin their lovely evening. But how could she explain how she was positive that this fairytale wasn't going to last? He had already declared that she deserved a fairytale, but Rose was sure she didn't. Somewhere, something would go wrong. It could be Alexander, it could be something else. Call it Murphy's Law, or Kismet, it didn't matter. She *knew* that eventually something would come along and ruin her happy ever after. "It doesn't matter," she said quickly. "I don't want to think about it." Looking up at him, she begged him without words. "Can we just enjoy?"

Ken's frown didn't dissipate, but he also didn't argue. "If you want."

"I want."

He nodded. "Then let's just listen to the waves and you can keep telling me about yourself."

Rose's groan was louder this time. "I think you know everything about me at this point."

"Why flowers?"

Ken's question caught her off guard. "What do you mean?"

"What drew you to flowers?" he asked. "You said it was something you picked up when you were married. But why? What about them fascinates you? And why bother to learn the language?"

Rose took a minute to consider his question. "Alexander used to send me flowers all the time," she began carefully. "They were an easy way to give me a gift and make me feel special, without much of an effort."

Disgust churned her overly-full stomach as she thought about how naive she had been back then. If she could go back in time and slap herself upside the head, she would.

"I'm struggling to see how flowers don't remind you of him," Ken said tightly.

They had paused on the boardwalk, their view of the ocean wide open. Rose rested her head against his shoulder. "His intent behind the flowers might have been dumb, but the longer I was surrounded by blooms, the more I came to appreciate their beauty." She pinched her lips together. "The more I realized how like them I was."

"What do you mean?"

"It's like I mentioned before," Rose explained. "Their beauty is fleeting. I'm self aware enough now to realize that to Alexander, I was simply a trophy. He liked the way I look and that made me valuable. The fact that I was young and stupid was a bonus."

"You weren't stupid," Ken inserted. "Inexperienced, yes. But not stupid."

"If you say so," she said.

"I do."

Rose smiled. "Fine, but back to your question. The lonelier I became in my marriage, the more I felt like the dying blooms. I had been given something beautiful, but it didn't last. It couldn't last. The romance didn't last. My first child didn't last. My happiness didn't last. Alexander's interest in me didn't last." A tear leaked from her eye and Rose straightened before wiping it away.

"Not everything fades away," Ken offered.

Rose gave him a sad smile. "Very little in this life lasts," she whispered.

"Most things last if we give them our time and attention."

"As long as our time and attention last," Rose argued.

Ken shook his head. "I think we're going to have to agree to disagree."

"Or you can just admit that I'm right."

He laughed. "I could say the same thing."

Rose leaned back onto his shoulder. "Yeah. Let's agree to disagree."

*****

Ken tried to content himself with Rose just leaning into his shoulder, but the task was nearly impossible. He'd managed to have a couple of quiet moments alone with Rose ever since she agreed to date him, but there was always the possibility that Lily would come skipping in on them at any moment.

Right now, he didn't have that worry. Lily was back at the house, Rose had admitted not only her feelings but that she trusted him, the night was cool, but not cold, the ocean was magnificent...what more could a man ask for than a kiss from the woman at his side.

Slowly, he moved the hand around her waist and rubbed against her arm. "Are you cold?" he asked softly.

Rose shook his head. "No. It's perfect out here."

Not quite yet.

Ken turned his and Rose's bodies until they were facing each other. His hands were looped around her low back. "I can think of something that would make this even more perfect," he said, staring straight at her mouth.

Even with his attention caught up on her lips, he knew her cheeks had to be flaming by now. She blushed every time he gave the slightest move toward flirting.

"You can, huh?"

"Yep." Ken pulled her in closer and brought his face down to hers. He could smell her flowery scent. Even with working in a flower shop all day, Ken knew that she wore a perfume with some kind of flower in it. He took in a deep breath. "What is that?" he asked, turning his head to draw his nose along her jawline. "You smell so good."

Rose let out a shaky laugh. "French Lavender."

"I'm going to buy stock in it," he whispered.

Rose's laughter grew. "You like it that much, huh?'

"Enough that I'll supply you with it for the rest of your life."

She pulled back just enough to look him in the eye. "You really think we'll last that long?"

Ken fought a sigh. They were right back to this topic again. He didn't know how to make her see that good things can last if taken care of. Maybe only personal experience would do so. If that was the case, he would be sure to give it to her. "Yeah...I do."

Rose pinched her lips together and her eyes dropped to where she was touching his chest. "And Alexander? What do you think will happen with him?"

That normal flare of anger burst to life in his chest at the mention of her ex. "I think that if he bothers to show his face in Seaside Bay, I'm going to nail him to the wall."

Rose's eyes widened as they darted up to meet his. "Ken," she breathed. "You can't do that. You never do anything outside the law."

Ken slowly shook his head back and forth. "The law is on my side."

"That's not how that sounded."

He shrugged. "I don't really care how it sounded. All I know is that he's a creep who doesn't deserve to look at you, let alone weasel his way back into your life. He broke the law and was convicted for it once. I'm not about to let him get away with it this time."

She blinked rapidly and looked out at the water.

Ken brushed hair from her forehead to behind her ear. "You deserve to live a life free of fear," he whispered, leaving a chaste kiss at her temple. "I'm determined to give that to you."

She turned back to him. "Are you saying you've become my personal protector?"

"Sweetheart, I was that a long time ago."

Rose laughed breathlessly. "I had no idea that coming to a tiny town on the coast would grant me such privileges."

Ken lowered his forehead to hers. "How about granting me a couple of privileges tonight?"

"Such as?"

"Such as letting me kiss you the way I've been dying to kiss you."

Rose's hand tightened on his shirt. "You haven't been happy with our kisses?"

A slow smile spread across his face. "Any kiss with you is wonderful. But every kiss we've had has been given with one ear tuned into your little five-year-old cutie who wouldn't quite understand if she caught us like this."

He could feel the exact moment she melted into him. Her hands slid up his shirt and locked behind his neck and her mouth came within millimeters of his. "Since you granted me the privilege of your protection, I think it's only fair I give something in return, right?"

"I did ask quite politely," Ken reminded her with a grin.

One of her hands crept into his hair and she tugged on him just the slightest bit. "Well, then...show me how a real officer kisses," she whispered just before bringing their mouths together.

She had asked for it, Ken definitely wasn't going to disappoint. Over and over again he kissed her, pulling her into his body and holding her in a way that he hoped let her know just how precious and protected she was.

He had thought of himself as her protector a long time ago, but it wasn't until recently that she had willingly let him take on the role. It was a part he would keep for life if she would only let him. Alexander was nothing but an annoyance that was keeping Ken from the future he wanted.

Ken's research showed him that the man was a coward. He had more money than courage and used that to purchase loyalty and muscle, then kept his hands out of it.

But since his release, Alexander had skipped town and no one knew where he was. That meant the guy had moved from annoyance to threat. Even though Rose's phone had been silent lately, it didn't mean Alexander was gone. It only meant he was biding his time.

There had been a moment when Ken thought their stint of living together might be over, but now Ken knew better. He'd spent half of his life studying criminals and becoming very good at his job. He might utilize his skills in a small town, but it wasn't because he wasn't capable of handling a big city. It was simply a personal choice that kept Ken at Seaside Bay.

Alexander was coming...and Ken would be ready for him.

And after good had triumphed over evil, Ken had every intention of seeing that Rose stayed in his house, but in a much different capacity than she was now.

CHAPTER 15

"Yoo, hoo!" The bell over the shop door jingled as Caro came in with a wide smile on her face. "Anybody home?"

Rose rolled her eyes and put her hands on her hips. "The store is open. Did you expect me to be gone?"

Caro grinned. "Well, you never know nowadays. Maybe a handsome police officer came and whisked you into the backroom for a bit of smooching."

Rose groaned and covered her face. "Caro..."

Caro's laughter was anything but repentant. "Ah, give it up, chica," the Southern woman drawled. "We've all known you had the hots for him for years. It's about time something came of it."

Rose shook her head. "I'm not having this conversation with you."

Caro marched up to the front desk. "Just who do you plan to have it with?"

Rose raised an eyebrow. "I didn't say I planned to have it with anyone. Maybe I don't want to discuss my private life." She felt some of her humor fall away. "Maybe I shared more of that than I wanted to already."

"Ah, sweetie," Caro crooned. "You need to get over the fact that we're family and we want to help. You've listened to all of us with our problems, even intervened with a few who didn't want to ask for help. Do you think less of us because of it?"

"Of course not!" Rose gasped. "Why would I think less of any of you?"

"Then why do you have it stuck in that pretty head of yours that we'll change our opinion of you?"

Rose sighed and leaned her hip against the counter. "Maybe because none of you were as stupid as I was."

Caro came over and gave Rose a fierce hug. "You might have been fooled, but you weren't stupid. Now stop calling yourself names."

"What else would you call it?" Rose argued.

"Honey, if you want to get down to the nitty gritty, every single one of us was stupid when we were young," Caro snapped. "Genni thought she was unlovable. Charli thought she had to beat the boys at their own game. Brook couldn't even see that the guy she was dating was the one she'd been in love with for years and even I thought the only way for my business to survive was to drive my soulmate out of town!" Caro threw her arms in the air. "We're all stupid! Deal with it!"

Rose couldn't help but chuckle a little. "I guess we all do dumb stuff once in awhile, huh?"

Caro nodded sagely, her lips pursed. "The worst part is, we'll keep doing stupid stuff until we die." She winked. "The point is to try to mingle some fun between the bad choices."

Rose laughed and shook her head. "You're ridiculous."

"And I'm also your best friend, so spill it."

Rose's eyebrows pulled together. "Spill what?"

"The deets, girl! I want to hear all about your date." Caro leaned in, her voice dropping dramatically. "And I want to hear if there was a kiss."

"What are we?" Rose asked as she spun and walked away. Her cheeks were twin flames. "Fourteen-year-old girls?"

"If we have to be," Caro replied, following Rose. "I probably won't fit in my jeans from back then and I definitely want nothing to do with the braces, but I don't mind pulling out my old Brad Pitt posters."

Rose began laughing again. She just couldn't help it. Caro was a hoot when she wanted to be and the lightness of the atmosphere felt wonderful. Rose's date with Ken had been fantastic. She had adored every minute of it, but even that was...intense.

Their relationship was starting off much more serious and in depth than most beginning relationships. More than likely that was due to the fact that Rose had spent so many years keeping a wall between them, while both parties had secretly fallen in love.

It was a near impossibility for them to start off as two strangers. They had too much history already.

"Caro," Rose warned. "You're ridiculous."

Caro shrugged. "That's fine. I can be ridiculous and still make the best chocolates this side of the Cascades." She waggled her eyebrows. "And Jack loves me whether I'm ridiculous or not, so..."

Rose's smile was starting to hurt her cheeks. "Thanks," she said sincerely. "I needed a good laugh."

"Yes, yes, you did," Caro agreed. "And now you need to tell me about your date."

Rose sat down on a bench that was normally used for decoration, but was currently free of planting pots. "You're really interested?"

"Are you kidding?" Caro cried. "Everyone is interested! If I'd let her, Charli would have demanded a movie night...but without the movie," Caro declared. "All we need is popcorn and your story and we're set for life."

Rose pinched the bridge of her nose. "I don't know how I feel about being the center of our group's gossip."

"Liar," Caro said easily. "We both know exactly how you feel." Caro planted herself at Rose's side. "Which is why I'm here instead of everyone." She reached into her purse and pulled out a small pink box. "Though I did bring snacks."

Rose smiled as she accepted a truffle. "Thanks."

"Anytime," Caro said around a mouthful of chocolate. "Now it's your turn to share."

Rose pinched her lips together for a moment before finally giving in. "Our date was...a dream."

"Oooh...good start."

For the next fifteen minutes, Rose relayed everything from them getting ready at the house to their time spent on the boardwalk. By the end, Caro was fanning herself.

"Holy cow, Rose!" Caro gushed. "Maybe I need to meet Jack all over again!"

Rose laughed softly and she wrung her fingers together. "I'm in trouble, Caro," she admitted in an almost inaudible tone.

Caro's humor was immediately gone. "What do you mean? Are you talking about Alexander?"

Rose shook her head. "No. Ken."

"What? Ken wouldn't hurt a fly!" Caro cried. "I mean, unless the fly was bothering you. Then he'd probably pound it into the ground, using his fists for good measure."

Rose was still shaking her head. "That's not what I mean. I'm in trouble because I'm in love with him."

"Ah, hon. Why is that a problem?"

Rose turned her head sideways to look Caro in the eye. "Because I thought I was in love with Alexander once too. What happens when Ken stops wanting me the same way Alexander did? Or what happens if Ken is hurt trying to protect me from Alexander? Or—"

Caro put up a hand and waited for Rose to stop. "You can't live your life on what if's," Caro said in a serious tone. "No one knows the future Rose." She set the box of chocolates aside and grasped Rose's clammy hands. "But we all have to live it and in some small ways, we can influence it." She smiled softly. "Ken loves you. You love him. And Lily loves everybody."

Rose huffed a small laugh.

"Take this happiness," Caro said, squeezing Rose's hands for emphasis. "The future can be dealt with as it happens, but if we make good decisions now...we can usually count on good things coming."

"I thought Alexander was a good decision," Rose argued.

"No. You were simply overwhelmed and deceived. And no one blames you for that," Caro explained. "But if you had been given enough time to think, you would've known he wasn't a good decision."

Rose took a deep breath. "So...what? I should just keep moving forward with Ken and pray that Alexander never shows up?"

Caro shook her head. "No. You should keep moving ahead with Ken and pray that *when* Alexander shows up, we have everything we need in place to put him back where he belongs. Because your future deserves to be free of this guy."

Rose took several calming breaths as she tried to let Caro's words penetrate. "I sure hope you're right," she breathed.

Caro tsked her tongue. "Honey, I'm always right. And we both know it, so there's no point in arguing about it."

Rose shook her head and hugged her friend. "Thank you."

"Anytime," Caro whispered in Rose's ear. "It's what friends...and family...are for."

*****

"Captain?"

Ken's head shot up from his desk.

Officer Windsor stood in the doorway with a smirk on his face. "Uh, I've got a lady out here who says she needs to speak with you."

Ken frowned. He didn't get visitors very often. "A lady?"

Windsor nodded. "Yep. Red-headed gal."

Ken smiled. "Let her in." He leaned back, eager to see why Rose would visit him at work.

Bright blue eyes peeked around the corner of the office door, but they weren't at the level that Ken had expected.

Ken chuckled and shook his head at Windsor. "Lily," he signed. "Come in!"

Lily rushed inside, leaping into his lap and burying her face in his chest.

Ken's amusement immediately disappeared. He glared at his officer. "What happened?"

Windsor shrugged. "She's fine. But something at school upset her today and she didn't want to go home."

Ken sighed and nodded. "Thanks. Send Rose a text and close my door, will ya?"

Windsor nodded and shut it behind him as he walked out.

Ken held Lily for a few moments, rubbing her back, before forcing her to sit up so she could see him speak. "Are you okay?" he asked.

Lily sniffled, but nodded.

Ken cupped her face and wiped her tears with his thumb. It squeezed his heart to see her so upset. He didn't have a ton of experience with kids, but he spent time with his niece and nephews enough to know that sometimes it was the little things that upset them. "Can you tell me what happened?" Sign language still felt fairly clumsy to him, though he tried hard. Usually he made extra sure his mouth was forming the words well so that she could rely on lipreading rather than his stuttering fingers.

Lily's bottom lip poked out and Ken had to hold back a smile. She was just about the most beautiful little girl he had ever seen. She looked exactly like a porcelain doll his sister had had growing up. White, flawless skin, wild, red curls, and soft pink lips.

Lily was the spitting image of her mama.

And when those cornflower blue eyes met his, Ken was a goner. With both of them.

When she didn't respond right away, Ken helped her pull off her backpack and set it to the side. The bright pink unicorns were almost an eyesore, but he figured it was par for the course for a five-year-old.

"Are you hungry?"

Lily hesitated, then nodded.

He pulled open the bottom right drawer in his desk and grabbed a granola bar, which Lily had half gone in about ten seconds. Chuckling, Ken lifted her up and walked over to his mini fridge, getting her a bottle of water as well.

With Lily settled on his lap, he went back to doing paperwork, assuming she would speak when she was ready.

The granola bar was gone and the water sipped on before she finally spoke.

"Brayden made fun of me," she signed.

Ken frowned. "He did? What about?"

Lily's lip began to tremble this time. "He said you weren't my dad."

Ken froze. *Ah, shoot.* He hadn't counted on this, though he should have. Kids talked...a lot. It should be no surprise that Lily was placing him in that role. "And, uh, what did you say?"

She huffed and her hands began flying. "I told him we live with you and I saw you kiss Mama, but Brayden says that doesn't make you my dad."

Ken nodded slowly, trying to figure out how to help her understand the truth. Lily had never had a male figure in her life before and it sounded like she wanted one.

That makes two of us, Ken thought wryly. He would love nothing more than to make this little girl his, but there were still a few steps that had to occur first.

"Actually," Ken said slowly, "Brayden is right."

Lily's eyes filled with tears. "You don't want to be my dad?"

"Oh, no, no, sweetie," Ken hurried to say. "That's not it at all!"

She tried to climb off his lap, but Ken put her back into place.

"Now, hang on and let me explain," he said loudly, since his hands were busy holding her.

It took a moment, but Lily stilled.

"Any man who gets to be your daddy is going to be one lucky guy," Ken said. "But in order to be your dad, he also needs to be married to your mom. And I'm not married to her."

"Do you want to marry her?" Lily asked innocently.

Where the heck is Rose when you need her?

It seemed unfair that he was the one having this conversation instead of Rose having to deal with it. Still...Ken cleared his throat. Perhaps it was best coming from him.

"Your mama and I aren't ready to be married," Ken explained. "But we like each other. And maybe someday in the future, we'll decide that's what we want to do, but we aren't ready for that yet."

Well...Rose isn't ready. I've been ready for ages.

"Do you love my mama?" Lily asked, wiping her nose on her hand again.

Ken grabbed a tissue and cleaned her up. "I do."

"Does she love you?"

Good heavens, this kid wouldn't quit. No wonder his sister was always complaining about her kids driving her crazy. "That's something you'll have to ask your mom," Ken said, deflecting the question. He could feel heat creeping up his neck and suddenly he really wanted this conversation to be over with.

"Mama does love you," Lily insisted. "I know. She let you kiss her."

He held back a groan. "Do you want to color a picture?" he asked, scrambling for his computer. "I'll bet I could download something for you. We have crayons in the back corner."

"Teddy?" Lily asked hopefully.

Ken let out a relieved sigh. Teddy was the bear they kept around in case they had to deal with a scared child during a call. When Lily had visited before, she had played with the stuffed animal with great enjoyment. "Teddy is in the same cupboard." He pointed across the room. "That one."

Lily hopped off his lap and skipped over, their entire uncomfortable conversation forgotten in the wake of play time.

Ken almost checked his forehead to see if it was sweaty, but he refrained. How in the world a tiny child could make him break out in a sweat that not even hardened criminals could was a mystery.

Windsor's face appeared in his door. "Got it covered?" he whispered.

Ken gave him a nod. "For now."

Windsor grinned. "Rose is still working. She said if you need to drop Lily off, just say so."

Ken glanced at the now happy child, then back at his officer. "We're good. I'll text Rose if necessary."

Windsor gave a mock salute and ducked out.

Ken woke his computer and, keeping one eye on his charge, went back to work, feeling an odd sense of contentment at having her there. Lily might have some hard questions at times, but there was no denying how much he loved the little squirt and how much he enjoyed having her around. If all went according to plan, he just hoped he got to have her around much more than a few hours in the afternoon.

CHAPTER 16

"You really think all this is necessary?" Rose asked as she sat in the Seaside Bay police station. Her foot was bouncing like crazy, but Rose wasn't even aware of it. She and Ken were getting together to talk about the information he had found on Alexander.

Rose really wanted everything that had to do with his case behind her, but the more she trusted Ken, the more she realized that allowing him the full use of his resources was going to help them in the end.

"I do," Ken said gruffly, his eyes stuck on his computer.

Lily was playing nicely in the corner with a large teddy bear that she seemed familiar with. Rose could only assume she had played with it before since Lily enjoyed spending time at the office. "What all are you looking up?" Rose asked.

"The files on the case," Ken replied, though his tone said he was slightly distracted. "And word on his release." Ken finally turned to give her his full attention. "Obviously, he's not on parole or he wouldn't be allowed to leave the city. And not only has he left, but no one knows where he is. With the texts he's sent, I think we can safely assume he's working his way closer to you."

Rose nodded, her lips pinched into a white line. She stared at her hands. Having Alexander come her way was enough to send her running into the night, but her friends were right. She'd never have peace if she kept running. And she'd never find more protection if she was among strangers.

Her eyes drifted to Lily. Alexander didn't know about the child, and that frightened Rose the most. She was terrified that when he discovered Rose hadn't told him about the pregnancy, he would do something drastic, like try to take her daughter away.

"How likely is it that the courts will give Lily to him?" Rose asked before she thought the question through. A sharp pain made it almost impossible to breathe as she thought of having to fight in the courts again. Getting divorced was hard enough, holding onto her child might be impossible, especially since Rose had lied by omission.

Ken's head jerked up from what he was working on. "None," he said bluntly.

Tears filled Rose's eyes. "You don't think they'll take her away from me?" Her knuckles were starting to ache from the way she was twisting them together, but Rose didn't care. A little pain was actually helping her focus at the moment. Her fight or flight instincts were screaming.

She didn't want Alexander here, in her little bubble of paradise. She didn't want to have to deal with this again. She didn't want to go to court. She didn't want Lily to be exposed to a man like Alexander.

"Rose," Ken said firmly.

She met his gaze, though it was difficult. Ken looked ready to tear something apart. Rose just hoped it wasn't her.

"No one is taking Lily away," he said carefully. "Her father is a convicted criminal and she has a healthy, happy life with you. There isn't a judge in the world who would view Alexander's case favorably, if he even dared try to attempt something so stupid."

Rose opened her mouth to argue, but Ken interrupted.

"Not even with his amount of money," Ken said in a tone that brooked no argument. He tilted his head. "Is there any chance that he would...simply take her?"

Rose's bottom lip trembled and she bit it between her teeth. "I don't know," she admitted hoarsely.

Ken sighed and scrubbed his hands up and down his face. "Well, that puts a different spin on things." He pursed his lips. "How desperate was he for a child?"

Rose shrugged and picked at a loose string on the arm of the chair she sat in. "He wasn't necessarily. I think it was more just another way to keep me under his control."

Ken nodded. "That makes sense."

"Plus, Lily is a girl and she's..." Rose trailed off, hoping Ken would finish the sentence without her needing to. Rose wasn't the least bit ashamed of her daughter's lack of hearing, but that didn't mean others felt the same way.

Alexander would more than likely view Lily as broken. And since she was female, she wouldn't be any use to him in the business...Rose hoped.

Ken grunted in disgust. "Then it sounds to me like we have nothing to worry about."

"Maybe."

Ken's eyebrows went up. "Why maybe?"

Rose wiped her face and took a deep breath to calm the shaking within her body. "Lily is useful to him...in order to get to me." Rose couldn't look at Ken as she said the words. They sounded too callous and egotistical all at the same time. She knew men considered her beautiful, but Rose didn't often feel that way. Being viewed as an object and coming to realize it was her exterior that had been the key to helping her break out of the cycle of poverty almost made her despise the way she looked.

Even now, Rose dressed nicely, but she never tried to show off and she rarely put on more than the basics of makeup. Her date with Ken had been one of only a handful of exceptions to her blend in rule.

Over the years of being by herself, a voice inside of her had grown stronger and stronger. One that wanted to be seen for her abilities, her kindness, her choices, rather than whatever she'd managed to be given in the DNA raffle. Rose would much rather be known as a competent flower arranger than a beautiful woman.

"That is one possibility to consider," Ken said as if the words were a foregone conclusion. "We'd be stupid to assume otherwise." He leaned back in his seat and folded his arms over his chest. "I think the key thing we're missing here is exactly *why* Alexander is coming." He held up his hand to stop Rose's immediate response. "We're assuming he's after you because of the money or because he feels he owns you, but all our theories are based on past behavior."

Rose shrugged. "What else do we have to go on?" she asked.

"Nothing, exactly," Ken responded with a shrug. "But we also need to realize that Alexander's probably not the same man he was five years ago...and that could be for better or worse."

Rose sighed and slumped in her seat. She rubbed her throbbing forehead. "I thought we were doing this research to give us a better understanding of the situation. Why does it feel like all it's done is bring up more questions?"

Ken nodded. "I know. Believe me, I know."

"I'm sorry," Rose said softly. "I'm not trying to diminish how this affects you." She gave him a tired smile. "I've been so grateful for you...in more ways than one. I don't think I could trust Lily and my safety to anyone else."

Ken leaned forward, his eyes intense, and Rose knew that if they were somewhere else, he would be kissing her. "I wouldn't trust your safety to anyone else," Ken said in a low tone. "I'm just grateful I'm in a position to do more than the average guy."

Rose nodded. "Right." She took in a long breath, letting it expand through the tightness in her chest. "So...what have you learned and where do we go from here?"

*****

Ken was grateful Rose was able to calm down and get down to business. Watching her cry was killing him, but with Lily completely oblivious in the corner, he didn't want to risk upsetting the whole room by rushing over to hold Rose and wipe her tears. Not to mention if he was holding her, he most definitely would be kissing her, and then they'd get nothing done at all...or at least nothing that would help them with Alexander.

"I think I've got the gist of the case," Ken said, forcing his eyes back to his computer. "Alexander was convicted of illegal money lending," Ken muttered, his eyes going over the case files. "It sounds like they had a hard time pinning him with anything else, since he had a tendency to let his muscle handle the intimidation side of the business."

Rose nodded. "Yeah. He was forever in meetings, but he rarely did the dirty work himself." She huffed. "Except when it came to me."

Ken felt his anger build at her words. Guys like Alexander were cowards, but the problem is, they were usually smart cowards. A person didn't run that big of an operation and keep away from the law without having the intellect to keep it going. "Well, he's already been taken down once," Ken said. "We can do it again if he pushes the line." Ken pushed the buttons necessary to print out a few things. "Now that he has a record, not just a file, the courts will be quick to take him back if necessary."

Rose nodded jerkily.

Ken could see she was still frightened and he didn't blame her. They were talking about Rose's safety and her peace of mind, but they were also talking about Lily's. Ken's skin crawled at the idea of either of them in trouble. He couldn't and wouldn't let that happen.

"We should probably come up with a plan of attack," Ken said softly. This was always a tricky part with any unsafe situation. It was better to be prepared, but it was also hard emotionally to plan for difficult situations.

Rose's hands were being pressed between her knees. "What do you suggest? Alexander hasn't even texted in almost a week." She bit her bottom lip. "You don't think it's possible he's moved on, do you?"

Ken could hear the hope in her voice and he hated to be the one to dash the illusion, but that's exactly what it was. He dropped his voice, making sure Lily couldn't understand what was being said. "More than likely, it means he's closer than ever," Ken explained. "It's not uncommon for a stalker to go quiet right before he strikes."

Rose's face drained of color and she swayed in her seat.

This time, Ken didn't hold back and he rushed over to kneel by her and help support her. "Breathe, sweetheart." He took exaggerated breaths with her. "That's it. In and out. In and out."

Rose's hand came out to clutch his. Her skin was cold and clammy, giving away her feelings as if her face wasn't enough to go on. "How do I keep my daughter safe?" she asked tightly.

"By staying with me," Ken said in a forced calm tone. "We don't know what he wants, but I don't believe he'll be content to say hello over a cup of tea."

"You said yourself he could have changed," Rose argued, an edge of desperation in her tone.

"If he wanted to reconcile in a civil way," Ken said, "I don't believe he would have sent you texts that can be construed as threatening."

Rose closed her eyes and her chin dropped to her chest. "I know you're right, but I wish you were wrong."

Skinny arms wrapped around Ken's neck from behind and a tiny body bounced against his back.

Ken forced a grin as he looked over his shoulder. "Hey, Peach," he said to a smiling Lily. "Have you been having fun?" he signed.

Lily nodded, then let go of his neck. "I'm bored."

Rose laughed and shook her head. "Having fun but bored. How can you be both?" she teased.

Lily pushed a chunk of red curls out of her face. "I was having fun. Now I'm bored."

Ken nodded and he climbed to his feet. "You can only play with Teddy for so long, huh?"

Lily bounced on her feet. "Right."

Ken glanced down at Rose, who had composed herself very quickly considering the circumstances. He hated to admit it, but she probably had a decent amount of practice in that. "I don't know about you," he began, "but I'm getting hungry for dinner. Should we grab some hamburgers and go back to the cabin to watch a movie?"

Lily bounced up and down. "With fries?"

Ken chuckled and rubbed the top of her head. "Of course! It's not hamburgers without fries."

"Yay!" Lily began to skip toward the door. "Come on!" she urged. "Let's go!"

Rose stood and stretched a little. "Thank you," she said softly.

Ken nodded in acknowledgement. "Sometimes a good old fashioned burger and fries really does help," he said with a grin.

Rose's smile grew, easing the ache in Ken's chest. "I suppose it does, but I'm a little more of a milkshake person myself."

Ken put a hand on the small of her back and led her down the hall. "Ah, but the real question is...chocolate or vanilla?"

Rose's mischievous grin over her shoulder was enough to bring Ken to his knees. "Neither," she said in a flirty tone. "Butterscotch."

Ken was still smiling as they arrived at his car and he opened the door for both of his passengers. "Buckle up, ladies, it sounds like we have quite a few appetites to settle tonight and it might take us a bit."

Lily's giggles could be heard through the car door and Ken enjoyed them all the way to the driver's side. Once again, he recognized just how used to this situation he could get.

But first...they needed to get Alexander out of the way. Permanently.

CHAPTER 17

Rose smiled as she listened to Lily laugh at the movie they were watching. Her laughter was like a balm to Rose's sore heart. She hated discussing Alexander and the horrible choices she had made while living back East. It only brought up bad memories and made Rose sink into a depression. But she understood why Ken pushed her the way he did. If they didn't understand the first set of troubles, being ready for the second round would be all the more difficult.

Rose just wished it didn't have to include all the biggest mistakes of her life.

Ken's hand landed on her neck and began to massage. "Don't think so loud," he whispered. "It's hard to follow the movie."

Rose laughed softly and let her head hang down. Oooh, the massage felt good. Every time Ken touched her, it felt good. Now that she had finally let down her guard, she had no idea how she had managed to hold him off for so long. He seemed to be able to anticipate her needs before she did. His caring and attentive behavior was more than she could have ever asked for and she had to admit she was a little surprised that he had stuck around as long as he had. Who would spend five years waiting on a broken woman with a special needs child?

Kenneth Wamsley.

He became more like a superhero every day.

"Just relax," Ken whispered again. "Nothing is happening tonight. We'll take time tomorrow to work on our game plan. For now, just enjoy the movie, your daughter, and the butterscotch milkshake made especially for you."

Rose glanced over her shoulder. "But not you?"

Ken's smirk was nothing if not playful. "That's a given. I didn't figure I needed to say it."

Rose laughed again, then allowed herself to lean back into the couch, resting against his shoulder. His hand grasped hers and Rose relaxed completely. Within only a few minutes, her head slipped sideways and she began to fight keeping her eyes open. She was warm, content, and felt absolutely safe. Trying to stay awake in those circumstances was nearly impossible.

"Mama!"

Lily's voice brought Rose out of her nap and she blinked several times. "Sorry," Rose rasped. She straightened and rubbed her face a little to wake up her brain. "Did you enjoy the movie?"

Lily nodded enthusiastically, then followed the action with a wide yawn.

Rose smiled. "I think maybe it's time for bed," she said. Standing, Rose took Lily's hand and began to walk her down the hallway.

Lily tugged on Rose's hand. "Wait!"

Rose looked down, her eyebrows raised.

"Uncle Ken!" Lily held out her hand to Ken, who was still sitting on the couch.

Rose held her breath as Ken looked to her for permission. He wasn't usually involved in Lily's bedtime routine, since it was easier to just keep it similar to what the child was already used to. Plus, Rose had been hesitant to let him get so involved in their lives in a way that would get Lily's hopes up.

Now, however, she found herself softening. Ken wasn't going anywhere, of that Rose was certain. And if he could ever help them break free of the Alexander fiasco, Rose was feeling quite confident that this thing between her and the handsome police captain had a strong chance of becoming permanent.

She nodded, giving him permission to come join her and her daughter, and the look that lit up his face was enough to send butterflies through Rose's stomach. Her free hand pressed on her belly, as if that would calm the teenager-like reaction.

Standing up from the couch, Ken swaggered their way, his eyes on Rose the whole time. He held out his hand to the waiting little girl, only then looking down at her. "What's first? Brushing teeth?"

Lily nodded and happily pulled both adults toward the bathroom.

Ten minutes later, Rose watched from the bedroom doorway, struggling with a mix of jealousy, fear, and overwhelming love as she watched Ken say prayers with Lily, then tuck her into bed.

"Night, Peach," Ken signed, then leaned down for a quick kiss on Lily's forehead. He stood and walked toward the door as Rose scrambled into the hallway.

Quietly, Ken closed the door behind him, then pinned Rose in place with his gaze. "She's wonderful," he whispered in a low tone.

Rose nodded, her eyes slightly misty. "I know. She's the only good thing to come out of my previous life."

Ken grinned and shook his head. "That's not true." Slowly, he moved toward her, until he had crowded Rose up against the wall. His strong arms caged her in and his large presence made her feel small and feminine.

"Oh?" Rose cleared her throat when the word broke. She'd never had anyone affect her like this. It was equal parts exciting and terrifying.

Ken's head shake was slower this time. "Nope." He rubbed his nose along her temple. "The strong, independent, and compassionate woman you've become is also a product of the trauma you went through," he whispered. "And as much as I want to kill Alexander for hurting you, I'll be forever grateful for all you've become."

Rose's knees were weak and she grabbed his arms for support. "Thank you," she breathed.

Ken brought their mouths closer. "Thank you," he whispered, right before cutting off all talking for the next several minutes.

*****

Ken had just settled in for a few moments of peace with Rose when she jerked against him.

Rose pulled back from their kiss and laughed softly. "Sorry," she whispered, tucking a piece of hair behind her ear. "My phone just buzzed in my pocket and it scared me." She jolted again, then frowned. "Holy cow. That's a lot of texts."

Ken pushed himself away from her. It was probably a good idea to cool off anyway. It was night and he shouldn't push the boundaries too far. "Might as well check on it," he said gruffly.

Rose glanced up at him with amusement. "You sound like a little boy whose favorite toy was taken away."

Ken rolled his eyes. "Maybe it was." Even in the darkness of the hallway, he could see the color creep into her cheeks. As he watched her, however, the color immediately drained when she read the texts. "Rose? What happened?" She didn't answer, so Ken grabbed her phone and began scrolling through the half dozen messages. A curse word slipped from his lips. "Is this the same number as the other texts?" he growled. When Rose still didn't answer, he jerked his head up to look at her. "Rose?"

Her hands covered her face and she shook her head. "How did he get those?" she whispered, her words muffled from her hands. Her hands dropped. "HOW DID HE GET THOSE?"

Ken put up his hands. "You're going to wake Lily," he said in a practiced calm voice. It was the same voice he used when dealing with overwrought victims when he was on the job.

Right now Ken's insides were roiling. The pictures of him and Rose and Lily together were as much of an invasion of privacy as someone could get. Now he knew a little bit of what Grayson went through on a daily basis.

The last text was the worst, however.

Who is this? Have you started a new family?

As Ken watched, another text came through.

Not for long.

Rose was openly crying now.

Without looking up from the phone in case another message came through, Ken reached out and gathered Rose into his chest. He was grateful she didn't put up a fuss. Her entire body trembled against him and Ken squeezed a little tighter. "It's going to be okay," he whispered. "We'll fix this."

"How?" Rose asked. "How can we win? We didn't even know he was in town."

"He might not be," Ken offered.

Rose leaned back so she could look him in the face. "What do you mean?"

Ken sighed. "He could have hired these out. He's definitely having you followed, but that doesn't mean that he's the one doing the following." Pinching his lips together, Ken thought hard for a minute. "In fact, based on his past, I would say he's *not* the one doing the pictures. His MO is definitely about hiring others to do the work. He's probably barricaded inside a hotel somewhere, keeping his face from the public, while he has others do the hands-on stuff."

Rose shook her head and let her forehead fall against his chest. "It doesn't matter. He still, obviously, has more power than I do."

"We're not giving up," Ken said tightly. "We just got started, Rose. Let me do my job and we'll take him down."

Rose jerked her head up. "He can't get to Lily, can he?" She tore herself from his arms and leapt across the hall to throw open the bedroom door.

"Rose," Ken whispered, tugging on her arm. "She's fine. My security system is in place. No one can get in without us knowing."

Rose's chest was heaving as she watched her daughter sleep peacefully.

He couldn't blame her. Sometimes a person just needed to see something in order to believe it. "She's fine," he whispered. "Let her sleep. You and I need to make a few phone calls."

Rose didn't move for a few moments, but eventually she nodded and backed out of the room. The door clicked shut and Ken took Rose's hand, pulling her into the dining room so they could set up camp at the table.

He picked up his laptop and set it on the table before calling the precinct. "Windsor?"

"Yeah, Captain?"

"We've got movement on Rose's case. I have a bunch of texts and pictures I'm sending your way. Start seeing if you can track where they came from."

"On it."

Ken hung up and immediately began forwarding the messages to his officer.

"What can I do?" Rose asked softly.

Ken glanced up. "Do you mind getting me some water? Then we need to discuss getting you a lawyer."

Rose frowned, but went to grab the water before she asked any questions. After setting down the glass, Rose slipped into a seat across the table from him. "Why do I need a lawyer?"

Ken kept his eyes on the computer. "We're going to need a restraining order," he muttered.

"Ken!"

"Yeah?"

Rose reached out and touched his arm. "Why do I need a lawyer?"

"We need to find a way to get Alexander out of your life or back behind bars," Ken explained. "We already have some evidence of stalking. A lawyer will collect the info and have it ready to take to court when we're ready to do so."

Rose slumped in her seat. "I can't imagine that a stalking charge will keep him out of my life for very long."

Ken shook his head. "It won't, but it will help create a history of using the law to keep him away from you. And I'm hoping the stalking charge is just a fall back. I'd like to have something stronger to throw at him to send a more impressive message, but if nothing else, we're prepared to start with the stalking."

Rose nodded. She tapped her fingers on the table. "Who do we have in town? Just Mr. Filchor?"

Ken nodded. "Yeah, but Grayson's brother is a lawyer and I think he might be a better choice."

"Why's that?"

Ken glanced up. "Because he'll be a little more knowledgeable about situations like this. We don't see much stalking in Seaside Bay. California has a lot more high profile situations like this."

Rose's face fell and Ken paused. Sometimes he got carried away by work and forgot to pay attention to the people around him.

"What's wrong?" he asked. He immediately wanted to smack himself. What *wasn't* wrong was a better question, but there was something happening right this moment that was bothering her, and Ken wanted to know what it was.

Rose shook her head. "Forget it."

Ken leaned across the table and took her chin, until she looked at him. "No. What is it?"

Rose's eyes were filled with tears and she looked defeated, even though they hadn't even started to fight yet. "There's no way I can afford Grayson's brother."

Ken almost said he would take care of it right then and there, but he knew Rose too well. "Let's not worry about that right now," he said carefully. "We'll take that on when we need to." There would be no later. Ken would take care of the bill. He was a single man with a good job and it had been that way for a long time.

No one would call him wealthy, but he wasn't hurting either, and taking care of Rose's lawyer bills would be the least he could do. After all, if he had his way, he would take care of her forever. A few bucks to keep her safe was absolutely nothing.

CHAPTER 18

Rose's head was pounding so hard that she could barely process everything that was being said. Grayson's brother, Carson, was on the phone talking rapidly about what information he would need sent to him and how Rose should handle things going forward. It was beyond overwhelming, but she also knew it wasn't something she should skip.

"Are you still there, Rose?" Carson asked.

"Yeah, I'm here," Rose responded. She knew her tone gave away her exhaustion, but she didn't have the energy to hide it.

Carson chuckled. "Hang in there," he encouraged. "I'm sure it feels like life will never be the same right now, but we'll get through this, okay?"

Rose nodded. "I mean, yeah. Thank you." She rubbed her sore forehead. "I'm grateful for all your help. I'm sorry if I'm a little distracted."

"Don't worry about it," Carson rushed to say. "I promise I understand."

A smile pulled on Rose's lips. "I'm sure you do. I don't know how you deal with junk like this all the time and still manage to smile." Carson's end of the line was quiet just for a split second too long and Rose realized the man wasn't as unaffected as he pretended to be. Her heart pinched that she was pulling him into the ugly mess that was her life. "I'm sorry," she whispered. "I wish I didn't need your help." After a second, she realized how that sounded and she hurried to correct herself. "I mean...I'm so grateful for you, but I wish you didn't have to deal with all this. I mean...someone needs to, and you're obviously good at it, but—"

Carson's laughter cut her off. "Rose...you can stop. I get it. And I'm glad I have what it takes to help you with this, but I totally understand wishing it wasn't happening in the first place." He sighed.

"Someone has to deal with the ugly part of life. I wasn't pretty enough to get slobbered over like my brother."

Rose laughed as intended, but she didn't agree at all. Carson, who had been the best man at Brooke and Grayson's wedding, was every bit as *pretty* as his brother. Carson was slightly smaller in stature and build, but not by much. Grayson's signature blue eyes were the only real difference. Instead of bright blue, Carson's eyes were more gray, which blended wonderfully with his dark Latino features. The woman who eventually caught Carson's eye was going to be lucky indeed.

That woman, however, was not Rose. Not only was her heart already taken, but her life was falling apart as they spoke. For just a few days, things had been perfect. Alexander had disappeared and her and Ken's relationship had solidified. It was a dream come true.

Until those pictures ruined it all.

Why can't he just stay gone? Why can't he leave me alone?

If she had the answers to those questions, then perhaps they could set the case to rest, but no one seemed to be able to figure it out for sure. Alexander was a narcissistic jerk and that was all Rose had to go on.

Her mind fluttered to the notebook she kept hidden in her mattress. It might just be the key to ending it all, but just as before, Rose was terrified that if she gave up the information she held on her husband, it would cost her something she wasn't willing to pay.

"I have a feeling you don't struggle in the women department," Rose teased.

His laughter grew. "Maybe not, but don't tell my brother. If my cover is blown, I'll have no way to bring him down a peg or two when his britches get too big."

"Your secret is safe with me," Rose responded automatically.

"And yours is with me," Carson said in a serious tone.

"Thank you," she whispered.

"We're going to get through this," Carson assured her. "Send me the info I requested and I'll get the case started. And follow Captain Wamsley. That man is your best chance at getting through this untouched."

"I will," she promised. Ken was a much safer bet than pulling out that notebook.

"Alrighty then. Anything else you need before we end this call?"

Rose took a deep breath. "Yes, actually. We haven't discussed payment at all." She hated the way the words tasted on her lips. They were necessary, but Rose knew full well the answer was going to hurt. She didn't have a lot put away, but hopefully it was enough to start a payment plan or something.

"Let's not worry about that right now," Carson said evasively.

"I hate to be pushy, but I will feel better if I have that under control," Rose responded. "Or at least a plan to eventually have it under control."

"What if you donated what you can to Bronson's Fathers and Sons charity?" Carson offered. "That way everyone wins."

Rose frowned. "Except you," she argued. "Carson, I'm not comfortable with you not being paid for this. While I'm grateful you're taking on the case, I'm not so far gone in my life that I'm willing to take charity."

"This isn't charity," Carson said quickly. "I promise. You just worry about keeping you and that little doll of yours safe and the bill will take care of itself."

"Carson," Rose said, her irritation bleeding through. "What aren't you telling me?" She could tell by the way he kept dancing around the subject that there was something she didn't know. What that was, Rose could only guess, but since this was her case and her life, she had every right to know what was going on behind her back. Especially since it involved her lawyer.

Carson sighed. "I'm not supposed to say."

"Either you tell me or I'll take things to another lawyer."

"Rose," Carson said on a sigh. "This isn't that big of a deal."

"It is to me," she said quietly. Rose couldn't explain it, but she hoped Carson would understand. She had paid her way ever since leaving Alexander. It was a part of the person she was determined to be.

A man had swept into her life and provided everything a princess dreamed of, but the longer it went on, the more Rose realized she wasn't a very good princess. Feeling like she relied completely on others made her feel helpless and like she was trapped back in Alexander's lair. She wouldn't go back to that. She couldn't. If Carson refused to give her a bill, Rose would just start sending him payments until he did.

She was not going to be beholden to anyone.

"All right," Carson finally conceded. "But now I'm going to be looking to you for protection, because Ken is way bigger than I am."

Rose stiffened. "Ken? What does he have to do with this?"

"Ken asked me to send the bill to him."

"Oh, no," Rose said. "No, no, no." She stood from the chair in her office and began to pace the small space. "He is not paying for me," Rose said through gritted teeth.

"I'll let you work that out with him," Carson said. "Just remember when you talk about it that his actions were done because he cares for you."

Rose squeezed her eyes shut and held herself up on the back of her chair. "I know," she forced herself to say. She knew. She even understood. But she didn't agree. "Thank you for telling me. I'll contact you again soon. If there's any other information you need, please let me know."

"Rose?"

"Yeah?"

"It's all going to work out okay."

"I sure hope so," she said before hanging up. She dropped the phone on the desk and took a moment to breathe deeply. Come tonight, she and Ken needed to have a talk. And it wasn't going to be pretty.

*****

"Boss?"

Ken looked up from his desk. "Any news?"

Officer Curby, who had taken over for Windsor for the morning shift, shook his head and leaned against the door frame. "The trace was a bust. They lost the signal up in Washington."

Ken pinched his lips together. "So he's close?"

Curby shrugged. "Maybe. I would at least venture to say he's not still over on the East Coast. But without a hit, we don't know for sure where he was texting from."

"Understood," Ken said firmly. "Up the amount of drive-bys at the school and shop."

The officer nodded. "On it."

He slipped down the hall and Ken was left to his quiet office once more. Now if only his brain was as peaceful. Instead, his head swirled with worry, anger, and frustration. He wanted this thing with Alexander done and to see the man behind bars again. How dare he try to scare Rose! How dare he poke into her and Ken's life and especially bring Lily into it.

The anger that coursed through his body at the thought of that creep having Lily photographed was enough to make Ken's skin feel hot to the touch. He was also upset on behalf of Rose, but Lily was so small, so defenseless. It brought out every protective instinct within his body and filled his mind with the ugly pictures of his sister's passing.

Every time he closed his eyes, Ken could see Clara's too-still body in the casket. The makeup they had used wasn't quite enough to hide the bruises and damage done from the car, and the vision made Ken sick to his stomach.

His hands clenched and his emotions grew until he thought he would explode. Slamming his fist on his desk, he ground his jaw and growled. He couldn't fail again. He couldn't let another female within his care fall victim to people who cared little for human lives.

This was exactly why he had become a police officer. To save those who couldn't save themselves. To protect the innocent. To bring peace and justice to those who didn't have the power to do it on their own.

He never would have imagined that his entire future depended on his fulfilling those promises. If he failed Rose the way he had failed Clara, Ken knew he wouldn't be able to handle it. He *needed* to catch Alexander and give Rose the future she deserved.

His phone buzzed, pulling Ken from his hazy thoughts. He glanced at the text.

We need to talk.

Frowning, Ken pushed the call button. "What's wrong?" he asked as soon as Rose answered.

"I just spoke to Carson a few minutes ago," Rose said in a frustrated tone.

"Oh, good," Ken said, not quite understanding what she could be upset by. He had spoken to Carson earlier and it sounded like they would all be on the same page without any trouble.

"I asked him about my bill," Rose said, leaving the remark slightly open ended.

"Okay." Ken wasn't going to offer anything she didn't already know. He had known she wouldn't be happy about him interfering with the money aspect of things, but he wanted to see what Carson had said before he began to argue with her.

"You're not paying for my lawyer."

Well, crud. Apparently, Carson wasn't as good at keeping secrets as a lawyer should be. "Rose," he began.

"No," she interrupted. "This isn't up for discussion. I will pay my own way and that's the end of it."

"Rose," Ken groaned, pinching the bridge of his nose. "Let me help. I know that can't be an easy thing for you to take on."

"My finances aren't your concern," Rose snapped. "I have paid for everything ever since I left the East. I'm not about to start relying on someone now."

Her words hurt, much more than Ken had expected they would. He knew she would object, but this was more than that. He could hear the emotion behind her words. But he was the type of person who took care of people and she had admitted she didn't have the money for this. After discussing things with Carson, even Ken had been shocked at what something like this would add up to. There was no way Rose had that kind of cash saved up and Ken refused to let her pay on it for the next ten years. Rose had paid enough because of Alexander. She didn't need to give up her financial security as well.

"This isn't about relying on someone," Ken began. "This is about the smartest choice for right now."

"It's not happening, Ken," Rose continued. "I'll pay my own way."

He closed his eyes and sighed. "Why don't we finish this discussion at the house tonight? Speaking over the phone probably won't help anybody."

"There's nothing more to talk about," Rose said firmly. "As far as I'm concerned, this conversation is over. I appreciate that you want to help, but your role as a police captain is the best thing you can do for me. You've already been generous enough."

"I'll see you tonight," he said, feeling suddenly exhausted. They weren't going to resolve this by shouting over the phone. Shouting actually wouldn't help resolve it at all, and it would be better to speak about it in person. Maybe Ken could convince her to let him pay and let her believe she could pay him back later.

If they got married, which he hoped they eventually did, then she wouldn't end up having to pay him back at all.

He straightened in his seat. That was a good plan. If he could just hold her off long enough for the case to finish and him to convince her to marry him, then they could put this whole lawyer bill behind them.

Ken nodded. That's what he would do. He wouldn't deny, he would just delay. Then they could focus on more important things than money. Like how to catch someone who seemed a little too good at hiding.

Ken went back to his computer. There had to be a way to track Alexander down. His behavior toward Rose was escalating and that was exactly when criminals began to make mistakes.

He clicked on a link and suddenly a name and phone number appeared on his screen. It hadn't occurred to Ken to talk to the detective who had put Alexander away the first time. Maybe the man could shed some light on Alexander's preferred methods and repetitive behaviors.

Pushing his fight with Rose aside, Ken grabbed his phone and placed the call. It was time to dig a little deeper. Then and only then would he be able to present himself to Rose and Lily as a viable candidate for a husband and father. Until he solved this case, Ken knew he would never be worthy of them and would never be able to move on. And the time had come for all of them to move on. This had gone on long enough.

CHAPTER 19

Rose closed the shop right on time that night and headed for home quickly. She had been so agitated all afternoon she could barely function. A rational part of her brain knew that Ken was only trying to help, but the traumatized part of her felt like she was dealing with Alexander all over again.

Her own wants and needs were being bulldozed so that someone could "take care" of her.

She didn't want to be taken care of. She didn't want to rely on others for survival. She enjoyed her freedom and independence and even if she and Ken ever looked at marriage, Rose knew that she wouldn't allow it to be the same type of marriage she had previously come from.

That kind of relationship should be an equal partnership and after having a few hard knocks, Rose knew she was willing to fight to have it that way.

She waved goodbye to the officer who had followed her home and walked inside to the smell of roasting chicken. Her heart pitter pattered just a little when she realized that Ken was cooking for her. It was a chore they had been sharing, since both of them worked, but tonight had been her night on duty.

She set down her purse next to the door and walked to the kitchen entry. Ken was standing at the stove, Rose's pink apron tied around his waist, with Lily on a step stool to his left.

"Easy does it," he said in his low, rumbly tone. He held her hand, guiding it while the little girl stirred something in a pot. "If we go too hard, it'll splash all over us."

"That would be hot!" Lily declared.

Rose smiled a little at her daughter's enthusiasm. Lily was a bright, inquisitive child and she had never let her hearing disability stand in her way. It had been a privilege to watch her learn and grow over the years. It was something that Rose knew Alexander would never have appreciated. In fact, Rose had a suspicion that Alexander would have rejected Lily because of her disability, though Rose had never mentioned that out loud.

He doesn't know he's a father, Rose reminded herself.

The pictures he had sent came back to her and Rose stiffened. Maybe he did know he was a father. No...the texts had seemed to indicate that Alexander thought Rose had had a child with another man. For now, that would work in her favor, but in the long run, it didn't necessarily keep Lily safe. If Alexander thought that using Lily to bend Rose to his will would work, Rose knew he would do it.

"Mama!"

Rose came out of her thoughts just in time for Lily to run into her thighs. "Hi, sweetie," Rose said loudly.

Lily looked up and grinned. "We're making dinner!"

Rose nodded. "I can see that." She glanced up at Ken. "I thought it was my turn tonight."

He shrugged. "It was. But we both thought you had enough things to stress about." He motioned between himself and Lily.

"And you don't?"

Ken gave her a half smile. "No stress. Just privileges."

Rose rolled her eyes. "Oh, my. Does that work on all the ladies?"

"Wouldn't know," Ken said, turning back to the stove. "I've never tried it on any of them."

Rose flushed. She knew that Ken hadn't dated anyone since she'd arrived in Seaside Bay. Not that all of that time had been her fault, but as they'd gotten to know each other, Rose had never once seen him stray or flirt with other women. For a man she wasn't dating, he had been amazingly loyal.

"Come eat!" Lily pulled Rose toward the small dining table.

"Are you sure there's nothing I can do to help?" Rose asked. She didn't like feeling useless. It just reminded her of why she was ticked at Ken to begin with. Though, it was hard to stay mad when he was going out of his way to help her feel better.

"It's done," Ken assured her. "Lily and I just need to plate it and then we'll be good to go."

Rose twiddled her thumbs for a couple of minutes before they were all in their seats and grace was offered. The dinner was quite good. It was a chicken and rice dinner, almost Middle Eastern in its flavors and a far cry from their usual coastal fare.

"This is really good," Rose complimented as she wiped her mouth. "Thank you, both." She winked at her daughter, who giggled. When Lily went back to her plate, Rose turned to Ken. "I'm surprised she's eating it," Rose mouthed.

Ken nodded. "My sisters always ate what they helped make, so I figured it would work on Lily as well."

Warmth swirled in Rose's core. She could only imagine how wonderful of a big brother this man had been. It was no wonder he felt so responsible for his sister's death. Ken was the type of guy who took responsibility for everything around him, and his sister's passing would have hurt immensely.

Despite the frustration she still held in the back of her mind, Rose couldn't help but admire his stance. Alexander ran his business and life completely differently. He wanted credit, but took no responsibility. Others did his work for him, but Alexander got the glory. Ken took no glory, but definitely shouldered the responsibility.

Was it any wonder that the police captain had stolen Rose's heart eons ago? Whether or not their happy story would continue remained to be seen, but for now...her emotions for him only seemed to expand with every new thing she learned.

*****

Ken could see the fight going on in Rose's eyes. She looked torn and Ken assumed it had to do with their earlier conversation about money. His gut was positive that when Lily went down for bed, the gloves would come off.

"You two cooked, so I'll clean up," Rose said, jumping to her feet and putting things away.

"We'll help, Mama," Lily offered, carrying her plate to the sink.

Ken joined them, and side by side, they put away dinner and got the dishwasher running. The scene was decidedly domestic, and Ken found that it helped fill a little piece of him that had been missing.

Longing for Rose had kept him from feeling whole for a long time, and now she was in his life, but there was still an unseen wall between them. He was enjoying her kisses and had taken her on their first date, but danger was always lurking around the corner.

It was clear that until Alexander was dealt with, their future would always be precarious. and Ken was growing impatient for it to feel more secure.

Then she can't argue about you paying her bills, he thought to himself.

"Ken?"

He looked up from where he'd been wiping the counter.

"A word?"

Lily had disappeared and Ken could hear the television going, so he assumed she was preoccupied for the moment. "Sure," he said with a smile. He probably wasn't going to be smiling in a minute.

Rose checked in on Lily, then led him down the hall.

Ken folded his arms over his chest, preparing himself to do battle.

"I wanted to make sure we were on the same page after our chat this afternoon," Rose said, putting her hands on her hips. Apparently, she was feeling a little defensive as well.

"The one where I pay for things?" Ken nodded. "Yep. We're good."

Rose's face turned red.

He probably shouldn't have started their conversation that way. It was a little on the boorish side, but unfortunately his patience had been wearing thin for several days. He didn't want this to be something they worried about. Alexander was far more important.

"Kenneth Wamsley," she said in a tight tone. "That is *not* what we discussed at all."

He couldn't help but smirk a little. "You called me by my whole name. Should I be scared?"

Rose threw up her hands. "I feel like I'm talking to Benny!" she said.

His grin grew. "He and I are friends, you know."

"Yes, I'm aware," Rose said wryly. "But I also know that when Benny acts like this, he drives you crazy." She raised an eyebrow. "So why do you think it's fine to do it to me?"

Ken relaxed. "I know," he said softly. "But seriously, Rose. I don't even want to discuss this with you. I have the money. It's not a hardship. Let me help."

"You are helping," Rose argued. "I'm living with you. You're already paying more than your fair share for groceries. I'm relying on you all day as you help me keep my daughter safe." She shook her head. "So, don't act like I haven't already met you in the middle."

"Rose," Ken said softly, stepping forward until he could brush his fingers on her cheek. "Don't you see? I *want* to do all those things. I want you here. I want to keep you safe. I want to be involved in your problems. I want to help shoulder them and take care of you and Lily."

"The last time a man took care of me, he abused me and threatened me with bodily harm," Rose said tightly.

Ken dropped his hand and stepped back. "There's no way you can compare me to that creep."

Rose closed her eyes and her chin fell to her chest. "No," she said softly. "I know you're not like Alexander." Her head came back up and her expression nearly broke Ken's heart. "But what does that matter if the end result is the same?"

Ken scowled. "What does that mean?"

"It means that when you push your way, no matter how politely the request, it means that my needs and wants get left behind." Rose backed up a couple of steps. "I spent years setting aside what I wanted in order to try and make Alexander happy. I assumed that because I wanted something different from him, there had to be a problem with *me*." Her finger jammed into her sternum. "But I've grown up since then," Rose continued. Her eyes were misty, but the tears didn't fall. "I've learned that I can give a lot before I break, but that I am always happy and healthiest if I don't wait that long. Sometimes I need things to happen a certain way because *I* need them that way."

All of Ken's defensiveness began to drain away. He hadn't quite looked at it like that. All he wanted to do was protect her, whether it was from physical danger or financial upheaval. He hadn't even bothered to consider how this would feel from her end, and that was something he was quickly growing sorry for.

"I don't demand my way all the time, but this…" Rose swallowed hard. "This is one of those important things to me," she finished softly. "When I finally found the courage to get away from Alexander, I promised myself that I would never again let myself be in a position where I relied wholly on others. I might not have a big bank account and I'll more than likely never be wealthy, but that doesn't mean I can't take care of myself."

She straightened her spine and shook her head to toss her hair behind her shoulders. The righteous indignation in her stance was a glorious thing to watch and Ken found himself entranced by the strength of character she showed while explaining herself. She was being firm but vulnerable at the same time and once again, it made him realize how much he didn't deserve her.

"I understand that you want to help," Rose continued, speaking over Ken's thoughts. "But please remember that this is *my* life and in order to be healthy, I need to have boundaries. Those include taking care of my own bills, Ken. So while I appreciate that you wish to help, I'm asking you...as a friend...as more than a friend...to let me handle this."

There was nothing for Ken to do but nod. "I'm sorry," he said sincerely. "My intent was never to take away your choices or bulldoze you into my way of thinking." He sighed. "I guess I've always been a little thick headed when it came to seeing other people's sides," he admitted, rubbing his suddenly hot neck. "I'll do my best to be more careful about it."

Rose nodded, then stepped up and cupped his face before leaving a light kiss on his jawline. "Thank you," she said softly. "I'm not sure I can adequately tell you how much I appreciate all you've done for us."

Ken put his hand over hers. "I'd do it all again in a heartbeat."

With a soft smile, Rose pulled away and walked around him to join Lily in the family room.

Ken watched her go, but for the first time since their little family had arrived, he didn't feel the desire to join in. He had moved Rose into his house to offer her protection, but he supposed that a naive part of him had thought how wonderful it would be to play "house" for a while. And it was, for the most part. But Ken was quickly starting to realize that a relationship to the depth that he wanted with Rose was far more than him just taking every burden from her shoulders and stealing kisses in the shadows.

His mind was swirling with a hurricane of emotions he wasn't quite sure how to handle. He had always been a fairly simple guy, and nothing about his current situation was simple.

Deciding a few minutes to himself were probably the best thing he could do right now, Ken headed to his bedroom. He'd leave the door open in case Rose or Lily needed anything, but perhaps a little bit of time rethinking his normal tactics wouldn't be a bad idea.

CHAPTER 20

Alexander had gone into hiding again. After sending that slew of pictures and asking weird questions about her "new family", he hadn't texted again. Rose could almost convince herself it was all a random joke.

Except that Ken was convinced his silence only meant he was closer than they thought. He already had eyes in place, the only thing left was for Alexander to show up himself. That thought had Rose jumping every time the bell on the shop rang or her phone went off with a message.

"Why can't we just get this over with?" she grumbled to herself as she stuffed a rose into an arrangement. "Ouch!" She must have missed a thorn because her thumb was now bleeding. Continuing to grumble under her breath, Rose sucked on the wound as she headed to grab a tissue.

Discovering her box was empty, she picked it up and nearly chucked it across the room. Why was everything going wrong today? Murphy's Law was working overtime.

Pushing open the door to her workspace, she headed out to the front. They usually kept a box of tissues at the front counter. Halfway across the room, Rose froze. All the air was sucked from her lungs and she could feel the blood drain from her head.

No. No, no, no!

Her chest began to heave and black spots danced along her peripheral vision.

"Hello, Rosalinda." Alexander's smooth tenor hadn't changed in five years and even if Rose hadn't been able to see him standing right in front of her, she would have known his voice anywhere.

"Oh, do you know Ms. Ingalls?" Susan asked. She finished punching a few buttons on the register. "Here's your receipt, sir."

Alexander never took his dark eyes from Rose as he accepted the piece of paper. "Thank you," he said. "You're very kind."

Susan flushed and turned to look at Rose. The flush drained and the older woman frowned. "Rose? What's wrong?"

"What are you doing here?" Rose managed to push out, though it felt like walking through concrete. Her body was still as stiff as a board and refused to obey her the way she needed it to. She wanted to run back to her work room and call Ken. Or maybe run to the street and see if an officer was close by. Anything!

But instead, she stood in one spot, unable to look away or react to the man smirking at her.

"Interesting," he crooned, taking his bundle of flowers and stepping around the counter to come closer. "I thought for sure you'd be happy to see me." Alexander stopped a few feet away, but leaned in. "It has been five years, after all."

"Which is not long enough," Rose snapped. She felt some of her muscles begin to loosen. The relief that brought was overwhelming. In just a few more seconds, she was positive she would have full control of herself again.

"Rose," Susan whispered in shock.

Alexander tsked his tongue and shook his head. "That's not a nice way to treat your husband."

"You are *not* my husband," Rose argued. "We've been divorced for a long time."

"And I can't blame you for that," Alexander said in a calm tone that was starting to grate on Rose's nerves.

How dare he taunt her, then show up and act as if nothing had changed between them! The anger building inside of her helped get rid of her debilitating fear and she shook out her hands, shifting her knees in a way she hoped he wouldn't notice.

"After all, waiting for a spouse who was spending time in jail definitely wasn't a good use of your time." He tilted his head. "But I have to admit, I hadn't expected you to rush off and find another man so quickly."

Rose ground her teeth, but didn't respond. If he wanted to think she was married to Ken, that was fine. It only made her unavailable. The bell over the door jingled, but Rose couldn't look away from her situation. She hoped Susan was able to take care of whoever it was without too much trouble.

"But then I got to thinking." Alexander tapped his bottom lip. "The little girl..." He raised an eyebrow. "The one who looks just like you...was too old to be the product of a new marriage." He sneered. "Not to mention, you never wear a ring."

The anger that had been helping relieve Rose's stiffness started to dissipate. She didn't like the way he was bringing up Lily, and his words were starting to sound a little too close to the truth. "What do you want, Alexander?"

He gave her an innocent look and spread his empty hand out to the side. "All I want is what's mine."

"Nothing here is yours," Rose said, though the breathy tone of her voice betrayed her fear.

"You don't think a paternity test would confirm otherwise?"

"You can't have her," Rose cried, clenching her fists.

Alexander's eyes went to her hand. "Rosalinda, darling..." He walked up and took her hand, rubbing his thumb along her knuckles. "You're hurt."

Three times Rose tried to pull her hand away from him, but each time, Alexander just held her tighter.

"Ah, ah, ah," he crooned. "We wouldn't want to get blood on your floor, now would we?" Keeping eye contact, Alexander brought her fingers to his lips and kissed the wound on her thumb. "Try to take better care, hm?" Dropping her hand, he began to fuss with the flowers in his arm. "I don't like my things broken."

"I'm not yours," Rose whispered. The fear was winning again at the moment, though her mind was screaming for her to run and find help. Why wouldn't her body obey? Alexander had almost full control at the moment and Rose hated the feeling of helplessness she was exuding. It was as if she hadn't learned anything at all from her years of independence.

Alexander chuckled, the sound somehow crossing the bridge between amused and menacing. "My dear Rosalinda." The smile dropped from his face. "You will always be mine."

The sound of a car door had Rose's eyes darting toward the front of the shop.

"It appears the cavalry has arrived," Alexander said sarcastically. "I'll see you soon." Without another word, he handed her the bundle of flowers. "I think you'll find those to your liking," he whispered before sidestepping her still body and disappearing through the back.

It was only moments later that Ken burst through the front door. "Where is he?" he shouted.

Rose didn't answer. Instead, her eyes were fixated on the bundle in her arms. With each flower she noticed, her stomach churned stronger and stronger. Alexander knew all about her fixation with flower language, and now he was using one of the greatest joys of her life to send a message that made her sick.

"Rose." Ken's voice had dropped. "Was he here?"

She nodded, her body beginning to shake. The paper around the flowers crackled as it shook in her hands.

"Where is he?"

"He went through the back."

Ken hesitated, then nodded and disappeared himself.

As soon as she was alone, Rose dropped the flowers on the floor and crumbled. Her energy was spent and her hope was now gone. She'd trusted that with Ken and the others helping her, they could make this work, but now Rose wasn't so sure. In only a few minutes' time, Alexander had very handily managed to show that, as usual, he was one step ahead of her. He was one step ahead of everyone.

*****

Ken burst into the alley, searching everywhere for movement. His hand hovered next to his gun, as he had no idea what exactly he would be facing with this guy.

His heart was beating nearly through his chest and the part of him that was in love with Rose was screaming that he needed to go back inside and check on her.

It had been easy to see that she had been through a horrible shock. Her white skin was paler than normal and she had barely acknowledged his existence, taking several seconds to recognize what he'd even said.

It took several minutes to make sure the alley was clear and once done, Ken found himself equal parts frustrated and relieved. Alexander was gone, but not in the way Ken wanted. Still, having the all clear allowed Ken to go back inside and check on Rose. He needed to know what had happened.

Susan had been running down the street, presumably on her way to the station, when Ken had driven by. He'd immediately pulled over, then taken off again for the shop. It had to have been Alexander. There was no other explanation for what he'd heard was happening.

"Rose?" Ken asked as he came in the back door. She didn't answer, so he walked out front to find her in the same place he'd left her, except that she was in a heap on the floor.

Susan was kneeling next to her, petting Rose's head and muttering soothing words.

"I've got her," Ken said, coming down to Rose's level. He tilted his head toward the door. "Why don't you turn the sign and lock up?"

The older woman nodded jerkily, then glanced at Rose once more before climbing to her feet and doing as Ken had asked.

"Rose?" He took her chin and forced her to look his way. Her eyes were glazed with shock and Ken knew it would take a little while to get her to come back to the present. "Did he hurt you?" He tilted his head in order to get a better look at her, but he didn't see a wound of any kind. "Rose? Are you hurt?" Ken spoke louder, though he made sure to keep his tone pleasant. His eyes caught on a smear of blood on her hand and he pulled it up, examining the small cut. It didn't look like something she would have received from Alexander.

Rose shook her head. "No," she rasped. "I'm not hurt."

He rubbed the spot for a second. "Good." He stood up and bent down to pick up Rose. "Susan, please call the station and let Officer Curby know what's going on. I'm going to take Rose in the back and help her come out of her shock."

The employee was wringing her hands together, but she nodded.

Ignoring the fact that he was smashing flowers under his boots, Ken walked to the back room and set himself down in a chair he hoped would hold his weight. Without so much as a peep of protest from her, Ken settled Rose on his lap and tucked her head into the crook of his neck. "I'm here now," he whispered, rubbing her back. "Everything's going to be okay."

For several minutes, Ken kept doing his best to help Rose calm down and come out of her frozen state. He had seen victims in situations like this before and he knew she probably needed to go see a medical professional, but Ken couldn't quite bear the thought of letting go of her. He could hold her and keep her warm until she was able to be present. That would be enough.

Slowly, he felt her trembling body begin to ease under his ministrations. Her breathing deepened and the shaking slowed down. Finally she put a hand against his chest. "Thank you," she whispered.

Ken gave her an extra squeeze. "Anytime." He waited a moment more for her to really relax before asking, "Can you tell me what happened?"

Rose nodded and leaned up. "Yeah." She took in a shuddering breath and wiped at her face.

Ken hadn't even known she was crying, since she had been facing away from him. He hated seeing her like this. The strong, capable Rose who had put him in his place just yesterday was gone and in her place was a frightened, broken woman. She was barely recognizable.

"I didn't hear him come in, since I was working in here," Rose explained. She spent the next several minutes describing her encounter with her ex and by the end, Ken was struggling not to hit something.

"Did he say anything about where he was staying or where he might go next?" he asked tightly.

Rose shook her head. "No. But he sent a message through the flowers."

Ken raised his eyebrows.

"The buttercups stood for unfaithfulness," she began, "the yellow carnations say he's disappointed in me, the geraniums mean stupidity."

Ken grunted.

"And the nasturtium stands for...conquest." Her voice had dropped and Ken found himself squeezing her tighter against him.

"Did he say anything else?" he ground out. This guy had gone too far.

"Just that he would see me again soon."

"Not if I have anything to say about it," Ken snapped. He forced himself to calm down when Rose winced at his tone. "We might need to shut down the shop and have Lily skip school for a few days until we get this all settled," he said.

Rose blinked a few times as the words penetrated. "You think we need to hide?"

Ken shook his head. "Not hide, exactly. But we need to be in control of where he can get to you. Lily is vulnerable at school, just like you're not safe here at the shop. Which was proven by the fact that even with extra patrols, no one was around when he strolled on in."

Rose slumped, her eyes falling shut in defeat. "Knowing Alexander, he knew exactly what he was doing. He probably timed his visit to be between the patrols."

"That's likely," Ken said, his mind working feverishly to figure out how he was going to nail this guy. He didn't want to wait until Alexander had made a move. He didn't want someone to have to be hurt before they could put him behind bars. He needed to take this guy out now.

Rose jerked upright. "Lily!" she cried, turning to Ken. "We need to call the school now! We need to pick her up! What if he went straight there? He knows she's his daughter now!"

"We're already on it."

Both Ken and Rose snapped their heads toward the voice. Officer Curby stood in the doorway, looking slightly sheepish. He scratched his chin.

"Uh...since Cap was helping you, Ms. Ingalls, we thought it best after hearing Sue's story to call the school. They have her in the principal's office until one of you two pick her up."

"We have to go now." Rose jumped to her feet. Her movements were overly frantic and Ken was honestly afraid she was going to hurt herself.

"Take a deep breath, Rose," he instructed, rising with her and taking her arms. He waited until she looked him in the eye. "We're going to go together, right now, to pick her up. She's safe and well cared for." Ken spoke very deliberately because Rose was still not acting rationally, and that was completely normal after a traumatic event, but he also knew she'd be mortified if she made a crazy decision while she was in this state of mind. "After we have her, we'll go back to my house and hunker down for the night. Okay?" He raised his eyebrows as he waited for her to process what he said.

"Okay," Rose breathed. She turned to Officer Curby. "Thank you," she said hoarsely. "I appreciate you thinking of her."

Curby nodded. "We're all here to help, Ms. Ingalls. We won't let this guy get away with anything."

Rose nodded and let Ken direct her outside to his squad car. When she was seated in the passenger side, Ken leaned in and helped her buckle since her hands were still trembling uncontrollably.

It only took five minutes to arrive at the school, but Rose couldn't seem to sit still the entire ride. After explaining that Lily would be absent for an indefinite amount of time, Ken drove his girls home and locked them all in the house.

"Who's hungry?" he hollered, heading straight to the kitchen after he had set the house alarm.

"How can you eat?" Rose asked, her voice quiet enough that Lily wouldn't pick up on the words.

Ken gave her a reassuring smile. "Right now my only thought is for Lily," he explained. "When she's content and taken care of, then I'll put my focus on Alexander and what I need to do. But until that point, I don't want her upset any more than she already is."

Rose slumped against the wall, pushing her hands through her hair. "I feel like such a failure," she admitted.

"Hey, hey," Ken said, rushing over to her side. "You're not a failure. You're here, Lily's here, I'm here." He tilted her chin up. "No one is hurt. Everyone is safe. There is no failure in that."

"I froze," Rose rasped. "All these years I've planned what to do if I ever saw him again. Everything from a slap across the face to breaking his nose." A dark chuckle slipped past her pale lips. "I even considered what it would be like to simply forgive him."

Ken's anger flared at that. He wasn't ready to forgive. He wanted justice first.

"But when it actually happened, the first thing I did was turn right back into that frightened little mouse that he manipulated for so many years." Rose shook her head. "What's wrong with me?"

"Rose," Ken said a little harsher than he'd intended. "Nothing is wrong with you. Now, we're going to focus on getting Lily taken care of and occupied, and then you and I are going to talk. Okay? Come on, now. Your daughter needs you."

Rose took in a long breath, then nodded. "You're right. She needs to come first." Straightening, Rose headed down the hall to their shared room, where Lily had disappeared.

Ken went back to the kitchen, hoping a quick treat would be enough to distract the child from the current situation. He had no idea, however, how he was going to handle Rose. A sugar high wouldn't be nearly as helpful in this case.

CHAPTER 21

The longer the afternoon went on, the more agitated Rose became. Ken's presence had slowly helped her feel safe, and with that safety came the confirmation of how horribly she had handled the situation earlier.

She was embarrassed, she was angry, she was ready to plan a way out of this situation, but Lily had decided she was far too excited to go to sleep and Rose was at her wit's end.

"I've got her," Ken said, relieving Rose of her nighttime duties. "Go grab a cup of something warm to drink and we'll talk when I come out."

Rose nodded her thanks, kissed Lily's forehead, and walked out of the bedroom. She normally wouldn't have just handed Lily over, but Rose knew she wasn't controlling herself very well at the moment. She needed a break and Ken was the only way for her to get it.

Ken didn't have a tea kettle, so Rose warmed up a mug of water in the microwave before dunking a bag of chamomile in it. Anything that might help her calm down would be a welcome addition to her life at the moment.

"She's asleep," Ken said as he came into the kitchen.

"That's impressive," Rose said, turning and resting her lower back against the countertop. She held the hot mug in her hands, soaking the heat into her brittle bones. She had never quite gotten full control of her body ever since this afternoon. The heat helped calm her tight muscles and Rose closed her eyes, taking a deep breath of the fragrant tea. "What are we going to do?" Rose asked before even opening her eyes. When Ken didn't answer right away, she looked at him and raised her eyebrows. "Ken?"

His face had gone from tired to hard as granite. "*We* aren't doing anything," he all but growled. "You are going to stay safe and I am going to get this guy out of our hair."

"Oh, no, you don't," Rose argued, coming to sit at the table with him. She set down her mug and leaned in. "We already talked about this with the money. You don't get to just take over." She held up a hand before he could argue with her. "I know I didn't handle things well this afternoon. I had almost convinced myself that he wasn't coming. That we would be able to go back to our regular lives and that somehow I had only imagined it all." She rubbed a hand over her face. "I know how stupid that was, but still...I let today catch me off guard." She pushed out a loud breath. "But I won't let it happen again." Straightening in her seat, she met his glare head on. "So I ask again, what are we going to do?"

"My answer hasn't changed," Ken said in a low tone. "This is a matter for the police. Your only job is to stay safe and keep Lily happy. My team and I are the ones who are going to handle the creep."

"Ken...I can't not be involved," Rose argued. "He's my problem."

"He's entering stalker territory," Ken shot back. "Once he crossed the legal line, he's no longer your problem, he's a problem of the law enforcement in whatever area you're in. In this case, it's me."

Rose rubbed her forehead. A killer headache was trying to invade and she didn't have the strength to fight it. "I can't just sit back and do nothing," she whispered.

"No one is asking you to do nothing," Ken said. His large, warm hand came across the table to rest on hers. "I'm asking you to take care of yourself and Lily so I can focus on getting Alexander behind bars."

Rose let her head fall back. "How do we know he won't just do this again?" she asked. She looked him in the eye. "So we pin him for stalking. Somehow I doubt that gets him put away for very long. Am I supposed to spend the rest of my life fighting to put him in jail every couple of years?"

"We went through this before," Ken said slowly, as if he were talking to a toddler. The action irked Rose more than it should have.

"First we need to get him off your back, then we'll put him away for a bigger crime than stalking." Ken's lips pinched together. "I'm so close to a breakthrough, I just know it!" He slammed his fist on the table, shaking Rose's mug. "There are so many red flags in his past, and all that's lacking is the right piece of evidence. If we can just find something concrete, we can put him away for good."

Rose picked up the cup and cradled it again. Her hidden notebook was sitting heavy in her gut. Should she pull it out and give Ken what he needed? But Alexander didn't know she had it. If he found out, he'd probably do something drastic and Rose couldn't afford the possible consequences. No...it was better to let Ken find what he needed on his own. That was his job after all.

Plus, right now she was working to hold onto her temper. While she appreciated "police-Ken" for being so protective, she also hated the anger that sometimes came up when he went into protective mode. She was never concerned that he would hurt her, Ken wasn't the type, but she feared that he would hurt someone else. Especially if he ever got a hold of Alexander.

"Sorry," Ken grumbled, rubbing his eyelids with his fingers. "All my research points to Alexander being involved in a whole bunch of crimes that carry heavy sentences. I'm positive that he was in charge of them all, but I'm lacking any concrete evidence."

Rose bit back the confession about her notebook and nodded sadly. That notebook was the only piece of insurance she had. She knew Alexander would do anything to keep it out of police hands. If all else failed, it had been her one hope for freedom. She couldn't give it up now. "I get it. Many of his cronies went to prison, but no one ever seemed to be able to touch Alexander." She took a sip of her drink, scrunching her nose when she realized it was starting to get cold. So much for it being soothing.

A buzz on her phone had Rose looking over to the kitchen counter. She sighed and started to rise, but Ken held out his hand.

"Sit. I got it."

Rose let herself relax, though it was hard. Ken was constantly taking care of her, and she was confused on how she felt about it.

He grabbed her phone, his eyes glancing at it quickly before he started to walk back her way, before he froze. Slowly, Ken raised her phone to look at it again.

Rose watched a flush rise up his neck and a muscle in his jaw start to twitch. Lifting his head, he tossed her the phone. "Lock the door behind me!" he shouted, running to the front door.

"What?" Rose scrambled to read whatever message had come through and immediately felt sick to her stomach.

Honey, I'm home.

Putting a trembling hand over her mouth, Rose held back the bile that wanted to emerge. She stumbled from the table, the chair falling backward, but Rose didn't even look at it. Her legs barely carried her down the hall. Her motherly instincts told her that Lily was fine, they would have heard something if Alexander had been able to get into the house, but her heart wouldn't listen to logic. Not right now.

Throwing open the bedroom door, Rose froze. The soft sounds of Lily's breathing floated through the air, easy to hear and recognize. No other movements came from the room and slowly, Rose's heart began to calm.

Until the pain-filled grunt of a man could be heard from outside.

"No," she breathed. Her heart began to race in concern for Ken just as badly as it had for Lily and Rose hurried out the front door just in time to see Ken rush at Alexander and tackle him to the ground. "KEN!" she screamed.

The two men grunted and shouted as they exchanged blows and wrestled on the gravel.

"Ken! You have to stop!" Rose cried, rushing out and pulling on his shoulders.

"Get back inside!" Ken shouted, jerking free from Rose's hold.

"No! You're going to kill him!"

Ken's fist stopped mid air and he seemed to come back to himself just a little at her words. Growling, he stood and brought Alexander up with him.

Alexander's nose was bleeding and one eye was swollen shut, but once upright, he scowled and found his feet. "Let me go," he said in a threatening tone, jerking against Ken's hold on his shirt.

"You're coming down to the station, buddy," Ken sneered.

"On what charges?" Alexander said with a sarcastic laugh. "Taking a nighttime walk?" He wagged a finger in Ken's face. "It's you who needs to go to the station. For harassment. Someone's about to lose their job." Alexander smiled, the look gruesome with the blood staining his teeth. "Go on. Take me in. I haven't broken any laws."

"We'll see about that," Ken said fiercely. "Rose. Go call the station. Windsor is on duty tonight."

Rose hesitated, but finally nodded. Alexander's words had sent a fear through her that brought up all the concerns Rose had had before she moved in with Ken. She knew she wouldn't be able to live with herself if anything happened to him. And now it looked like her worst fears were coming true. And it was all her fault.

*****

Ken sent a quick prayer heavenward that Rose had obeyed. It had sounded like she'd gone in the house, and Alexander's eyes had come back to his, but unless he looked over his shoulder, there was no way for Ken to know for sure.

"You've stepped in it this time," Ken muttered, refusing to look away from Alexander.

Alexander laughed again and wiped his sleeve across his mouth. "My lawyer will have me out within a few hours." His eyebrow went up. "What about yours? Fancy losing your job over her?"

"Rose is worth any sacrifice," Ken ground out. He shouldn't keep talking to the guy, but Ken couldn't seem to help himself. When he had read the text, Ken had been sure he would find Alexander lurking outside and sure enough, a silhouette against a tree had been visible just enough for Ken to run after.

It had been a little too easy to catch Alexander and Ken had a fleeting concern that it had all been a set up. When he'd gotten closer to Rose's ex, Alexander had begun to speak. His taunting and crude way of speaking about Rose had finally sent Ken over the edge and he'd tackled the guy, with an intent to arrest, but the fight had gotten out of hand and both had ended up throwing punches, though Ken wasn't quite sure who had hit who first. He was sure, though, that he had been the one to end it.

Wetness dripped down his chin and Ken was sure his stinging lip was split and bleeding. A small price to pay in order to keep Rose safe.

"Who's going to take care of her when you're behind bars, hm?" Alexander continued to mouth off and Ken felt his temperature rising again.

His free hand clenched into a fist, but he held himself back. That suspicion that this had been a set up continued to grow in magnitude. Alexander was right. If Ken got in trouble for the fight, Rose would be without protection.

"Ken?"

He tilted his chin, but still didn't look away from his catch.

"Officer Windsor is on his way."

"Good," Ken said gruffly.

"Good to see you again," Alexander called out to Rose. "You've got such a cozy little set up out here."

"Stop speaking," Ken said, giving Alexander a little shake.

"It's a free country," Alexander sneered. "You can't stop me from talking." His eyes went back to where Rose probably stood in the doorway. "How's our daughter?"

"Rose, wait inside," Ken said, his hand clenching and unclenching again. If his officer didn't hurry, Ken was going to do something that would really bring him trouble.

"No," she said firmly.

"Oh, ho! The little woman finally has a voice," Alexander cried with a laugh.

A squeaking sound came from Ken's teeth as he ground his jaw together. He knew this was a trap, but Ken was falling for it anyway. A soft hand landed on his arm.

"Don't do it," Rose whispered.

"What? No welcome home kiss?" Alexander asked. "After all these years, I would have thought you'd retain some of those manners I taught you."

Rose's hold tightened when Ken's muscles bunched. "You've got him," she whispered. "Don't make this worse."

Ken felt like a raging bull. He *hated* guys like Alexander, who thought they were above the law. That they had the power to manipulate everything in their favor. Someone like that had killed his little sister and now another was trying to take away the woman Ken loved. He was sick and tired of creeps like that hurting the people in his life, and he was dangerously close to making sure this one could never hurt another person again.

Blue and red lights flashed in the darkness, illuminating his front walkway, and Ken forced his free hand to relax. It was going to be okay. Windsor was here and they would take care of Alexander, getting him behind bars, even if it was only temporarily. It would be enough time for Ken to find a way to lock this guy up for good.

"Captain," Windsor said by way of greeting as he rushed up. He immediately grabbed Alexander's hands and pulled them behind his back, stating the man's Miranda rights from memory. "I've got him, Captain," Ken's officer said firmly.

Ken struggled to force himself to let go. His knuckles were locked down and letting go felt wrong, like he was giving in.

Officer Windsor stepped up and got in Ken's face. "I have him, Captain. Let him go and I'll take him to the station."

Ken took a deep breath and used every bit of self discipline he had to force his fingers to loosen. It wasn't until Alexander was tucked safely in the back of the patrol car and it had started down the street that Ken blinked and his whole body shuddered from the adrenaline coursing through his system.

"Let's get you cleaned up," Rose said softly, pulling on his sleeve.

Ken let her lead him inside and he sat down at the table, waiting on her ministrations. The split on his lip was the worst, though the bruise forming on the cheekbone on the left side of his face was a close contender.

"What were you thinking?" Rose rasped as she cleaned up his knuckles.

"Excuse me?" Ken asked.

"You can't just go around beating people up!" Rose cried. Her burst of anger immediately crumbled and she slid to her knees in front of Ken, covering her face as she began to sob.

Ken groaned, his entire body stiffening in pain, as he leaned forward to grab Rose's arms. "Come on," he said, pulling her up and into his lap.

"I'm not sitting here," Rose argued, trying to stand. "You're too hurt."

Ken held her tight. "It hurts worse to have you pulling away," he snapped. "So let me hold you and in a minute we'll both feel better."

Rose finally settled down and Ken let himself enjoy the feel of her in his arms. He would never get tired of this sensation. And maybe now that Alexander was on his way to being taken care of,

Ken could finally start to plan how he could convince Rose to make this permanent.

In the quiet of the room, Ken's phone buzzed, but he ignored it. Until it happened again. And again.

Sighing, he reached across the table, shifting Rose so he could reach it. "Hello?" he said in a hoarse tone.

"You need to come down here, Captain," Windsor said quickly. "This guy is planning to bring charges against you and it'll be better if we have all the involved parties in one place."

Ken closed his eyes and deflated. This was exactly what he was afraid of. Alexander had planned this from the start. "I'm on my way," he said, hanging up.

"What charges?" Rose asked, standing up from his lap. "What is he going to charge you with?"

Ken bit his tongue as he stood, the aches and pains of the fight feeling heavier at the moment. "Probably assault."

"And then what?" Rose demanded. "What will that do to you?"

Ken looked down at her and thought about lying, but he couldn't bring himself to do it. He pushed a breath out his nose. "If worse came to worst, I could lose my position at the station. But!" he shouted when Rose began to get hysterical again. "It won't come to that. As an officer, I have a little more leeway than your average citizen." He walked over to the counter to grab his keys. "It'll be his word against mine and the courts are more than likely to favor me over an already convicted criminal."

Rose sat at the table, her face ashen, looking like the world was on her shoulders.

Ken put a hand on her cheek. "Set the alarm and I'll see you soon." Walking away while she was in such distress was one of the hardest things Ken had ever done, but he also knew they'd never move on if he didn't finish this once and for all.

Alexander needed to know he didn't have all the power, and Ken was perfectly willing to be the sacrifice to teach him that. Alexander's reign of terror was over. Ken would see it done.

CHAPTER 22

Rose sat at the table in confusion for the next fifteen minutes. She wanted to go see what was going on at the station, but she also wanted to grab Lily and run.

The fight between the two men had been ugly and Alexander's threats were ringing in Rose's head enough that she felt completely responsible for Ken's rash behavior. His bruises and split lip were bad enough, but if he lost his job and ruined his reputation over her, Rose wasn't sure how she was going to survive it.

She had experienced guilt before. Heavy guilt. Crushing guilt. The kind of guilt that made a person want to give up on living. She'd felt it when she discovered she wasn't enough to keep Alexander's attention. She'd felt it when she left after the divorce and never told him he had a daughter. She'd felt it when she lost the first baby and Alexander had called her a failure. She also felt it each time she looked at Lily, knowing that the child was being kept from knowing who her father was.

The weight had almost killed her at times, but in each instance, Rose had chosen to live on someone else's behalf. At first, it had been Alexander's. She was his wife. He deserved her best effort. Then it was her daughter. Lily deserved a life free of pain and abuse, even if that meant hiding Rose's past.

But now, Rose didn't know where to turn. If she was only taking care of Lily, the best thing to do would be to run and keep her away from all this ugliness. Ken, however, was burrowed too deep in her heart to not be considered as part of her life. If Rose stayed, who wa to say that she wouldn't continue to get into horrible situations with Alexander?

Rose knew her ex-husband. She knew he didn't stop until he got what he wanted and at the moment, that seemed to be her since the topic of her divorce settlement had never come up. But she was positive that Alexander would continue to push Ken until he got the policeman out of the way.

And then what?

Did he think he and Rose and Lily would just be one happy family? Did he think she would welcome him back with open arms after he destroyed everything she loved? Did he think that Rose would believe he had changed during his time in prison?

She choked on a sob and buried her face in her hands. It was all wrong. She had had such hope for a while and now it was gone, drowning in a sea of despair.

A knock on the door had Rose nearly leaping from her seat. She quickly wiped her face, then cleaned her mascara smeared hands on her pants. Cautiously, she walked to the door.

"Rose? It's Caro!"

A rush of air burst from Rose's lungs as she hurried over to let in her friend. Rose reached out, grabbed Caro's arm, and pulled her inside, locking the door behind her. "What are you doing here?" Rose hissed.

Caro's bright blue eyes were wide with shock. "Uh, Ken called me from the station. Asked if I would check on you."

Rose put her back to the door, her body too shaken to continue to hold itself up. "Did he tell you what happened?" she rasped.

Caro nodded, sympathy oozing from her gaze. "Sweetie, I'm so sorry," she whispered in her heavy Southern twang. "It sounds like a nightmare."

A harsh, inappropriate laugh broke free and soon Rose couldn't stop laughing. Slowly, she slid to the floor while tears dripped down her cheeks. Once she landed, the laughter turned into sobs and Rose pulled her knees into her chest and dropped her forehead onto them.

"Oh, Rose," Caro said, climbing to the floor so she could sit next to her friend.

Rose should have pulled away when Caro's arms came around her, but she couldn't find the energy to do so. "It's all so wrong," Rose choked out.

"I know," Caro said softly, rubbing her back. "I know."

"I hate Alexander."

"Shhh, honey, I know."

Rose shook her head. "I hate Alexander and I'm in love with Ken."

Caro's laugh was without humor. "I know that, too."

"This whole thing is all my fault," Rose continued.

Caro paused and pulled back. "What?"

Rose pulled her head up with great effort and didn't even care that she probably looked like a tomato had been squashed on her face. "This is all my fault. Ken being at the station. The fight with Alexander. The stalking, the—

Caro's face hardened. "Now, you wait one gosh darn minute, here, Rosalinda Ingalls."

Rose sniffed but obeyed.

"None of this is your fault. Do you hear me?" Caro snapped. Her eyes were flashes of blue fire and Rose was momentarily mesmerized by her friend's righteous anger. "That bozo who calls himself your ex-husband manipulated you years ago. You were strong enough to break free once, don't you *dare* let him come back here and take over your brain again."

"But—"

Caro put up a hand. "Did you ask him to marry you?"

Rose shook her head.

"How about loaning money? Did you encourage that?"

Again, Rose shook her head. She knew exactly where Rose was headed with this, but the guilt was still eating her up inside.

"The texts? The stalking? The overall creepy factor of everything he's ever said?" Caro practically shouted. She plowed on before Rose could answer. "How about asking him to come here? Did you encourage his attention in any way? Seek him out? Tell him to come save you from Ken?"

"You know I didn't," Rose said almost inaudibly. Her voice felt raw and hoarse at this point from so much crying.

"Then how in the—" Caro pressed her lips together. "There's a child in the house, and even if she can't hear me, I'll refrain from saying what I want to."

Rose almost laughed, but the humor didn't quite outweigh her current grief.

"How in the ever-loving world could any of this be your fault?" Again, Caro raised a hand. "Nevermind, don't answer that." She shook her head. "People who are determined to take on others' guilt will always find a way to spin it back to themselves."

Rose jerked back, pain hitting her chest. "That's not fair."

Caro raised a single eyebrow, a look she had down pat. "Oh, really? So, I what? I'm supposed to just agree with everything you say because you're my friend?" Caro scoffed. "What kind of friend would I be if I didn't take the time to let you know how stupid you're being?"

Rose turned away. She didn't want to listen to this.

"You're letting him win," Caro continued.

Rose stiffened.

"You beat him once, and now you're willing to let him win again, all because you like feeling responsible."

"Can you blame me?" Rose shouted, her anger exploding over her despair. "Someone has to be responsible! I spent years being thrown around and being told what to do. If I don't shoulder the weight of the situation, then it controls me!"

Caro nodded slowly. "And therein is our problem."

Rose sighed and let her head fall back against the door.

"Because there's two of you doing that now, and instead of sharing the burden, you're both fighting over who gets to hold on...and that's leaving you in a vulnerable position." There was a pause. "And Alexander knows too well how to take advantage of a vulnerable situation."

The two women were silent for several moments, Caro's harsh, but true words swirling through Rose's head.

Guilt, shame, fear... Why was it that negative feelings so easily outweighed the good? Rose had experienced joy, love, laughter and even hope, but every time Alexander came into the equation, she lost her hold on the good parts of life.

Her hands slowly tightened into fists. She was so tired of it all. So tired of letting the very name Alexander run her life. Tired of missing out on more joy and laughter because of something that happened years ago. Tired of wondering if she would have to leave it all behind. Tired of trying to plan five steps ahead just so she could keep breathing.

"He can't win," she whispered.

Caro turned to look at her.

"All these years I thought I was getting stronger," Rose continued. "But all this time, I've never truly been the brave person I thought I was. Yes, I broke loose, but I never actually broke free." She turned her head to stare at Caro's misty blue gaze. "Because I let fear rule it all."

Tears dribbled down Caro's cheeks, but she still didn't speak.

"He took years of my life..." Rose swallowed hard, knowing if she said these next words, she needed to back them up with action. "He can't have any more."

"What are you going to do?"

It took a couple more deep breaths before Rose could even form the words. "What I should have done five years ago." She pushed herself onto shaky legs. "Anything it takes to put Alexander away for good." *And anything it takes to keep Ken in my life for good.*

But Caro didn't need to know that yet. Ken needed to be the first person Rose told that to and now that she had made the decision, a small trickle of anticipation began to swirl in her belly.

She knew Ken would fight until there was nothing left to fight for, and Rose was determined to give as much or more than he was. Because for the first time ever, she wasn't alone. Between her friends and the man she loved, Rose knew she would never be alone again. And with a little encouragement, she was determined that that knowledge would always be stronger than the fear.

*****

Ken's head was ready to explode. The pounding against his skull was enough that he wanted to go to sleep and never get up, but he couldn't afford to do that right now. Alexander was doing exactly what Ken had expected him to do. He had immediately called for a lawyer, then spent the rest of the time shouting from the rooftops that he had been a victim of police brutality.

According to the slimeball, Ken was going to be served a lawsuit, the likes of which Seaside Bay had never seen before. Alexander was going to take Ken's house, his life savings, his reputation, and his badge. It wasn't until Alexander had also claimed he was taking Rose and Lily that Ken had had to be restrained.

At the time it had ticked him off, but now that he was a little more clear headed, Ken was grateful for his officer's interference. Punching the guy out wouldn't have looked good to the judge.

"You need to call a lawyer yourself," Officer Windsor said from Ken's doorway.

Ken squinted with gritty eyes. "I will."

The officer tilted his head. "Are you going to tell me what happened? Up until now I would have said you were the type who never lost your cool, but I just had to pull all your bulk off a guy who's probably forty pounds less than you."

Ken groaned and rubbed his temples. "I know."

"What happened?"

Ken sighed. "Exactly what it looks like. A fight."

"I got that, but I want to know what started the fight. *Who* started the fight?"

Ken shook his head. "I actually don't even know. I raced outside after Alexander sent a text to Rose and found him on my property."

"Go on."

Ken gave his employee a look. "Why do I feel like I'm the one being interrogated?"

"Because you're not stupid," Officer Windsor said. He folded his arms over his chest. "Things have been a little crazy trying to get the guy to shut up, and we never got your statement. I'm getting it now."

Ken nodded, but the movement hurt, so he quit moving. "I don't know who threw the first punch, I was too angry to notice. But I do remember eventually taking him to the ground and we wrestled for a bit, each hitting the other." He sighed. "Rose screamed and ran up, pulling on my arm and telling me to stop."

"Did she see who started the fight?"

"I don't think so," Ken said. "She was inside when it started."

"Okay. What else?"

Ken shrugged. "There's not much else. Rose pulled me into rational thought again and I stood, holding Alexander's shirt so he couldn't get away."

Officer Windsor sighed and pinched the bridge of his nose. "None of that is going to look good for the lawsuit."

Ken shrugged again. "I don't care. As long as Rose and Lily are safe, that's all I need."

"You say that now, but when you lose her because you have to start wearing stripes, you might feel different."

Ken understood what his friend was saying, but he wasn't inclined to agree. Losing Rose would hurt, but knowing he had finally protected one of the women in his life…that was enough to give him sweet dreams for many years, even if they were filled with an insatiable craving for her kiss.

"This isn't about Clara," Officer Windsor said softly.

Ken stiffened. "I never said it was." And yet, that's exactly what he'd been thinking.

Windsor shook his head. "I'll write up what you told me, but I would recommend you don't go very far, and definitely don't do anything else stupid."

Ken nodded his understanding and waited for the officer to leave before slumping in his seat. His forehead felt like someone was taking a hammer to it and he rubbed it once again. Glancing down, he began opening drawers. Surely there was something in there he could take, even if it kept him up all night.

Finding what he needed, Ken poured a couple of pills into his hand, then stood and grabbed a bottle of water from his mini fridge. After chugging half of it and swallowing the medicine, he rested the cold bottle against his forehead. It felt good against his heated skin.

In the quiet, his mind began to wander and he wondered a little more on the idea of Rose leaving him over this. He had hoped that getting Alexander taken care of would give them the opportunity to stay together permanently, but he had to consider the idea of it being the opposite.

His anger had probably frightened Rose and he couldn't blame her. When Alexander had threatened Rose, it had broken a key piece of Ken's rational brain. The part he had buried after his sister's death had obviously been simmering and growing during its exile, rather than dissipating into nothingness.

Now, Ken had given it the perfect opportunity for that untamed rage to take center stage and look where it had gotten him.

Sighing, Ken picked up his phone. He knew it was late, but he really should take Windsor's advice and get a lawyer. Unfortunately,

Carson was the best one Ken could think of, even if he was in California. Plus, it would be best to wrap up both Ken and Rose's situation together if possible.

"Hello?" Carson's voice was lower than normal.

"Carson?" Ken asked. "It's Ken Wamsley."

There was a shuffling on the other side of the line. "Did something happen to Rose?" Carson hurried to ask. "Has Alexander made a move?"

"You could say that," Ken said on a sigh. "Rose is fine...physically, anyway. But Alexander came to the house and I..."

Carson groaned. "Please don't tell me you two got into a fistfight."

"You really don't want me to tell you?"

"What is it with you big macho types who think you can handle everything with your fists?" Carson grumbled.

Ken could hear noises in the background and assumed the lawyer was getting dressed. "Sorry," Ken quipped. "It's always worked before."

Carson snorted. "I've met you, Ken. I know you don't normally do this." He sighed. "I'll either get the next flight out or drive up if it's going to be too long. Hunker down with Rose and when I get there, we'll hash it all out, okay?"

"I owe you one," Ken said softly. And he was serious. Carson was going above and beyond at the moment, for people he only knew as acquaintances. Just because his sister-in-law was a close friend of Ken and Rose's, didn't mean Carson needed to treat them as family.

"Hey, it's what I do," Carson joked. "Now, hang tight. I'll be there soon."

CHAPTER 23

Despite making up her mind about her next steps, Rose's legs still felt like complete jello. Her determination wasn't quite enough to help break the hold that fear still held over her muscles and limbs. She was about to give up her one piece of insurance. Something she had held onto for five years and had risked her life to obtain in the first place.

Now she was determined to use it to save someone else, but a small voice in the back of her head kept arguing that giving it up meant her own life was forfeit. If Alexander had any idea of the information she had gathered, he would have her taken care of so fast, she wouldn't even see it coming.

Stepping out of her car to walk up to the station felt like she was trudging through mud. The scared side of her was screaming in desperation that if she took Lily and left, everything would resolve itself. Alexander would stop coming after Ken. Ken would move on from his feelings for Rose. The legal issues would disappear and the people that Rose loved would be safe from her baggage.

Unfortunately, or fortunately, depending on how a person looked at it, Caro had spent a half hour disabusing Rose of her martyr-like attitude.

Rose felt much more in control of her mind, enough to understand that Caro was right, even if the scared, young woman who had reemerged during this whole disaster said otherwise. It was time to take control of her life and stop letting others dictate it for her.

Taking a deep breath, Rose forced herself to keep fighting for control of her emotions and to open the station door in front of her. The whole building was lit up with lights, and almost every officer their small town employed was working at the moment. Rose winced, knowing once again she had had a hand in this.

You didn't ask Alexander to do this, Rose thought to herself. *He made choices, and though they affected you, they were not yours.*

Praying she would eventually be free of the guilt from the situation, Rose walked up to the front desk.

"Ms. Ingalls!" Officer Windsor said in surprise. He jumped to his feet. "Are you okay? Has something else happened?"

Rose shook her head. "I'm fine." *As fine as I can be anyway.* "But I couldn't stay at home, not knowing what was going on."

The officer rubbed the back of his neck. "There's not much to report at the moment. Mr. Callister is locked up for the night, his lawyer is expected in the morning. Captain is in his office." Officer Windsor chuckled. "I'm hoping he fell asleep on the couch, but..."

Rose nodded and gave a tremulous smile. "He's not one to lie down on the job, is he?"

"No, ma'am," Officer Windsor agreed. He tilted his head to the side. "I am going to need a statement from you, but I had assumed it could wait until morning. Is someone watching Lily?"

Rose nodded. "Caro's there."

"Ah." The man nodded thoughtfully. "Well, while you're here, let's get that statement done and then I'll send you back to Cap's office."

Rose wrung her hands, the file folder under her arm burning her skin. "That'll be fine," she said softly. She had come with the intention of speaking to Ken, but the officer was right. She did need to give a statement. Hopefully her words wouldn't end up hurting Ken's chances of getting cleared of all charges.

"This way." Officer Windsor guided her to a side chair where the noise was a little less prominent. "Now...let's start with you telling me what happened tonight from your point of view."

The next twenty minutes were spent retelling the story yet again and Rose found that by the end, she was utterly sick of it. The more she spoke, the more her adrenaline began to ebb and she found herself straightening in her seat. It was time to end this.

Caro's scoldings and advice were on a loop through Rose's head. The more Rose considered how she had been acting, the more angry she was. This wasn't her. This frightened, impotent woman who cowered and shook with every shadow that passed over her wasn't the woman Rose had built herself to be.

She had survived an abusive marriage.

She had left the only home she'd ever known and struck out on her own, pregnant and with limited finances.

She had broken ties with a criminal and started a new life for herself.

She had raised a beautiful little girl, who was happy, carefree, and healthy.

She had also met the man of her dreams. She'd experienced his kiss. She'd come to know what the strength of his arms felt like when wrapped around her. She had seen his fierceness in protecting those in his care. She had watched him become a part of her life. A part that was just as precious to her as Lily was, and Rose refused to let Alexander take those things away from her.

She was a survivor.

And now she was also going to be an accuser, because despite everything she'd gone through, she had also managed to build a case against Alexander that would put him away for good.

"Is that all you need, Officer?" Rose asked, her voice more in control than before.

He looked up from his notebook with a raised eyebrow. "I suppose so...for now."

"May I go check on Ken, please?"

Officer Windsor grinned. "I think he'd like that."

Rose ignored the blush creeping its way up her neck and cheeks and gave the friendly man a regal nod. Then standing, she brushed back her hair, wiped her fingers under her eyes, and marched down the hallway.

No matter what the future held, it was time to get a few things straight in the relationship between her and Ken.

She gripped his doorknob, taking one last deep breath, and then pushed her way inside.

Ken jerked his head in her direction. "Rose!" he said, jumping to his feet.

She didn't miss the way he cringed slightly. His bruises probably hurt like the dickens. "Do you have a minute to talk?" Rose asked politely. She didn't feel like being polite, but this was a two-sided situation. Ken needed to have his say as well.

Ken nodded slowly. "Yes." He indicated a seat in front of his desk. "Did something else happen? Where's Lily?"

"Caro came to the house," Rose said simply, shutting the door behind her.

Ken relaxed in his own chair. "Good. I was hoping she would."

Instead of sitting like Ken had asked her to, Rose moved swiftly around the desk, grabbed Ken's face with her hands, and kissed him.

It wasn't the most elegant of exchanges, but all the independent, fierce, determined emotions that were coursing through her body definitely came out in the way she handled him.

It only took seconds for Ken to adjust to her actions and hop to his feet in order to wrap his arms around her. When he returned her hunger and matched her passion, Rose nearly lost her purpose to the sensations and emotions coursing through her system.

Nearly.

Putting a hand to his chest, she tapped it and pulled back just enough to breathe and speak. If all went well, she had every hope that there would be plenty of that kind of affection in her future, and sometime soon, they wouldn't have to stop.

"Sorry," she said hoarsely, softly rubbing the split in his lip.

He shook his head and opened his mouth to play off her apology, but Rose jumped back in.

"I love you," she whispered.

Ken's eyes widened and he stumbled backward into his chair.

Rose took a calming breath, her heart now racing for a different reason than it had been earlier. "I love you and I want a future with you. But it can't happen with Alexander looming over us." She bent over to pick up the folder which had fallen during their little...conversation. "I have something that should help us do that."

*****

Ken blinked a couple of times, trying to keep up with her conversation. "You have what?"

"I have a folder containing names and dates of crimes and murders that Alexander had his hand in. Even though he didn't usually commit them himself, he was the ringleader." She held out the folder. "And this proves it."

Ken's eyes were wide and he could barely breathe as he took the offering. "You've had this the whole time?"

She nodded.

"Why the he—" He cleared his throat. "Why didn't you say something before?"

Rose took a couple of breaths before answering him. "It was my insurance policy," she explained softly. "I ran off so fast the first time that I just kept it with me, planning to use it if Alexander ever tried something underhanded to get me back. I would be able to threaten him with jail. I didn't tell anyone because I didn't want him to know. If Alexander had any idea of what that folder contains, he'd have had me killed, wife or not." She took another shuddering breath. "But I think I've finally reached a point where I want my future more than I want my safety."

Ken slowly stood up, but he didn't allow himself to touch her again yet. This was so much to process. All this time. All this time she'd had the ability to put Alexander away and she hadn't said a word. Ken wanted to rant and rave, but he also wanted to hold her close and never let her go again. He struggled to hope that the end was really going to be so easy. "And what future is that?"

A small smile crept across her face and her eyes softened. It was one of the most beautiful sights Ken had ever seen. "You. I want you as my future."

Words would only get in the way at this point. Without saying anything, Ken wrapped his arms around her once again and proceeded to show her exactly how he felt. How he had felt for so long. But there were new feelings attached to his emotions now. Determination, compassion...and pride.

He had never been more proud of Rose than he was right now. Knowing she had kept her and Lily safe for a long time already made her a strong woman. Knowing she refused to keep running and wanted to put a creep behind bars made her even more so.

"You're amazing," Ken breathed against her jawline.

Rose laughed breathlessly. "No. I'm just stubborn."

"That too," he admitted, earning him a slap on the shoulder. He laughed. "It often takes stubbornness to be courageous."

Rose rolled her eyes. "That doesn't make me feel any better."

Ken stepped back, took her hand, and led her over to the couch on the wall of his office, pulling her down to sit next to him. What he really wanted was to pull her into his lap and continue what they'd already been doing, but the temperature in his office seemed to be steadily rising, so he figured it was time to slow down for a bit. "I need to know exactly what you have. Everything you've been hiding from me. Did you actually see a crime? Or is this all paperwork?"

Rose swallowed hard and her face paled, but she nodded jerkily. "I heard a situation and that's what led me to gathering the rest of this," she whispered. "I began to sneak into his office and copy documents when he wasn't home and ended up with quite the stack by the time I left."

"How come the police didn't find those documents?" Ken asked. "They would have searched the house after Alexander was arrested."

Rose nodded. "Yes. But he had destroyed a bunch and the rest were in places they would never be able to find." She smiled sadly. "I only knew where they were because I watched everything."

Ken sighed. "Okay. Can you start from the beginning?"

She closed her eyes, as if imagining a scene and Ken kept a tight hold on her hand, offering what little support he could. "Alexander was late for dinner. Very late," Rose began. "He had held me up in the past, but I was really starting to get irritated, so instead of going to bed and ignoring it, like usual, I decided to head down to his office to see why he wasn't coming."

A shiver rocked her body and Ken pulled her into his chest, wrapping his arms around her as if to hold her together. He knew from working with other victims in the past that recalling a traumatic incident could be extremely emotional for someone.

"His office was clear on the other side of our house," she whispered into his shirt. "So it took several minutes of walking to get there." There was a pause before she continued. "Even from the hallway I could hear the screaming and the shouting."

Ken squeezed tighter. His heart was ready to explode with every word she spoke.

"The noises weren't coming from his office, but another door," Rose whispered. "I walked up and put my ear to the door and heard Alexander's voice. He was as smooth as ever, sounding for all the world like he was speaking to an acquaintance at a party, rather than whatever was going on in that room."

When she stopped again, Ken kissed the top of her head. "You can do it," he encouraged. "Almost there."

Her body was trembling and her hands clenched in his shirt. "I heard a man shout for a little more time, but Alexander said he'd had enough. Then the man began to say the word 'please'. Over and over and over again…"

She was openly crying now and Ken squeezed his own eyes shut, biting his tongue to keep from telling her she could stop. She couldn't stop. They needed this out if they were going to have a chance for any kind of future.

"The last 'please' was screamed so loud I almost didn't hear the gunshot," Rose said thickly. "But right after the noise, everything stopped. The stillness felt eerie after so much shouting." She swallowed audibly. "My legs were shaking and sweat was running down my back, but I knew I needed to get out of there." Rose took a deep breath. "Right before I managed to move, I heard Alexander say, 'Clean this up.'"

Ken let his head fall back against the couch. "Did he see you?" Ken asked hoarsely.

Rose's head shook against his chest. "No. My fear outweighed my shaky limbs and I was able to run away before the door ever opened."

"Thank heavens for that," Ken said, kissing the top of her head again.

Rose pushed against his chest and sat up so she was looking at him. Her blue eyes were brighter as they swam in tears and her skin was tinged in red. "The next morning I found an article in the paper talking about a man's homicide. He was killed by a gunshot wound," Rose said, her voice still low. "It had to be the guy Alexander had killed. I knew for sure that I couldn't stay at that point, especially since I had recently learned I was pregnant," she said.

Ken nodded. "I get it," he said. "But why not use that to put Alexander away the first time? You had to know that money charges weren't going to be enough to keep him away from you for good."

Rose's pink lips were pinched into a straight white line. "I know, but at the time, I was so scared that he would kill me if I testified, and

I had to protect my baby." The pooling tears began to slip down her cheeks. "I'd already lost one, I couldn't stand to do it again. I gave my lawyer a few tidbits about his loan practices, enough to help, but left the police to do the rest."

"So he never figured out that you were the snitch about his loan shark business?"

Rose shook her head. "Not that I know of. My lawyer said he made sure everything I gave was completely anonymous. Everything on record should have only shown that I was divorcing Alexander, not helping put him away."

Ken pushed a hand through his hair. "Why didn't you offer the testimony anonymously as well?" He shook his head. "I'm sorry. The cop in me just won't stop, but in the end it really doesn't matter. This is where we are now, and this is exactly what we need to put him away for good."

Rose leaned back from him and wrung her hands in her lap. "You'll help protect Lily, won't you?"

Ken jerked toward Rose and cupped her face in his hands. "I'm protecting you both," he said fiercely. "You and Lily. You're a pair. You're *my* pair, and when this is all over we are absolutely talking about making an honest woman out of you and then moving you from Lily's room to mine."

Rose's smile was teary but stunning. "I would love that, but only if Alexander is no longer a threat." She sucked in a deep breath through her nose. "I've already risked you and your life enough just by dating you."

Ken shrugged. "And what a wonderful time it's been. Besides, if my job wasn't threatened once in a while, I wouldn't count myself a good cop." He stood. "Carson will be here in a few hours. Until then, I'm going to look through the file. Why don't you grab some sleep?"

"Can I do it here?" Rose asked softly. "Lily is with Caro and Jack, and I don't want to go back to the empty cabin."

Ken moved to his cupboard and grabbed a blanket. It wasn't very big, since it was meant more for a child, but it would do for now. He walked back and wrapped it around Rose's shoulders. "Lay down," he said. "I'll be here."

Rose nodded and slid sideways, tucking her feet on the couch. Her face was tight at first as she closed her eyes, but Ken waited until he saw her relax and her breathing even out. She had obviously been exhausted and he was grateful she trusted him enough to sleep when she was scared. It was a heady sensation, but one he had no intention of breaking.

Walking back to his desk, he sat down. The responsibility hung heavy on his shoulders, but it was a feeling Ken enjoyed. He now had the missing piece of the puzzle. It was time for Alexander to disappear from their lives for good.

CHAPTER 24

Carson Cordova slapped his briefcase on top of Ken's desk and opened it with efficient fingers. He really was nearly as handsome as his movie star brother, Rose couldn't help but notice. She hadn't seen Grayson and Brooke in several months and it nearly felt like having a celebrity in their tiny little town.

"You've got the testimony all signed?" Carson asked, his voice smooth and businesslike.

Ken nodded. "Yeah. She took care of it this morning."

"Perfect." Carson dug around then turned to Rose. "Were you hurt last night?"

Rose shook her head. "Just Ken."

Carson raised an eyebrow. "Are you sure I can't help you claim emotional distress? I love slapping guys like this with as many charges as possible." He winked. "It makes me look good at my job."

Rose laughed softly and tucked a piece of hair behind her ear. She probably looked insane this morning. Her eyes were dry and gritty, her face was probably still red and puffy, and who knew what her hair had decided to do. She hadn't had a chance to look in the mirror yet, but it was easy to tell the curls were chaotic at best. "I think putting him away for murder should be enough."

"That and dropping the police harassment charges," Carson said with a nod. "I have a feeling his lawyer isn't going to be pleased with that little addition to the plan." Carson's head jerked up. "Has he arrived yet?"

"The lawyer?" Ken clarified.

Carson nodded.

"Nope," Ken said. "I think he's expected in another hour or so."

"Hmm..." Carson said with a nod. "Duly noted."

Rose looked back and forth between the two men. "Is that significant?" she wondered.

Carson shrugged. "Not necessarily. But keeping an eye on their behavior can help me figure out their game plan. If Alexander wanted out of here, he would have been out within fifteen minutes of being locked up. There's no way he didn't have his lawyer on standby."

Rose stiffened. "Standby? You mean he *planned* to get arrested?"

Carson gave a low chuckle and put his hands on his hips. "A guy like that? Oh, yeah. More than likely he's aiming to get lover boy, here, out of the way so you have nowhere to run."

Rose put a hand to her nauseated stomach. Just when she thought her ex couldn't get any worse. He didn't seem to care how many people he hurt along the way as long as he got what he wanted. If only she hadn't been so stupidly naive as a young woman!

"Whoa," Ken said, rushing to her side. He wrapped an arm around her and led her to a chair. "Put your head between your knees for a second," he directed. "I'll grab some cold water."

Rose jumped when a cold bottle landed on the back of her neck, though she couldn't argue with the fact that her nausea began to dissipate. "Thank you," she said, sitting up.

Carson gave her a sympathetic look. "Sorry," he said, scrunching up his face. "I don't always filter the way I should."

Rose shook her head. "You did nothing wrong. I guess I just didn't think about how low Alexander would go to get me back." She shuddered. The idea of going back with her ex was enough to make her want to run again, but Rose pushed the sensation down. She had been determined last night to see this through. Her daughter was safe at the moment, and Alexander was behind bars, even if only temporarily. It was a starting point.

But it was enough.

Carson grumbled under his breath, then went back to digging things out of his briefcase. The man moved at an almost manic pace, obviously not the type to sit still very well. "Okay, first things first," he said. "I know it's stupid, but we need to make sure all our paperwork is in order and then I need to speak to the guys who first put our creep away back East." He looked at Ken. "Can you get me some names and numbers?"

"Already done," Ken said. "I've chatted with the police chief over there, getting a few of my own questions answered."

"Excellent." Carson looked sympathetically at Rose. "The next couple of days are going to be rough, but if I do my job well, after a few hours in purgatory, you'll be able to breathe easy for the rest of your life. Are you ready?"

Rose swallowed hard, then nodded. "I appreciate you coming," she said softly. "Thank you for taking this on."

"I'm always willing to help friends," he said with a wink. "And putting away murderers is an extra bonus."

Ken cleared his throat when Carson continued to smile at Rose. Carson looked completely unrepentant when he turned his attention to the police captain. "Can't blame a guy for trying," he said with a grin.

Ken glared. "While I understand the sentiment, I think I've already shown what I'm willing to do when it comes to protecting her."

"Ken!" Rose scolded.

The men didn't even acknowledge she had spoken. Carson gave Ken a fake salute. "Loud and clear, Cap. Loud and clear."

Ken's stoic face melted into an amused smile. "Just so we understand each other."

Rose was mortified. Carson had barely been flirting and these two men were acting like it was serious. She wanted to smack them both upside the head.

"Crystal clear," Carson said with his own laugh. "I suppose it would be a conflict of interest anyway."

Rose groaned and put her face into her hands, which seemed to only cause more laughter. She looked up and gave them her best mom glare. "If you two are done being men, I think we have work to do."

Carson raised his eyebrows at Ken and shrugged. "She might be asking too much. I can only be what I am."

Ken nodded. "I plan to marry her. Think of all that's going to force me to be."

Rose was still too emotionally distraught to handle this. She jumped to her feet and began to march to the door, but thick arms wrapped around her from behind before she could get very far.

"Sorry, hon," Ken whispered in her ear. "We'll stop."

She spun in his arms. "This is serious!" she cried. "Mine and my daughter's lives are on the line, plus your job, and you two are joking like fraternity brothers!"

Ken's amused face dropped all humor. "We were only breaking the tension," he soothed. "But I'm sorry. It was too soon." He led her back to the chair. "We'll get down to business."

Carson looked severely chastened as well. "Sorry, Rose. Wasn't trying to make you feel like I wasn't serious."

Rose sighed and rubbed her forehead. "No, I'm sorry. I'm just on edge. I know you two didn't mean anything by it."

Ken rubbed her back and left a kiss on the top of her head. "Regardless, let's get this done. We'll both feel better when we're free."

Rose couldn't agree more.

*****

Ken was going to fall asleep on his feet. Staying away all night was starting to catch up with him, but Ken knew he wouldn't quit just yet. Alexander's lawyer was meeting with him at the moment and more than likely, would call for a meeting with Ken or Carson soon as well.

"You need a nap," Rose whispered, running her fingers through his hair.

Ken closed his eyes and let his head fall back on the couch. "Yep."

"Why don't you take one now?"

"Nope."

"What do you mean, nope?" Rose scolded. "You're tired. You're not going to be able to go on like this much longer."

Ken cracked one eye open to look at her as he grinned. "Sometimes I can definitely tell you're a mom."

Rose huffed and pulled her arm back, folding both arms over her chest. "You're ridiculous."

Ken chuckled and took her hand, holding it between his own. Despite his smiling and laughter, he needed to stay connected to her. It was one of the few things keeping him sane right now.

Her phone buzzed and Rose looked down. "It's Caro again."

"Better answer it," Ken warned. "She'll only keep calling, plus with Carson on the phone, it's probably a good time to give her an update."

Rose sighed and nodded, still staring at the phone. "I know, but it's hard to want to drag them into this."

"They're your friends. They're already a part of this whether you want them to be or not," Ken said softly.

Rose nodded again and took a deep breath. "Hey, Caro. Is everything all right? Is Lily okay?" Rose paused. "Oh. Mm, hm. Yeah...sure. I'll hang up." She pressed the end button and waited.

Ken nudged her shoulder.

"She's doing a video call for Lily," Rose said. She smoothed her hair. "Hopefully five-year-olds aren't good at seeing distress."

Ken kissed her cheek. "You look beautiful, that's all that's going to matter to Lily."

Rose gave him a tired smile, then answered her phone. "Hey, sweetie!" Rose's smile was tight and strained, but Ken was sure Lily didn't notice. She was too busy signing and speaking as if she hadn't seen her mother in a month instead of a few hours.

"Chocolate milk for breakfast?" Rose exclaimed. "Wow, what a treat!"

Ken chuckled. Caro was going to regret the sugar pumping if she had to hang onto Lily for the rest of the day.

"Yeah, he's here," Rose said, turning to Ken. She raised her eyebrows, silently asking him a question.

Ken nodded and took the phone. "Lily!" he said in a happy tone. "How's my favorite girl?"

"You weren't here this morning!" Lily accused, poking out her bottom lip. "I wanted to make pancakes."

Ken's amusement became real as he laughed softly. "I know," he said. "But I had an emergency at work."

"You're at the station?" Lily asked, eagerness lighting up her adorable face.

Ken nodded.

"Can I come?"

Ken shook his head, feeling bad when Lily's pouting became more pronounced. "Not today, sweetheart," he said. "But you know that I love having you here. You can come next time."

"Okay," Lily said sadly. She waved and signed off before handing the phone to Caro.

"Wow. The kid knows how to pull the heartstrings, huh?" Caro said with a grin.

"Don't fall for it," Rose warned from over Ken's shoulder.

He turned the camera so both of them were on the screen.

"She's a conniving little thing," Rose continued. "If you're not careful, your whole inventory will come home with her when this is all over."

Caro laughed louder. "Sounds like a girl after my own heart."

Ken grinned. "Are you doing okay with her?" he asked.

Caro nodded. "Oh, we're fine. And if for some reason we're not, I'll just start passing her down the aunt and uncle chain. It'll be a good six months before you two need to pick up the parent mantle again."

Rose relaxed into Ken's side. "Thank you," she whispered.

"That's what we're here for," Caro said, her voice still chipper. In the next instant, she glanced over her shoulder and her tone dropped. "All right, the pretty princess is out of the room. What's going on?"

"We're in waiting mode," Rose complained.

Ken grimaced and nodded. "We're still gathering the case and waiting for a chance to speak to Alexander's lawyer."

"How long do you think the stalker charges will put him away for?" Caro asked.

Rose hesitated and glanced at Ken. He shook his head at her, then answered Caro. "We think we have something better, but again, we're waiting for some answers from Boston."

Caro pouted. "So it's leave your friends in the dark time? I hate that!"

Ken rolled his eyes. "You're an adult, Caro. I'm pretty sure you can handle it."

"Maybe, but that doesn't mean I have to like it," Caro snapped. Her eyes opened wide. "Oh, by the way, Benny and Ally get back this afternoon. He'll be really sad he missed all the action."

Rose groaned quietly.

"Good bye, Caro," Ken said wryly.

"Okay, okay, okay," she said, putting a hand up. "Sorry. I won't tease like that. But seriously, please let us know what you can. Lily has more helpers than she needs, so don't worry about her, but Rose...do worry about yourself, okay?" Caro's concern was palpable even through the phone screen.

Rose nodded. "We're doing the best we can," she responded.

"Good." Caro's blue eyes pinned Ken in place. "And you, big guy. I know you're a macho man who's willing to do anything to protect and serve, but we want you around for the long term as well, got it?"

Ken couldn't help but look at Rose as he answered. "I'm doing the best I can."

"Right. And now I'm leaving before the phone explodes in flames from that look," Caro teased. "Keep us updated!"

The screen went black and Ken found he didn't feel the least bit embarrassed by the way it had ended.

"Do you promise?" Rose asked.

"What?" He frowned.

"Do you promise you're trying to stick around? You're not going to just sacrifice yourself for me and Lily?"

Ken shook his head and brushed his knuckles against her jaw. "You wouldn't have liked my answer to that earlier this morning, but with your testimony, I'm confident we're going to be just fine. All of us."

Before he could kiss Rose, sealing the deal, Carson spoke.

"All right, love birds. Meeting is on." He was stuffing his papers into his briefcase. "Mr. Lincoln Thompkins and his client will be ready for us in just a couple of hours."

Ken snorted.

"Two more hours?" Rose asked. "Why is it all taking so long?"

Carson grinned. "Actually, they're ready to meet now. I'm holding them off because I've got something up my sleeve that I think will bring this to a close much faster if we can just delay for a bit."

Rose looked to Ken and he shrugged. "If that's what you think is best."

"I think it's best we put this guy away for good," Carson responded. "And letting him squirm for a bit will not only be fun, but worthwhile in the end. Trust me."

CHAPTER 25

After stepping out into the hallway, Rose had a sudden panic attack. "Hang on," she said to Ken and Carson, then quickly dashed into the bathroom. If she was going to have to face Alexander and be willing to stand her ground, she needed to not feel like something that had crawled out of the swamp.

Taking a few minutes to refresh her face with cool water, scrub her teeth with her finger. and tame her hair the best she could, Rose looked at herself in the mirror and gave herself a small pep talk. "You're strong," she encouraged. "You can do this. For Ken and for Lily...and for yourself."

Her cheeks flushed after saying his name and Rose found herself smiling. It had taken her a long time to be willing to look at a future with this man, but she couldn't be more grateful for his persistence and willingness to work at her speed. She'd put him through the wringer, but Ken had never faltered and never pushed.

Rose was sure it was impossible to love a man as much as she was growing to love him. She had been attracted to him from the start, but it had taken more time for the attraction to turn to something more and with her past and present fears, she had held it off as long as possible, but the end result, she decided, had been inevitable.

Taking one last steadying breath, she came out of the restroom and nearly ran into Ken's chest. "Are you all right?" he asked, his voice low and concerned.

Rose nodded. "Yeah. I just...needed to not look like I slept on your couch." She scrunched up her face. "You know?"

Ken chuckled and stepped aside so he could put his hand on her back and guide her along. "You're beautiful no matter what," he whispered.

"And you're biased," Rose shot back.

"If I said anything else, I'd be blind," he quipped right before they reached the interrogation room. "You ready for this?"

Rose shook her head. "Nope. But we're doing it anyway. I refuse to let him rule my life anymore."

Ken nodded and the pride in his eyes was a welcome sight. "Good girl," he muttered almost inaudibly right before pulling open the door.

"Carson Cordova," Carson said, taking over the room immediately. He walked past Ken with his hand out and headed straight to Alexander's lawyer.

Rose immediately felt wary of Alexander's counsel. He had that same "greasy" quality that Alexander did. His black hair was slicked back and his suit could have easily paid Rose's flower inventory bill for the month. His hooked nose overtook his face in a way that kept him from being classically handsome, but it gave him a fierce, determined look instead, much to Rose's dismay.

"Lincoln Thompkins," the man said, his voice cultured in a way Rose hadn't heard since she'd lived on the East Coast. People were a little more natural in Oregon and it was one of the things Rose loved.

What she saw was what she got.

Mr. Thompkins glared at Ken. "You must be Captain Wamsley."

Rose noticed Carson put a hand on Ken's shoulder, whether in warning or to restrain, she wasn't quite sure, but either way, she knew it was probably a good idea since Ken's face had taken on that granite look that told her he was ready to rip something apart.

Ken nodded curtly, but didn't speak.

Dark eyes then turned to Rose. "Ah...the lovely Mrs. Callister."

"That's not my name," Rose said before she could think better of it. The man had probably been trying to agitate her and she'd fallen right into his trap.

"My client goes by her maiden name, Ingalls, which you're well aware of, Mr. Thompkins," Carson said easily. "I'd hate for our meeting to be over before it began simply because you cannot bring your client to face reality."

Rose bit the inside of her lip when Alexander's bruised face began to flush a deep red. His skin was a smooth brown and when he grew angry, the subsequent red was enough to make him look like an overripe eggplant. To his credit, however, he didn't speak, which wasn't like Alexander. He liked to hear himself talk and liked even more to watch others react to whatever he said. If he was being this quiet, it was because they had a plan.

Mr. Thompkins put his hands in the air. "No harm was meant, counsellor. I'll update my notes."

Rose barely held back from rolling her eyes, especially when Carson snorted.

Mr. Thompkins looked less than impressed. "Shall we begin?" he asked with a practiced smile.

Carson nodded and Rose folded her hands in her lap. She was positive a bunch of words were going to be going over her head, but if she just remained quiet, she hoped to be able to understand the majority of the proceedings.

"Go ahead," Carson replied, his own smile looking like a shark ready for his next meal.

Rose shivered slightly and leaned back in her chair. She was so grateful that in her usual line of work, she was surrounded by plants who weren't out to break her down. She couldn't imagine what it was like to have a job where your main purpose was to prove other people were wrong.

"My client is pressing charges of police brutality," Mr. Thompkins said, reaching into his briefcase to grab a file full of papers. "Last night Captain Wamsley brutally attacked my client, repeatedly punched him in the face, and caused serious damage."

Carson clucked his tongue. "You failed to mention that your client had trespassed onto my client's property," he said.

"My client's wife was in the house," Mr. Thompkins stated, causing Rose to stiffen, though this time she managed to refrain from replying. "He had every right to go after her."

"Last chance," Carson warned. "She's not his wife. The divorce was final years ago. If you're going to keep pressing something that isn't true, then we're done."

Mr. Thompkins sighed. "A divorce hasn't changed his feelings for her."

"Doesn't make it legal," Carson returned. "She's not his wife and that wasn't his property. The law is on my client's side."

Mr. Thompkins cleared his throat. "Then maybe we should discuss the fact that my client's daughter, whom he didn't know even existed until recently, was in that house."

Rose felt herself blanch at the blunt accusation.

"Your client," Mr. Thompkins sneered, his eyes flickering to Rose, "kept a secret from mine for over five years." He tilted his head to the side, smiled, and spread his hands. "Now, we both know there's going to be repercussions for that and any jury is going to side with a father who was concerned for his daughter."

"They might," Carson admitted, much to Rose's dismay. "But after they hear that the father didn't know about the child because he was in jail on charges relating to abuse and illegal money lending, I think they'll change their tune."

Rose relaxed ever so slightly when Mr. Thompkins' jaw clenched. He didn't like that Carson had a good point and it made Rose glad. As long as Mr. Thompkins and Alexander were upset, it meant they knew they weren't winning.

Which meant Rose and Ken were.

*****

"I don't see why we can't get along, here," Mr. Thompkins said in his whiny voice.

Ken wanted to plug his ears. The guy screamed "used car sales-man" and Ken could spot his type a mile off. It seemed fitting that someone as slick as Alexander would have a lawyer who was equally as slimy.

But the whole situation ticked him off. Ken hated playing games and that's exactly what this was. He knew they had the information they needed to put Alexander away, but Carson had to wait for the right moment to present it. Otherwise, it could ruin everything and leave Ken and Rose with charges still hanging over their heads.

"It wasn't right to keep that information from him and you know it," Mr. Thompkins argued, his voice losing some of his practiced tone.

"We're not here to debate the rightness of something," Carson said back. He looked completely relaxed in his chair. "We're here to talk about legality." Carson's gray eyes drifted to Alexander lazily be-fore coming back to his lawyer. "It's not illegal to not tell the father about a pregnancy."

"Maybe not, but being in my client's good will might be neces-sary, if she ever hopes to marry and have the child adopted by anoth-er man."

Alexander made a strained noise and Ken watched his knuckles clench against the chair.

It made Ken want to puff up his chest and smirk. Apparently, the guy didn't enjoy the thought of someone else having their hands on Rose. Ken wanted to declare that he was the guy. That he had kissed Rose and definitely planned to make Lily his daughter. But the argu-ment was petty, and Ken knew it.

He was wound tighter than a spring at the moment and every lit-tle thing was setting him off. It wasn't like him. Ken knew himself to be a good policeman. He usually kept a cool head and was known for getting through difficult and high stress situations without ever rais-ing his voice.

Something had changed in the last few weeks, however. Ever since he had been given permission to take Rose under his wing and protect her from her past...his protective side had become a raging monster.

It had come to a head last night when Alexander had taunted Ken, speaking crude, disgusting words until Ken broke and the two men ended up in a tussle. Ken's need to protect Rose and Lily was becoming all consuming and he needed to get a grip.

Protection was important, but so was doing it in a way that he could be proud of. He'd sworn an oath to uphold the law and his love for Rose should be an excuse to do it better, not to let himself become a Neanderthal with a gun.

It's like I don't trust her.

The words shook him a little. He did trust Rose. Didn't he? When guilt began to seep into his gut, Ken knew the answer was one he didn't necessarily like. His mind flashed over the last couple of weeks and how many times Rose had had to call out his behavior.

How he'd tried to take over the financial burden without consulting her. How he ordered her to stay in the house, demanding obedience in order to keep her safe.

"I think we'll be able to work the courts in our favor on that one as well," Carson said confidently, breaking into Ken's sudden self loathing.

He couldn't believe how far he had gone in the wrong direction. He'd been so blinded by the need to keep her safe after failing his younger sister that he hadn't thought about how he was achieving that.

When this was all over, Ken knew an apology was in order. He couldn't claim to love Rose and then keep treating her the way he was treating her. She was strong, beautiful and even though there had been times when she was fragile, she had survived very well without him for a long time and she deserved credit for that.

His hand twitched in wanting to take hers, but decided it probably wasn't best to taunt Alexander, even if the childish side of Ken wanted to gloat.

"The courts don't strip rights very often," Mr. Thompkins said in a low tone.

"Maybe not," Carson agreed. "But I think we have something to convince them otherwise."

"And that is?"

Carson shook his head and glanced at his watch. "I'm not quite ready to reveal that. I'm waiting for the last piece to fall into place."

Ken scrambled to get his mind caught up on what was going on in the room. He shoved aside his need to berate himself and promised he would finish later. Ending this saga with Alexander needed to come first. His personal scolding could happen once he was at home.

"You've had several hours to pull this together," Mr. Thompkins said with a smirk. "If you haven't figured it out by now, it sounds like your case is on shaky ground."

Carson merely shrugged and Ken sighed internally again.

Back to the games.

"Our case, however, is not," Mr. Thompkins stated.

"And just what is it that you think would help your client feel better about getting caught trespassing?"

Mr. Thompkins left eyebrow rose high. "For the safety of the people, we're seeking for Captain Wamsley to resign from his position."

"No." Rose gasped.

Ken quickly looked her way, but he didn't miss the triumph in Alexander's eyes at the announcement. He wanted to assure Rose he'd be fine. Ken wasn't sure why Carson was biding his time with the murder charge, but he knew Carson was a good lawyer. If he felt the need to hold onto the signed testimony for now...then Ken would do his best to trust in that. On the other side of the coin, Ken knew Carson wouldn't let him lose his job. If that had been a true possibility, it would have come up during their prep time this morning.

"That's not an option," Carson said calmly. He folded his hands on the table. "It's Captain Wamsley's presence that actually keeps the people of Seaside Bay safe. In fact, it was his presence that kept Ms. Ingalls and her daughter safe last night. Removing him from his job would be a tragedy for all."

Mr. Thompkins scoffed in disbelief. "A police captain who uses his fists to solve his problems isn't one that belongs on the force."

"He was off duty," Carson pointed out.

"And yet he still should know better."

Ken saw Rose shifting in her seat. It was easy to see the clenching of her jaw and recognize that she wanted to argue, wanted to defend him. He felt his own anger dissipate a little at her protection. Ignoring the warning in his head, Ken reached over and took her hand, resting their combined fingers on his thigh.

The touch soothed himself as well as having a visible effect on Rose. Her shoulders loosened and she gave him a grateful smile before relaxing once more in her seat.

When Ken turned back to the current argument, Alexander, however, was definitely not as happy with the situation. He leaned over to whisper in his lawyer's ear, who subsequently glanced at Ken's leg where their hands rested.

"I believe it would be in everyone's best interest not to show any favoritism," Mr. Thompkins said with a tight smile. "Please instruct your clients to release their hold on each other for the duration of our meeting."

Carson's eyebrows shot up and he laughed harshly. "They're a dating couple. They have every right to support each other in the best way they know how. Your client holds no power over this and hasn't for over five years."

Mr. Thompkins' lips pinched, but he turned and whispered to Alexander, who grew redder by the second.

Now that Ken was working to see through his haze of anger, he felt a flicker of pity for the man. Alexander Callister had once held something very precious in his hands and instead of nurturing and savoring it...he had abused and nearly ruined it.

Yes, it had been his own choices that led to the situation, but Ken knew the guy's loss had been heavy. Alexander wanted it back, but it was too late. That kind of knowledge had to be hard to deal with and could easily break any man.

The acknowledgement and strange sense of understanding left Ken only that much more determined to see that he, himself, didn't make the same mistake.

CHAPTER 26

Alexander's obvious disdain only made Rose tighten her hold on Ken's hand. More than just putting her ex in jail, this meeting was about putting him behind her for good. She was done letting him have any control over her actions and choices.

When his dark, hateful eyes met hers, Rose took a deep breath, tilted her chin in the air, and challenged him right back. Gone was the girl who had cowered in his presence and refused to rock the boat. Only a few hours ago she had written down a testimony that should be the key to putting Alexander away for more than just a couple of years. And although Rose wasn't quite sure why Carson was drawing out this meeting, rather than just jumping to the point, she was willing to let the lawyer lead. She wasn't, however, willing to let her ex have any say in that.

"So you've decided we should let the jury decide in this matter?" Mr. Thompkins prodded. "You do realize that with the upheaval in our country today, they aren't going to look favorably on a police captain who abuses his power?"

"You're right, they wouldn't," Carson answered. "But that won't matter because not only did my client *not* abuse his power, but your accusation will never see the light of a courtroom."

Rose stiffened when she saw the triumph in both Mr. Thompkins and Alexander's eyes. They thought this meant they were going to win. She was more positive than ever that Alexander's whole plan was to get Ken out of the way. He had been the one obstacle keeping Alexander from approaching Rose the way he wanted to.

"I'm glad that you're seeing sense," Mr. Thompkins said with a pleased smile. "But remember, we won't settle for anything less than his job."

Carson shook his head. "Unnecessary." He pulled out some pictures and pushed them across the table. "Are you aware that your client was sending threatening messages to Ms. Ingalls in the last few weeks?"

Mr. Thompkins glanced at the pictures and tossed them back down. "I suppose it's all how you interpret them," he stated with no emotion.

Carson's eyebrows went up. "Really? Then would you mind telling me what he was referring to when he said he was coming to take what was his?" He waited a beat before continuing. "Ms. Ingalls is in possession of nothing from your client that the United States court didn't allow her to have. So what was he after?"

Mr. Thompkins pinched his lips before turning to whisper to Alexander, who answered back in angry undertones. The two men went back and forth several times before Mr. Thompkins turned back to the rest of the group. "We find this to be a personal matter that he doesn't wish to discuss in public unless it becomes absolutely necessary."

"A jury isn't necessary?"

"We aren't in front of a jury," Mr. Thompkins explained. "If we find ourselves in a courtroom, he will tell his side. Until then, it's not vital to the charges we're speaking of."

Carson chuckled. "Actually, it is."

Mr. Thompkins and Alexander both frowned. "In what way?"

"It helps me decide whether or not to simply stop at the charge of murder, or whether or not we can add other charges such as stalking, cyberstalking, harassment…"

Mr. Thompkins' mouth flapped open and shut a few times while Alexander leapt from his seat and cursed. "What kind of setup is this?" he shouted, pounding his fist on the table. "I didn't kill anyone!"

Mr. Thompkins pulled his client back into his seat and quickly told him to be quiet before glaring at Carson. "You've made an awfully big jump, Mr. Cordova. I thought we were discussing police brutality charges."

Carson nodded. "We were, but I warned you they would never make it to court."

"I haven't heard of any recent or suspicious deaths in the area," Mr. Thompkins said carefully. "Exactly who are you accusing my client of killing?" He waved a hand behind him when Alexander started to complain again.

Carson dug casually through his briefcase again as if he had all the time in the world. He pulled a large file out and opened it slowly.

Rose could see that the nonchalant attitude was eating at both Mr. Thompkins and Alexander and she wanted to grin. Carson quite obviously knew how to pull off a grand surprise. Both men had been caught completely off guard by the accusations.

"Let's see here," Carson said, his eyes skimming the paperwork. "I believe his name was Leroy Guzman." He glanced up. "Does that name sound familiar?"

Alexander folded his arms over his chest. "I don't know who you're talking about."

Mr. Thompkins cleared his throat and threw his client a warning glare.

"Let me refresh your memory, Mr. Callister," Carson said with a smile. He pulled out a piece of paper and set it in the middle of the table. "Leroy Guzman was a small business owner. He ran a bread store in downtown Boston, after emigrating from Mexico. However, like many beginning business owners, he needed money to get started, money which he didn't have." Carson began to tap his fingers on top of the table in a slow, methodical pattern. "Luckily, or unluckily he would later discover, he was referred to a man who was willing to give him a loan." Carson raised an eyebrow. "But at a cost." He leaned forward, arms folded and resting on top of the table. "Would you like to guess who that man was, Mr. Callister?"

Alexander sneered. "If you expect me to keep track of every no-body who ever borrowed money from me, then you're delusional. That would be like you knowing every client you've ever had by name."

"Except this was just a few years ago," Carson said, looking at the paperwork as if checking his reference. "The death was reported on-ly a few weeks before you went to jail for your loan shark activities." Those gray eyes came up. "Are you telling me you can't remember a few years ago? How in the world do you remember your ex wife? You haven't seen her in five years either."

"Enough," Mr. Thompkins said sharply when Alexander opened his mouth to fight back. "Get on with your point, counsellor."

Carson smirked. "My point is, Mr. Guzman's body was found with a bullet hole in his head, dumped just outside Boston city lim-its. Friends testified that he had been behind on his payments and one night had been...collected...by a couple of large men who were taking Mr. Guzman home to have a talk with him."

"Loaning someone money doesn't mean my client had anything to do with this so called chat."

"Are you sure?" Carson offered. Rose watched intently as Car-son's eyes darted back and forth between the two other men. "Last chance to confess before it's too late."

Mr. Thompkins rubbed his forehead. "You're speaking in riddles, Mr. Cordova. Either drop this ridiculous line of conversation or share why this has anything to do with my client."

Carson stood and walked to the door. "A recent witness has come forward that puts your client in the room with the deceased on the night he was not only questioned and tortured, but eventually killed." Carson grabbed the doorknob and looked over his shoulder. "And on that note, I think you should meet some friends of mine."

*****

Ken's eyebrows rose high on his forehead as the small room was suddenly flooded with men and women, all in uniform, but definitely not from his precinct. He jumped to his feet, pulling Rose with him and backing up until they were out of the way. Ken made sure he was partly in front of Rose without blocking her completely.

"What is this?" Mr. Thompkins shouted over the rising noise in the room. He and Alexander were both standing up and for the first time since this whole fiasco started, Alexander looked worried.

It's about time, Ken thought to himself. The guy had stayed overly confident for much longer than Ken would have thought. Especially with Carson dragging it all out for so long. Ken still wanted to ask his friend what had caused such a delay, but he could wait until it all died down. He watched as several of the officers approached Alexander and began reading him his rights. The man's hands were cuffed and he was pulled from the room while he and his lawyer shouted profanities not fit for anyone's ears.

"Captain Wamsley?"

Ken came out of his thoughts and stood tall. "Yes?"

"I'm Chief Thurston." The man held out his hand.

"Jeremy Thurston?"

The officer nodded. "Yes." He jammed a thumb over his shoulder. "These are a few officers from my precinct, including the homicide division." He grinned smugly. "We came to take Mr. Callister back home on charges of murder and breaking parole." His smile grew. "We've been looking forward to taking Mr. Callister down for a long time, but he was too good at covering his tracks."

The officer's eyes went over Ken's shoulder to where Rose was waiting quietly.

"You must be Ms. Ingalls," the man said in a softer tone.

"I am."

Ken stepped aside, ignoring the fact that he wanted to shield her from it all. "Rose, meet Chief Thurston. He was the one in charge of the loan shark case against Alexander."

"Well...my men were, I didn't handle it personally." The older man smiled and held out his hand to shake Rose's.

She responded in kind. "Nice to meet you," she said.

"I can't tell you how excited the whole station was when we got word of your testimony and evidence file. I realize it had to be frightening to finally come forward with it, but we're grateful you're willing to do so."

Rose leaned into Ken and he wrapped an arm around her shoulders. "She's a pretty remarkable woman," he said, agreeing with the chief.

Chief Thurston chuckled. "I believe it." He turned to glance at the chaotic scene behind them. "Looks like they've got Callister just about ready to go." He turned back and nodded. "We're heading straight back, sorry it took so long to arrive, but we'll take it from here."

Ken nodded, still a little in shock from the bombardment. He shook a few more hands as the officers milled around, gathering the files they needed and speaking to those involved.

A half hour later, the group was gone.

Rose collapsed in a chair. "What in the world was that?"

Carson grinned and leaned his hip against the table with his arms folded over his chest. "That was the end of your association with Alexander Callister."

Her eyes misted over and Ken walked over to sit at her side.

"Can it really be that simple?" she asked. "Won't I have to testify?"

Carson nodded. "I'm sorry to say that you will, but that should be pretty smooth. You'll have all the protection you need and you won't have to face him alone."

"I'll go with you if you want," Ken offered. It took a great deal of restraint not to demand she not go without him. His overprotective side was still fighting him, but Ken was working to keep it in check. He'd been telling the truth earlier when he said she was a remarkable woman. Rose could handle anything she put her mind to, but if she allowed it, Ken wanted to help carry the burden. In fact, it would be a privilege to do so.

Rose gave him a tired smile. "I'd like that," she said softly.

Ken had to turn away or he was going to grab her and kiss her right then and there. Carson probably wouldn't enjoy the show nearly as much as Ken did. "So does this mean Alexander's charges of police brutality are dropped?"

"I'll wait for official word," Carson said as he put all his paperwork back in the briefcase. "But I think it's safe to assume Mr. Callister will be far too busy working to keep himself out of jail than to worry about trying to take your job."

Rose shuddered. "I have to ask," she said softly. "Why in the world did you draw out that process so long?" She shook her head. "It seemed like you were purposefully trying to upset him."

Carson chuckled with a slightly evil tone to it. "Yeah...that was fun."

"You enjoyed it?" Rose asked, her voice a little loud.

Ken squeezed her hand. "You're what my parents call an instigator," he accused.

Carson's grin was pure mischief. "I have no problem with that label."

Ken laughed softly while Rose groaned. "But seriously," she pressed. "Why?"

Carson rested his hands on either side of him. "Would you believe I was buying time for the police to get here?"

Ken froze for a split second before laughing. "That was it? You were taking the guy apart piece by piece just so the Boston officers could arrive?"

Carson nodded. "The taking apart probably wasn't necessary, but if I have to entertain a murderer, you can bet I'm not going to read him a fairytale and offer tea."

"Why not just have Ken's group arrest him?" Rose asked.

Carson shrugged. "This made more of a statement. We could have had Ken arrest Alexander at any time, but this way you got to show your ex that you weren't scared of him anymore, you built a united front with Ken, and you eventually closed the door in the guy's face."

Rose was quiet, but Ken nodded. "Thanks," he said. Carson didn't have to go out of his way to give Ken and Rose the chance for full closure, but he did and it meant a lot to Ken.

"Yes, thank you," Rose finally said. She stood and walked over to leave a kiss on Carson's cheek. "We owe you one."

When Carson began to smile and reached for Rose, Ken stood and cleared his throat.

Carson laughed and put his hands in the air. "She started it!"

Rose rolled her eyes. "Once again, you two are utterly ridiculous!" Shaking her head, she headed to the door. "I have a daughter to get home to."

Ken's heart fell. They had spoken a little about what would happen when this was all over, but nothing was official, and with the way she was heading out so quickly, he worried she would change her mind.

Rose paused in the doorway. "Are you coming?" she asked him.

Aaaand...nevermind. Feeling a sudden burst of energy, Ken hurried over to join her. "One of my officers will drive you to the airport whenever you're ready," Ken said without looking back.

"Yeah, yeah...get outta here," Carson called out after them.

Ken put his hand on Rose's lower back and together they walked out of the station, into the bright sunlight. The weather was indicative of his mood as they drove to pick up Lily, as if God himself were shining down on them with His approval.

Rose sighed and leaned back against her seat. "I'll be glad when we get home. I'm exhausted."

Ken wasn't sure what to say. Did she mean his house? Or her own apartment? He wanted to believe she meant where they were all living together, but he also didn't want to press his luck, so he made a noncommittal sound instead.

Rose's eyes had fluttered closed right before she murmured, "One of these days I'm going to give the cabin a woman's touch, though."

That was all the encouragement Ken needed. He gripped the steering wheel to keep from reaching for Rose and pushed the speed limit to get to Caro's. It was time for the whole family to be together. And in the very near future, he would see that they stayed that way permanently.

CHAPTER 27

Rose stood up from the passenger side of Ken's car and took a deep breath of salty, sea air. It had been a solid week since her last encounter with Alexander. Since she had agreed to stand up and testify and gave the information necessary to help put him behind bars for good.

Surprisingly, she found that her fear had dissipated quite quickly. She'd spent so many years hiding that she had expected to feel anxious about her upcoming time in court and even about her safety until that point in time, but none of that was happening.

She and Lily had moved back into the apartment and the biggest problem that had been plaguing Rose's mind was the fact that her life felt so empty without having Ken around all day long.

Every time Lily did something cute, Rose smiled and looked for Ken to share the moment with. Each time the apartment grew quiet at night, Rose wished she could curl up on the couch with Ken's strong arm around her and snuggle in for a while before bed. Even coming home after work to an empty apartment was wearing on Rose. She wanted to hear Lily giggling as she and Ken cooked dinner. Rose missed Ken checking in with her every hour and sending her cute, flirty texts that helped her make it through the day. She missed his sly smile when he did something cute with Lily. Basically, she just missed him.

They'd talked and he'd come over for dinner twice, but it hadn't felt like enough. Yet what more could they do? They weren't married and hadn't even talked about it since the situation with Alexander had come to a head. Rose assumed it would probably be put on hold until after the trial. She just hoped it wasn't one drawn out over the next several years. She wasn't sure she could survive quite that long.

"You chilly?" Ken asked as he walked around the car to take her hand.

Rose smiled up at him and shook her head. Her jacket was plenty warm and any time Ken touched her, her temperature was higher than normal, so no…she definitely wasn't cold. "Do you realize that this is the first time we've arrived at a bonfire together?" Rose asked as they walked through the sand.

Their group of friends used to spend every Friday night during the summer holding bonfires together, though over the last couple of years as each one of them got married, the gatherings had begun to become less frequent. At this point, it was more like once a month, but it didn't truly matter. Rose was just grateful for the chance to spend time with people she loved and could now let into her life in a way she never had been able to before.

"Benny said bringing Allison the first time was worse than meeting the parents," Ken teased.

"Considering his mother-in-law," Rose murmured, "that's saying something."

Ken blurted out a loud laugh. "Rose Ingalls," he scolded. "I don't know if I've ever heard you speak that way."

Rose made a face. "I probably shouldn't have said that. I'm sorry. It was unkind."

Ken shrugged. "It's not like we don't all agree with you."

"Yeah, but still…I'm sorry."

Ken pulled her closer and wrapped an arm around her shoulders before kissing her temple. "Easily forgiven."

Rose savored his touch. She really hadn't meant to say something quite so rude about Benny's mother-in-law. The only thing she could think of was her frustration at her own romantic situation slipping out, but that was certainly no excuse for bad mouthing someone else.

"You made it!" Caro squealed, jumping up from her seat and running to grab Rose in a tight hug. "I'm so glad this whole mess is over," she whispered into Rose's ear.

"Me too," Rose said, melting into her friend's embrace. Despite how close some of them had become, Rose had always held a piece of herself back. She knew there was a good chance that at some point, she would need to leave, not to mention the weight of holding onto her testimony was not one she wanted to burden any of her friends with.

Now, however, it all felt different. The wall of indifference was gone and Rose felt whole for the first time in ages. Tears pricked her eyelids as she stayed connected to Caro. Soon another set of arms wrapped around them, and then another...Rose didn't even bother opening her eyes to see who was joining the group hug. She just soaked up all the love and support that was being offered.

Several minutes later, the group finally broke apart and the women all laughed at each other while they wiped teary eyes.

"I have to admit that as long as I have pictured you and Ken finally getting together, I never imagined it would be over something like this," Charli said, rubbing her small baby bump. "Who knew it would take a criminal to force you to let Ken in?"

Caro huffed. "Well, seriously, who can resist a man in protection mode?"

"You!" Jack called from his seat near the fire.

The women all spun and Caro stuck her tongue out at her husband, who simply grinned.

Ken rubbed the back of his neck and Rose could see he was a little uncomfortable with the whole situation.

"He really has been a hero," Rose said softly, wiping her cheeks once more. "I wouldn't have survived without his help."

Ken shook his head and stepped up to tuck her under his arm again. "Yes, you would. You've been taking care of yourself and Lily for a long time. While I'm glad I was there to help, the more I look back on the situation, the more I realize how amazing it has been to watch you handle it."

"Well, shoot, cowboy," Caro said, fanning her misty eyes. "Most of us here are far too hormonal for you to go about being so sweet."

"Are you finally admitting you have an announcement?" Charli demanded.

Caro paused. "You mean you already knew?"

Rose laughed softly as Charli rolled her eyes. "Caro, even for you, you've been sassier than usual. We all figured something was going on and a baby was the most obvious choice."

The petite blonde put her hands on her hips. "Are you telling me that my dramatic moment has been ruined?"

"Pretty much," Mel said, wincing at her own statement. Her own stomach was poking prominently out from her T-shirt. "I think it's safe to say that we can all see the signs."

Rose looked around and had to agree. Since the entire group of friends had started their married lives within the last couple of years, it made complete sense that they were all starting their families at similar times as well.

It would be nice for Lily to have some young children to play with. Maybe she could even babysit eventually.

Rose's eyes drifted to Ken, who was smiling and laughing with some of the men at this point. *And maybe if I'm lucky, Lily will get to do that with a sibling, not just a friend.*

"So if I'm having a girl..." Caro tapped her lips. "Does this mean I get dibs on Charli's boy? Can we like sign an early contract?"

Charli groaned. "Those kinds of marriages went out of style ages ago, Caro."

"What about you, Mel? Wanna plan our kids' wedding?"

Laughter continued as the women floated over to their seats. Rose felt lighter than she had in a decade. She truly did have a future now and she was excited to see where it went. And she was even more excited because despite their difficult week, she was fairly certain it would eventually be spent with a certain police captain, who was quickly becoming more to her than she could ever explain in words.

*****

Ken had tackled criminals, locked up drunks, pulled women out of abusive situations, dealt with death and life and everything in between…but it wasn't until this moment that he was sure he knew exactly what true fear was.

His heart was ready to pound out of his chest, his forehead was slick with sweat, and his right hand was shaking almost uncontrollably.

"You ready?" Jack asked in an undertone.

Ken shook his head. "No. I think I'm gonna puke."

Jack chuckled. "Been there, done that," he said.

"How in the world did you all do it?" Ken muttered.

Jack grinned and the rest of the men laughed.

"What's so funny?" Rose asked as the women came into the circle. They each moved around until they were sitting by their significant others, including Rose at his side.

"Nothing," Ken quickly answered. He glared when Benny snorted and had to try to cover his reaction with a cough.

Rose frowned. "Seriously. What's going on?"

"I think the scaredy cat to your right has a question for you." There was a whacking sound, as if a person had been hit, and then silence.

Ken closed his eyes and hung his head as a hush went through the entire group. Leave it to Benny to get to the heart of the matter before anyone else was ready.

"Ken?" Rose whispered.

He pulled his head up and looked into her soft eyes and saw such hope that he knew no matter how much he wanted to give Benny a black eye at the moment…it was time. Slipping out of his seat, Ken got down on both knees and began to pull a small box from the inside pocket of his jacket. "Rosalinda Ingalls," he began. The words paused when she put her hands over her mouth and choked on a sob.

Ken smiled reassuringly at her. "I have been in love with you for a *really* long time."

Chuckles circled the group behind him.

"But, as much as it pains me to say it, it wasn't until recently that I truly understood what that love was." Ken took a deep breath as a single tear slipped down Rose's soft cheek. "At first I was just confused as to why you wouldn't let me in. Why, when I was positive you had feelings for me, would you hold us back from enjoying a relationship together?" Ken shook his head. "It really messed with me for quite a few years."

"I'm sorry," Rose whispered.

"No." He again shook his head. "Don't. Because I know now that I needed to change." He smiled and cupped her cheek, wiping away the wetness. "When I found out about your past, I was set on protecting you. Protecting you and Lily from everything that could ever harm you, and I took that too far. I pushed and prodded and kept you from being able to still be yourself." Ken sighed. "And for that, I'm sorry. But as I watched you challenge me and shift my way of thinking, I came to realize that just protecting you wasn't love. Keeping you safe is a loving thing to do, but letting you have the freedom to shine is better."

He pulled the box open and lifted out the ring, holding it in his palm and offering it to her. "Benny was right. I do have a question. I want to know if you'd be willing to let me keep learning and growing and allowing you to do the same. I want to know if you'll allow me the privilege of letting Lily call me Daddy. I want to know if you'll let me spend the rest of my life learning about real love and all the ways I can show that to you through every breath I take."

Sniffles were a prominent sound, along with the roar of the ocean as Ken waited for Rose to make her decision, but none of them were the sound he wanted. He wanted, more than anything, to hear Rose say the word "yes", but right now she was staring at him in what looked like shock and wasn't moving.

"Rose?" he prodded. "I got Lily's permission if that helps."

Her face crumpled and she buried her face in her hands. "You spoke to Lily?"

"Of course I did," Ken said, ducking his head so he could look into her eyes. "This would all affect her as well."

"Captain Wamsley," Rose said, pulling her head up and cupping his face. "You are the best thing that has ever happened to me. But I don't know if I would have recognized that if we had met when I was a young, ridiculous girl. If going through my past is what I had to do in order to be ready for you, then I would do it a hundred times over if it meant coming to this moment, every single time." She leaned in until their noses brushed. "I love you," she whispered, her warm breath fanning his face.

"But will you marry me?" Ken asked in exasperation.

"Yes."

That was all he needed. Ken closed the distance between them and ignored the slaps, hollers, and congratulations of the group as he focused on Rose. He was suddenly regretting having a public proposal as he wanted to keep Rose completely to himself for the next eternity or so. He couldn't imagine having to leave her at the end of the night, or however many nights it would take until they were finally married. The idea of letting her go nearly made him sick again.

"Marry me," he murmured between kisses.

"I said yes." Rose laughed.

Ken shook his head, pulling back just a little. "No. I mean right now."

"Now?" Rose cried. "Ken, it's a Friday evening. The county office isn't open."

"I can change that," he said temptingly.

"Oh my gosh," Rose said with a smile, resting her forehead against his chest. "You're not abusing your police powers to open the courthouse for us to get married."

"What? You could have done that?" Benny cried. Another smack sounded and Ken grinned at Ally, who smiled in return.

She shrugged. "We've been married less than a month and I still have to keep him in line."

"Honey, I think you signed up for a lifetime commitment," Caro said sarcastically.

"Ken," Rose said, pulling his attention back to her. "I know you've waited a long time. Far longer than you should have, but give me a week and then I promise we'll never be separated again."

"Three days," he bargained.

Rose shook her head with a smile. "A week."

"Two days."

"I don't think that's how this is supposed to work," Jack interrupted.

Ken looked at his friend and raised an eyebrow. "And how did you feel in this exact moment?"

Jack paused, then gave Rose a sheepish grin. "Two days is probably good."

The women all groaned collectively.

"At least let her find a pretty dress," Caro argued. "Plus, I'm gonna need time to bake all those goodies."

"And I have to order the flowers," Rose argued. "I want to be surrounded by flowers when we get married." Her smile was nothing short of breathtaking. "After all, it's what brought me to you."

Ken rubbed his knuckles along her chin. "Fine. One week, but speaking of flowers, I probably ought to give you this." He fished a folded piece of paper out of his pocket and handed it to Rose.

Her hands were shaking as she opened it and a small cry broke free when she saw the childish picture on it.

When Ken had spoken to Lily, she'd been determined to be a part of the evening and had drawn her mother, wild red hair and all, with a bouquet of flowers. Each flower held a very specific meaning, a bit of knowledge the five-year-old had obviously learned from her mother.

"Carnations for you being her mother," Ken began.

Rose nodded.

"Sunflowers for happiness."

Rose nodded again.

"Tulips and hydrangeas," Ken continued, "for family."

Rose's eyes came up to meet his.

"And red roses...lots of red roses," he teased, "for love."

Rose laughed softly and folded the paper carefully before putting it in her own pocket. "Did you know that red roses stand for something else?"

Ken frowned. "What did I miss?"

Her arms slowly went around his neck and Rose went up on tiptoe. "Red roses are also used to symbolize a father," she said.

"Why didn't we bring an entire crate of tissues?" Caro yelled. "These pregnancy hormones are no joke, people!"

Rose laughed at her friend's antics, but Ken was frozen. He loved Lily and knew that Lily loved him, but to know that her picture was just as much for him as it was for her mother...his heart did a funny little jump and Ken knew that a grand celebration was in order for the beginning of their tiny family.

"A week," he agreed. "And it's going to be the best, most joyous wedding Seaside Bay has ever seen." Before Rose could respond, he sealed the promise with a kiss.

CHAPTER 28

Rose put a hand on her stomach, but it did nothing to stop the flip-flopping. She couldn't believe she was doing this again. At one time, many years ago, she had most definitely been the blushing bride. But this time she was older, wiser, and loved her fiancé with a love so deep she was sure she would walk away half of a person if their relationship fell apart.

Surely, that kind of experience should have led to being calm as a summer day on the morning of her wedding, but it seemed to do the exact opposite.

"Did the lilies arrive?" Rose asked anxiously, fighting the urge to go see for herself. She had put this wedding together in such a short amount of time that some of the orders weren't arriving until the morning of. Now she was locked in the bride's room and flowers were still being unloaded and it was driving Rose crazy not to be out directing traffic.

Caro gave her best friend a wry look. "Honey, I'm pregnant, not stupid. The lilies are here, they're on the table you requested, they look divine, and if you ask me about the flowers again, I'm gonna claim momentary insanity and hit you with something!"

"I don't think a bruise is the 'something blue' she's supposed to have," Charli quipped as she slipped inside the door. She paused and eyed Rose up and down. "Rose, you are absolutely the most beautiful woman I have ever had the pleasure of knowing."

"Hey!" Caro cried as Rose tried to fight the blush creeping up her face.

Charli dismissed Caro's argument. "Yeah, yeah. We all know the Southern sass is fun, but seriously." Charli waved a hand at Rose and sent Caro an expectant look.

Caro reluctantly nodded her head. "All right, all right. You're right. But still...no knocking down the pregnant woman's confidence."

Charli sighed and rubbed her forehead. "I have a terrible feeling that Caro's pregnancy is going to last longer than anyone else's."

Rose bit her lips between her teeth to keep from laughing. She had noticed that as well. The dramatic Southern belle was definitely going to use every bit of her condition to her advantage.

"Is she ready?" Genni poked her head inside and gasped. "Oh my gosh, Rose," she breathed, coming the rest of the way in. "I hate to think what kind of time you're going to have with Lily when she's older because she looks just like you, and you look like an angel."

Caro huffed, but Charli nodded her agreement. "That's what I said!"

"How much room is left?" Hadlee called as she cracked open the door.

"Good grief!" Caro cried, throwing her hands up. "Is a bride's room not sacred anymore?"

"Not when you're as loved as Rose is," Charli shot back.

Soon the room was full with every woman Rose was close friends with. Some she had started her relationship with upon arriving in town and others she had gained as they married the men in her friend group, but in the end...it didn't matter.

Caro, Charli, Genni, Hadlee, Allison, Brook, and Melody...they were all there.

Tears pricked her eyes as she realized this was her family. This was what she would have been leaving behind if she had run. This was what made her life so wonderful. She was more grateful than ever that Ken had been so patient and yet so determined. He had talked her off the ledge several times, keeping her from running from her problems, choosing instead to face them head on in a way that ultimately ended it rather than delayed it.

"Hey! Where's the mini me?" Caro asked.

Mel held up a finger. "Just a sec. I think I know." She slipped back out of the room and it grew quiet for a few seconds before Mel was back. "I'm not sure we can contain so much beauty in one room, but we're sure going to try."

Rose melted as her daughter came into view. Lily's red curls had been tamed and shaped so they framed her oval face, looking exactly like a porcelain doll. The women all oohed and aahed appropriately, but Rose could barely contain her emotions.

Lily's light blue dress matched the bridesmaids in color, but was a much younger looking design and it was the exact shade of Lily's eyes, making them look almost fake as they stood out from her soft, white skin.

"Mama!" Lily cried, rushing to hug Rose.

Rose didn't care at all about wrinkles or handprints and dropped to her knees to embrace her daughter.

Lily pulled back quickly. "You look beautiful."

"And you look like a princess," Rose signed back.

Lily preened under her mother's praise. A second later, her face fell and the five-year-old looked uncertain.

"What is it?" Rose asked, her heart beating painfully against her chest. She had thought Lily was excited for today. She had certainly been celebrating all week.

"Is Uncle Ken really going to be my dad?"

The room fell into a hushed silence and Rose swallowed hard. "Uncle Ken is going to be my husband," she tried to explain. "He will live with us and help me take care of you. Whether or not you want to call him 'Dad' will be up to you."

There had been no word on whether or not Ken would be allowed to adopt Lily. Rose felt certain if she approached Ken about it, he would be happy to do so, but things were still so up in the air with

Alexander, so Rose wasn't sure when the opportunity would be available. She had hope, however, that it would eventually come to pass.

"Does he want me to call him 'Daddy'?" Lily signed slowly.

Rose's eyes filled with tears yet again. She knew the answer to this one. "I think he would love it."

Lily's face lit back up and she bounced on her toes.

Rose breathed a sigh of relief that that was the answer her daughter was hoping for and rose to her feet.

"Let's go now! It's time! It's time!" Lily cried.

"She's right," Caro hurried to say. She glanced at the group. "Okay, one hug and then it's time to get this woman down the aisle! Her groom has waited long enough!"

Rose laughed as she was engulfed by arms, laughter, and an overwhelming sense of love. These women were everything that was good in the world and together, they would raise their children side by side and maybe, just maybe, help make the world just a little better with their presence.

"Here we go," Caro said in an excited tone. She ushered the other women out and then brought Rose up last.

The line of women stopped at the chapel door and Charli, who was going first so that Caro could help Rose, grinned wildly. "Here's to our future," she whispered right before opening the door. Lily went inside, followed a few seconds later by Charli.

One by one, her friends began to slip inside and Rose suddenly had a panic attack. "My flowers," she hissed at Caro. "We forgot my bouquet!"

Caro's eyes widened and she looked around. There was nothing around to help save them. "I'm sorry," Caro whispered. "I have no idea where they are. Do you want me to stop the ceremony?"

Rose hesitated then shook her head. "No. It's not worth it for that." She straightened her shoulders and plastered a smile on her face. "Something was bound to go wrong, right? At least this one was sort of minor." Rose had put a lot of thought into her bouquet, but in the end, it was just flowers. Marrying Ken was the real prize. "Let's just go ahead and I'll count the decorations as mine."

"I'm so sorry," Caro said as their turn at the door came up. "I'll make it up to you."

*****

Ken nearly dropped the flowers in his hands when Rose came through the door. He had never seen such a vision. The stunning, white dress hugged the line of her body without being tight and trailed out starting at mid thigh, until she had a small train of lace skimming the carpet behind her.

Her red hair was a stunning crown to her glory as her curls were wrapped into an intricate design on her head that was far beyond anything Ken had ever seen before. He found himself slightly jealous of the wisps that floated around her face and neck, just kissing her skin as she walked.

His brother snickered from Ken's left and he realized he probably looked like a love-struck teenager. Still...if Rose was what he got stuck on, there were a lot worse things in life.

Instead of giving his brother the set down he deserved, Ken ignored the teasing and began to walk down from his place at the altar.

A murmur ran through the crowd and Rose's eyes widened as he approached.

"What are you doing?" she asked as they came face to face.

"First of all, I couldn't let you walk alone," Ken whispered. "And secondly..." He held out the flowers. "I had this made for you."

Rose's bottom lip trembled as she slowly reached out to take the offered bouquet. Ken couldn't take credit for the arranging of the flowers, but the idea had definitely been his. He wanted Rose to understand that he wanted to be a part of her life in all aspects, not just the ones that were convenient. So, while he might be all thumbs when it came to things like flowers and plants or other domestic type chores, Rose loved them, which meant Ken wanted to love them too. So he spoke to her in a way only Rose would understand.

"You did this?" Rose whispered thickly, her eyes sparkling with tears as she looked up in awe.

Ken's chest puffed up a little under her obvious adoration. "Well, I'm sure Caro will want credit for the arranging, but I picked out the flowers."

Rose sniffed and wiped at her eyes, while letting out a soft laugh. "Yes, I'm sure Caro will let me know she was involved." She looked back up. "Tell me about them."

Ken's smile was too big for his face, but he didn't care. His entire precinct was watching him act like a puppy dog, and none of it mattered. All that did was this moment and solidifying his relationship with his soon to be wife. "I had to include a couple of roses," Ken started. "Love and passion are certainly going to be a part of our marriage," he said with a grin as Rose blushed. "But I didn't want them to be the sole focus." He started pointing to individual flowers. "Orchids for fertility and elegance."

Rose cleared her throat.

Ken couldn't stop his chuckle. He loved the daughter they were going to share, but he definitely hoped they had more kids and there was no reason to hide it. "Sunflowers for adoration and loyalty." He moved to the next one. "Peonies for prosperity and honor. Lavender for serenity and grace." He moved the bouquet around so he could see the other flowers. "Tulips for love and hope. Carnations for admiration and good fortune. Aaaaannnd, jasmine for eternal love and positivity."

Rose fingered the tiny white flowers that were being used in between the big ones. "And these?"

Ken racked his brain. He was sure it had a meaning, but he was drawing a blank. Crud, he had practiced this a thousand times this week! How could he forget something now? Rose's lips quirked and Ken pulled on his tie. Why had he thought this would be a good idea?

A tug on his jacket had Ken looking down to find Lily. "It's baby's breath," she whispered, in her less-than-quiet whisper.

Ken squatted down. "Do you remember what it means?"

Lily smiled. "Love."

Ken smiled back. "Good job, Peach." He wrapped an arm around the small girl and stood with her tucked into his chest. "Baby's breath for love."

Lily put her hand on Ken's cheek and turned him to face her. "Just like I love you, Daddy."

The sob that broke free from Ken couldn't have been considered manly in any sense of the word, but considering the sighs and the fact that there wasn't a dry eye in the entire church after that comment, he felt positive no one cared. Gently grabbing Lily's head with one hand, he gave her a fierce kiss on her rosy, little cheek. "I love you," he whispered back. "And I'm honored to be your daddy."

He raised an eyebrow at Rose and nodded at the flowers. She nodded in return and Ken plucked a piece of the baby's breath out of the bouquet. "I love you," he said again, handing it to Lily.

"I'd like to make one correction," Rose added in a thick voice. "Baby's breath is *unconditional* love."

"Then I suppose it was the perfect choice," Ken responded, clearing his throat. He turned sideways and held out his left arm. "Shall we?"

Rose slid her hand into his elbow and beamed up at him. "We shall."

Ken knew it was untraditional. He knew having a child in his arms the whole ceremony was going to cause some tongues to wag. He knew that the town would be gossiping about Rose's situation for the next ten years, but he could deal with that.

After five years of patience, longing, and self discipline, the woman he had set his sights on was finally becoming his and there was nothing better than this exact moment in time. This moment at the altar when they were joined in holy matrimony before God and all the witnesses of the church. The moment where they were free of past problems and restraints. The moment where they could move forward with one heart and mind and face all the future held together.

"I now pronounce you man and wife," the pastor said with a wide smile. His eyes twinkled as he said, "You may now kiss the bride."

Ken shifted his hold on Lily and cupped Rose's face with his left hand. "Hello, Mrs. Wamsley," he whispered when their mouths were close together.

"Hello, my handsome husband," she whispered back.

"I'll never get tired of that," he managed right before closing the distance between them.

If the kiss went on a little longer than it should have, no one blamed them. Even Lily simply laughed and clapped as the couple struggled to pull away from each other.

"There will be more of that later," Ken said in her ear as he turned them both to face the crowd.

"There better be," Rose shot back while smiling at the crowd.

"I now give you, Captain and Mrs. Wamsley!" the pastor cried.

Ken held their combined hands in the air and started walking down the aisle, smiling and nodding at all the congratulations being thrown their way. Life wasn't perfect. The road to their happy ever after had been a clear indicator of that. But in this moment, for just a split second, he got a glimpse of a joy so full it felt as if perfection was possible. And lucky man that he was...it was in his arms, and he was never letting it go.

EPILOGUE
6 months later

Carson whistled as he walked to grab his mail. Life was going pretty good at the moment. Work was plugging away, there seemed to be no end to people who hated other people and wanted justice in court, giving him a hefty paycheck and too many tasks for daylight hours.

He paused at the thought. Really, if he broke it down, that wasn't a very good way to look at his life's work, especially because he enjoyed what he did. But still...

He shrugged. Who cared how he broke down his work? He paid his bills, had enough extra to have fun with, and he was enjoying almost every minute of it.

He grabbed the mail and slowly walked back inside his townhome.

"Hey, Carson."

With his hand on the knob, Carson turned to smile at his neighbor. "Emme!" He took in her stylish outfit of white shorts with a baby blue sweater hanging off her shoulder. "Don't you look nice."

Emme smiled enticingly and stuck out her hip. "Maybe one of these days you'll think I look good enough to have dinner with."

Carson winked. "I don't think that's the issue," he said. "I think you're already too far ahead for me to ever catch up." With a quick wave, he ducked inside and closed the door.

Emme was a beautiful woman, Carson would have to be blind to not see it. The problem? Like so many of the other women he met, they all knew he was related to Grayson Cordova. Hollywood heartthrob, recently turned director. His change in career, however, didn't change the thousands of women who wanted to meet Gray.

Despite Carson's earlier thoughts about how well life was going, if there was one thing Carson would change, it would be the fact that he couldn't seem to meet a woman who actually wanted to know him for him. They either enjoyed his money, or they wanted a crack at his brother.

"Stupid fame," he grumbled, tossing the mail on the counter. A bright red envelope caught his eye and Carson paused before pulling it out of the stack. "Speaking of..."

The letter was from Gray and Brook. Brooklyn was Grayson's lovely wife that he'd met while hiding up in Oregon during a time when Gray was recuperating from an onset injury.

Carson ripped open the card and frowned when he read the invitation. Apparently, his brother and sister-in-law were holding a Christmas party next month. A week-long Christmas party.

"You've got to be kidding me," Carson grumbled. He pulled out his phone and quickly dialed Jude.

Jude was Grayson's personal physical therapist, but with Grayson married and moving from house to house as he worked on different projects, Carson and Jude had become closer without Gray playing mediator between them.

"Hey man," Jude answered.

"Jude, the dude," Carson responded, knowing his friend hated the nickname. "What's up?"

Jude sighed. "Really? You're over thirty years old now. Don't you think the dumb nicknames have gotten a little old?"

Carson chuckled. "Ticking you off never gets old," he responded. Really, Carson enjoyed playing devil's advocate in every part of life, not just in teasing his friends. It was part of what made him such a good lawyer.

"You're impossible," Jude grumbled. "Did you have a point for this call?"

"Did you get today's mail?"

"You too, huh?" Jude said. "I was just looking at the invite and deciding how to politely decline."

"What?" Carson cried. "You can't decline!"

"Why not?"

"Because then I'll be left without a wingman!" Carson explained.

"You're a grown man," Jude said. "I have no doubt you can handle it. Besides, aren't you friends with a lot of Brook's buddies up in Seaside Bay?"

"Aren't you?" Carson shot back.

"I really only got to know Brook while I was there," Jude said. "Though I met the rest once at a bonfire...and at the wedding. They're all nice."

"They are, but they're also very married."

"Why do you think I was trying to get out of it?" Jude said with a laugh. "Like I want to walk around Gray's coastal mansion for a week being a third wheel to every person I meet."

"Which is exactly why you need to come," Carson groaned. "Otherwise, I'm the one walking around like that."

"Yeah, but you're family."

"Which is why *I* can't say no. Gray won't let me." Carson fell onto his couch. This was not how he had planned to enjoy his holiday break. A week in Oregon? In the winter? The people were nice enough, but geez. What the heck was he going to do for a week? Especially as possibly the only single man in the group.

Jude sighed. "Car, I really don't want to go."

"Me either," Carson grumbled. "Please...I'm begging. Don't leave me alone like this."

There was silence on the other line for a few seconds and hope shot into Carson's chest. If he could at least have Jude there, then Carson would have someone to play pool with or cover for him if he escaped out the back door to get away from all the happily hitched folks.

"I have to work..." Jude hedged.

"I'll pay you twice your normal salary."

"Really?"

Carson nodded. "Yep. Scout's honor."

"I don't even know if you were a Scout, but I just might take you up on that. I might need to get a new car, so if you rich lawyer types are passing out money just for spending time with friends, then that might be a good deal. Torture. But a good deal."

Carson grinned. "And people say money doesn't talk."

"It doesn't," Jude replied. "We just let it lead us by the nose." He huffed. "All right. I'll come, but you have to promise not to throw me under the bus."

"Scout's honor," Carson said for the second time.

"Again, I have no idea if you were a Scout."

"I plead the fifth," Carson answered with a grin.

"You would." Jude took a deep breath. "Fine. I'll confirm. But if I regret this, then next time you ask me to work on your back, I'm totally going to throw something out of alignment."

Carson winced at the thought, but smiled at his victory. "Duly noted." He calculated things in his head. "We've only got three weeks. Better let your boss know."

"Yeah, yeah. I'll make sure things are fine on my end. You just worry about getting your own butt there."

"Yes sir!" Carson saluted the phone. "I owe you one!"

"You owe me a new car!" Jude called out before the line went dead.

Carson flipped the invite onto the coffee table. He wasn't exactly thrilled at the idea of going, but having Jude there would make things better. And if Jude was naive enough to think that Carson wouldn't throw him under the bus if it meant avoiding the matchmaking of his family? Then it would only make Carson's escape easier.

Don't miss Carson's story!
Grab it now!
"Her Unexpected Mistletoe Kiss"

Follow ALL my new releases by joining my Reader Family!
You can do that HERE[1]

Lauraannbooks.com

---

1. https://dl.bookfunnel.com/j10fix95s7

www.ingramcontent.com/pod-product-compliance
Lightning Source LLC
Chambersburg PA
CBHW070920190726
48292CB00004B/1039